TALES FROM BIREHRA

A JOURNEY THROUGH A WORLD WITHIN US

RAFI MUSTAFA

WHIMSY PUBLICATIONS

WHIMSY PUBLICATIONS
19 Legacy Drive,
Markham, ON L3S 4C4
Canada

www.rafimustafa.org
rafi.mustafa@indusflow.com

Cover Photo by Tariq Sherwani

ISBN
978-1-9995631-1-0 (Hardcover)
978-1-9995631-2-7 (Paperback)
978-1-9995631-3-4 (eBook)

1.   FICTION, HISTORICAL

بشنو از نے چون حکایت می کند

از جدایی ها شکایت می کند

کز نیستان تا مرا ببریده اند

از نفیرم مرد و زن نالیده اند

سینه خواهم شرحه شرحه از فراق

تا بگویم شرحِ دردِ اشتیاق

هر کسی کو دور ماند از اصلِ خویش

بازجوید روزگار وصلِ خویش

رومی

Listen to the flute what it is saying,
It is complaining about separation.

"Ever since I was cut from the reed field,
Men and women weep when they hear my cries.

"I want a heart which is torn from separation,
So that I may explain the pain of yearning."

Whoever is plucked from his roots,
Is always longing to return one day.

- Rumi

For my grandchildren

Je me souviens !

Table of Contents

BOOK ONE
TIMELESS GLOBE

Birehra

Located on the southern tip of a two-mile-long dirt track was Birehra, a small, dusty village in northern India, whose population had stood at around 500, plus or minus a few souls, for over the past century. Those were the days when there were not many people in Birehra who had ever seen a train, let alone ride on one. There were no radios and no motor cars in Birehra. There was only one country outside India, and that was Vilayat, or "the Foreign Land." They said that the British had come from Vilayat, where they had tall buildings and roads made of glass, on which motor cars slid so smoothly that one could carry a bowl of water, filled to the brim, without spilling a single drop! The British had invented many things, including glass bottles, enamel pots, and wind-up toys.

So, what was significant about Birehra? Well, nothing! There was nothing about Birehra that one could care for. However, for the people of Birehra themselves, that was the place to be in and to stay in.

The northern end of the dirt track connected to an old bitumen road, with cracks and potholes, worn out due to years of neglect. The road was mostly occupied by bullock carts loaded with bales of hay. The sleepy bullocks chewed their cud and announced their presence by the dull sound of the bells around their necks as they pulled their carts at a snail's pace. They continued on their familiar path with no need for driving instructions. Their drivers napped on top of the hay, getting down from time to time to urinate by the roadside. An old rickety lorry, jumping up and down at every bump and hole, also travelled on the road once a day. It carried passengers between a small railway station called Kasganj and another small town known as Bilram. People coming to Birehra took the lorry at Kasganj and told the driver to drop them off at the dirt road leading to Birehra.

The one-way fare for the trip was one anna, which was insignificant even at that time. One could have sixteen such lorry rides for one rupee. Things were cheap in those days. Children were given one anna to spend the day at the annual fair set up across the fields. They got twelve pies in change, and for every pie, they could buy a pocketful of roasted peanuts or a handful of sesame sweets. For one pie, they could also get a ride on a wooden Ferris wheel that squeaked with every rotation, or they could buy a pinwheel with eight multi-coloured vanes. Apart from that annual event, nothing else ever happened in Birehra. People were generally happy and contented. The only problem that could be worrisome was for parents who had not yet been visited by a prospective suitor for their marriageable age daughters.

The exact location of Birehra was spelled out clearly on letters that the postman delivered to its inhabitants: To Karmoo the Water Carrier, Village Birehra, Post Office Dholna, Tehsil Bilram, District Etah, UP, Hindustan.

Everyone in Birehra belonged to one caste or another and lived in his or her own neighbourhood. There was a settlement of casteless untouchables at the village entrance, who picked up refuse from toilets and swept homes. People knew them as sweepers or Bhangies, branded as impure from the moment of birth - the lowliest of the low and the most pathetic caste system victims. They collected cow dung from the street to make circular cakes stuck to their walls, peeled off when dried, and then used to make cooking fires. Everyone who passed through the neighbourhood could smell the stench of dung fires.

Among the low-caste Hindus, there were Chamars, who tanned leather and made shoes, Julahas who spun threads and wove cloth, Kumhars who made earthen pots, pitchers, tumblers, and plates, and Dhobis who collected dirty clothes from homes and washed them at the pond. Every Dhobi had his own slab of stone on the bank of the pond. They soaked clothes in water and thrashed them on the slab until the dirt was beaten away. Stubborn stains were removed by cooking them in a stew of goat dung before bringing them to the pond. Each community lived in their own colony, ensuring that their dwellings did not encroach upon another community.

Then there were Sherwanis, the Muslim landowners whose ancestors came to Birehra four centuries ago. All Sherwani families lived in the centre of the village, surrounded by low-caste Hindu communities. Each Sherwani home was referred to as a Haveli or a mansion, regardless of its size. While most houses in Birehra were small shanties, built from mud and straw, the Sherwanis lived in brick homes, each surrounded by a compound. They owned small pieces of farmland outside the village, and even though they were not rich, they considered themselves elite since their ancestors had come from the north and were fair-skinned people. They spent the revenue from farming, mostly on taking care of the families of their workers.

Outside the Sherwani neighbourhood, there was an area where working-class Muslims lived. They worked as servants in homes and the fields. Apart from farmworkers, there were tailors, water carriers, shopkeepers, milk churners, washermen, barbers, shoemakers, and many other professions. They could come into the mosque inside the compound to pray and could even be embraced on the day of Eid, to celebrate the end of the month of fasting, but that was where the Islamic brotherhood ended.

There were no Hindus of upper castes in Birehra. They all lived in a colony called Nagla, located three fields behind Birehra. Among them were the Brahmins, the holiest of the holy and the custodians of sacred learning, who occupied the highest status in the caste system since they were created at dawn from Brahma's mouth, the creator god. They treated the Sherwanis as their equal due to their common Aryan roots.

Even though everyone fitted in his own pigeonhole and knew his status clearly, they were all treated with respect. Yet an untouchable was supposed to be respected. According to their age, children were taught to address people as bhaiyya, chacha, or daada, regardless of their caste or religion. After all, it was not by choice or lack of motivation that someone was a sweeper. He had to be a sweeper since he was born in a sweeper's home! With everyone knowing their proper place in the society, the village worked like a self-managing human body, in which every organ performs a specific function.

Every year the farmers waited for the first monsoon rain when they were ready to sow the summer crop. It rained continuously for several days until the sun came up. Every leaf turned bright green, and there was not a speck of dust in the air. Sparrows flew chirping from branch to branch, thousands of crows encircled above rooftops, cawing without pause, and eagles glided high in the sky under bright white clouds that were flying away from the village.

Girls put swings under tall trees and sang rain songs. Boys waited at a distance, winking at each other and commenting on the girls. Some of them ventured closer and started pushing swings for their favourite girls. Others waited with patience until they noticed that the girls had accepted the earlier group, and then they joined them one by one. They were careful in the beginning not to touch any girl, keeping their hands on the rope, except when it happened accidentally. Such accidents became more frequent as time passed by. Every boy assessed the reaction carefully. The girls enjoyed the thrill as the boys pushed their swings harder and harder. As their toes touched high branches, their hearts sank with every swing. The romance was in the air. Every boy felt his heart pounding in his chest every time the swing came back, and his palms touched the back of his girl!

Then came the time when the mustard crop filled the entire field with yellow blossoms. A bright yellow carpet was spread as far as the eye could see. Peacocks called their mates, and their pee-hoo could be heard for miles. Cows mooed, roosters crowed, birds chirped, nightingales sang, and donkeys brayed. The village was full of sounds and sights. There was hardly a moment when one did not hear one sound or another. There was no room for loneliness. How could one be lonely when there was so much life around him?

Birehra was a timeless globe. Nights followed days and days followed nights, but time stood still. There was no past and no future. There were births and deaths, love and betrayal, fights and reconciliations, but every event occurred in the eternal present.

A Touch of Untouchability

The business was booming for the *Doms* of Bombay. For the past 2000 years, they had been handling dead bodies and providing fire for the cremation pyre. That was their job. According to the ancient Hindu text of *Manusmriti*, which assigned professions to every caste, the Doms were the givers of fire for the purification of the body once it was devoid of spirit. Since death does not discriminate based on religion or caste, the Muslim gravediggers, too, were minting it, as death scooped up neighbourhood after neighbourhood. It had all started during the early summer of 1896, but nobody knew why the angel of death had suddenly started working overtime. Funeral processions followed one another to cremation grounds and graveyards, like caravans of camels in the desert. It was not until September of that year that Doctor Viegas diagnosed the disease that killed the port city's inhabitants by the thousands every week: bubonic plague. This realization resulted in a mass exodus, thus carrying the disease to the farthest corners of India.

Oblivious to the panic sweeping through the country, the people of Birehra were celebrating the birth of Khansab, the first and last child of Sherwani Sahib. Known for his generosity, kindness, and loyalty to his friends, Sherwani Sahib was the village's undisputed leader. However, his landholding acreage was far from grand, compared to several nearby landowners with significantly more acres. Towering at six-foot-four, fair-skinned, and armed with a pair of long moustaches pointing upward, he looked like a colonel from the British army, but deep down, he was an Indian through and through. At times, he felt like King Solomon watching over his kingdom from the mountaintop as his subjects went around performing daily chores in his fields. At harvest time, he distributed most of his income among his workers and maintained a modest living at home.

They said that the Sherwani tribe had originated in a small village called Sherwan, somewhere in Central Asia. Their Pathan ancestors came to India in the fifteenth century as soldiers in the armies of Bahlol Lodhi from Afghanistan. Recognized for their gallantry and ferocity, they occupied the front line; the enemy columns parted like the Nile when they leapt forward like hungry tigers. Their battle cry was enough to rattle the hearts of the bravest of their enemies. They served their employer well, and after the country had been conquered, they became renowned as advisers, commanders, accountants, and royal companions. In recognition of their loyalty, they were awarded estates and required to pay a portion of their revenue in taxes. It continued when the Mughals arrived and established their empire. When the Sherwanis switched from soldiering to farming, they mellowed down over four centuries. Even though they still claimed the legendary bravery of Pathans, the fact was that most of their men and women were just hot-headed. They quarrelled and screamed, but their fists never reached their opponents' noses.

The Mughals placed many men from the Sherwani tribe in high positions in their courts. When the British arrived on the scene, most of the Sherwanis pledged their allegiance to the new rulers and continued to pay taxes to the new government. The British gave them more land, but they felt embarrassed over the years when someone told them that their wealth was the result of their grandfathers licking their English masters' boots. The Sherwanis of Birehra insisted that they had been landowners even before the arrival of the British. They claimed that the great Mughal emperor, Akbar, had awarded the estate 400 years back. One of them was Sherwani Sahib's ancestor, who founded Birehra and hired the local Hindu population to work on his land. As time passed, some workers adopted their employers' religion to elevate their social status and receive preferential treatment.

As the estate passed from generation to generation, it was divided and subdivided among the descendants. Its size diminished with each inheritance until it was not enough to sustain their families. Some of them sold their land and moved to the city, but Sherwani Sahib was not one of them. At home, his mother, who was addressed as Khanum-a title reserved for a Pathan woman of noble descent-was in charge, and he followed her every command like any obedient son. Khanum was a dignified woman with an aristocratic demeanour. Even though she was mild-mannered, her servants and maids could not raise their eyes while speaking to her. The only exception was Bibi, who was a few years older than Khanum, took the liberty to advise her, or even scold her, taking advantage of her seniority.

Life was good, and Sherwani Sahib did not find much to complain about, except that he was childless after ten years of marriage. Khanum considered it beneath her dignity to suggest to her son that he get a second wife. She continued pretending that she had submitted to the will of God and never complained about her son being without an heir. At last, she smiled at the sight of her daughter-in-law vomiting in the morning. She gathered the expectant mother into her arms and said a prayer for a safe pregnancy as she kissed her on the forehead.

***

The moment had finally arrived. The news went out that a servant was on the way to summon the midwife from the neighbouring village. Those who had gathered in front of Sherwani Sahib's house to congratulate him were treated with sweetmeats and ice-cold sugared water with rose extract. However, the mood inside the house became sombre when it was found that, even though the baby was healthy, something had gone wrong with the delivery. The mother had suffered a postpartum hemorrhage. The midwife kept asking for more rags and old shirts to soak up the blood. She put bricks under the bedposts to lower the head, but the bleeding continued until the new mother turned pale and died quietly. The celebration suddenly turned into lamentation as the sad news made it out of the house.

Sherwani Sahib got busy arranging for the burial. He moved like a robot, giving instructions and embracing people as they gathered at his house for condolences. There was not a single tear in his eyes. He held off mourning for later. Khanum was busy, ensuring that the maids had laid out enough chairs for the women coming in to offer condolences.

After Sherwani Sahib returned from the graveyard, he entered the house and saw his newborn son for the first time. The motherless baby was sucking the end of a wick floating in sugared water but would eventually need feeding. Reluctantly, the midwife told the family that she had delivered another baby that week, but it was in the home of a woodchopper. "Maybe that woman can nurse both babies."

Khanum was aghast at the prospect of a Hindu woman of the untouchable caste, nursing her grandson. "Impossible! Unheard of!" she screamed.

"Let us calm down, Mother." Her son put his hands on her shoulders and asked her to sit down. According to a saying, when you are angry, you should sit down if you are standing and lie down if you are sitting. That will bring the anger down.

"I cannot see my grandson's lips touching the bosom of an untouchable," she whispered as if she were talking to herself.

"A Bedouin woman nursed even the Prophet," Sherwani Sahib reminded her.

"But she was not untouchable."

"Show me where it says that someone can be untouchable." Her son tried to keep his voice down to avoid sounding disrespectful to his mother.

"We are Pathans of noble caste," she replied. "What will people say?"

Sherwani Sahib did not respond. He wanted to give her time to cool down enough so that she could reason.

Khanum walked out of the room and went straight to the stairs leading to the roof. It was an open rooftop, with a low brick fence around it. She could see people working in fields around the outskirts of the village. A goatherd boy was chasing goats that had separated from his herd. He ran from side to side, moving his stick up and down while trying to bring the stray goats back in. Khanum spotted a playful field spaniel terrorizing a donkey. The dog ran around the donkey and barked while pretending to leap at it. Occasionally he ran away from the donkey and then turned back to leap at it. The donkey was tied securely to a post under a tree and jumped every time the dog came closer. It brayed bitterly, perhaps to draw its master's attention.

Khanum was absorbed in the view until she remembered why she was there. She had set up a roof garden with fragrant flowers, which she took care of diligently. Whenever she was under stress, she came upstairs and got busy, cleaning dried leaves and removing dead flowers. There was a row of flowerpots with rose, jasmine, magnolia, freesia, lily, and hyacinth along the fence. As the sun descended, a calm, gentle breeze started blowing and kissed the flowers before caressing her cheeks. She took a deep breath to absorb the sweet smell of roses. Khanum had associated a flavour with the fragrance of every flower. Jasmine was gently sour, magnolia was a bit astringent, and hyacinth reminded her of vanilla. Drowned in deep thought, she did not notice that the flowers were in full bloom, and their fragrance had filled the air, dancing wildly around her.

She got up and started pacing back and forth, rubbing her left cheekbone periodically. It was a sign that she was under stress. Whenever she was anxious, the left side of her face became numb, and she rubbed it repeatedly. She thought of her son, who was going through his grief. She remembered her daughter-in-law, who was like a daughter to her and had been buried earlier that day. *From Him, we come, and to Him, we shall return*, she thought. She had wept many a time in her life but had never wailed, as she believed that it was uncouth to scream uncontrollably. At that moment, however, she felt like crying bitterly. Then she thought of the little gift her daughter-in-law had left for her-her first and perhaps the last grandson. According to the pedigree of Sherwani Sahib, starting seven generations back, each generation was blessed with only one male child. As she walked along a row of flowerpots, she thought of her dilemma.

My grandson being fed the milk of an untouchable woman!

Who will believe that?

Our blood has stayed pure from the beginning!

What will people say? A child of nobility raised on the milk of an untouchable woman?

But what is the alternative?

Maybe it is a test for me.

She felt torn by the fierce battle raging in her mind. What makes someone untouchable? That was what her son was asking her, but she had no answer.

We are Indians, and that is the way it is.

What will the Brahmins of Nagla think? They are our friends.

Will our friends even want to touch my grandson?

Windmills were churning in her head, or was it her heart pounding in her ears? *Whoosh, whoosh, whoosh*-the noise inside her was maddening. She battled with question after question until she was exhausted. Finally, she gave up. "No, my son is right! There is no such thing as untouchability; no human can be untouchable!" She did not realize that she had said it out loud; her plants had heard her, the flowers had heard her, and the air around her had undoubtedly heard her. She walked down the stairs, and as she reached the bottom, she found herself composed. She turned to the midwife, who was preparing to leave. "Go ahead and tell the woodchopper that e will reward his family generously."

***

When the woodchopper's wife entered Sherwani Sahib's home, holding her baby in her lap, her face covered with the edge of her shawl, she sat down on the floor as it was customary for people of the lower caste. Khanum came forward and stood in front of her, looking down at her and the baby. "You can raise your veil," said Khanum.

The woman pulled up her shawl to uncover her face but kept looking down. She was a dark-skinned young woman with an innocent face. A tiny mole on the side of her chin made her look more attractive, despite the few smallpox spots on her face.

"What is your name?" asked Khanum.

"Harpirya," replied the woman. Her lips quivered as she answered.

"What have you named your son?"

"Bhagwan Das."

"Servant of God!" Khanum translated it. "It is a good name. I am sure your child will be true to his name when he grows up."

Harpirya did not respond. She kept wrapping and unwrapping the corner of her shawl around her finger just to keep herself occupied.

"You don't have to be shy in front of me. You can look at me," said Khanum with a smile.

Harpirya looked up but could not stand Khanum's gaze. She lowered her eyes again.

Khanum's heart softened as she watched the innocent girl sitting on the floor in front of her. She did not look old enough to be a mother.

"You should have no fear in this house," said Khanum. "You will be part of this family and treated with respect."

Harpirya nodded gently without raising her eyes.

"Let me look at your baby." Khanum came forward and looked down as Harpirya moved her shawl. The baby squirmed with his eyes closed.

"You have a beautiful child."

Harpirya's lips quivered.

"We are grateful that you have agreed to share your milk with a motherless child." Khanum had dropped her guard. Her pride had given way to humility. She could not have ever foreseen that she would have to treat an untouchable woman as her equal. When she saw Bibi arriving there with the baby, she got up with a start and walked back toward the stairs leading to the rooftop. She was ready to engage in new battles with her demons.

Harpirya nursed Khansab for one year. When he and Bhagwan Das crawled together and learned to snatch toys from each other, Khanum watched them, sometimes with disgust and sometimes with wonder. Had God played a joke on her? A woodchopper's son had become the milk brother of her grandson, one born in the hut of a Hindu from the untouchable caste, and the other in the home of a Pathan of noble caste. Was it God's way to humiliate her for her pride?

***

Twenty years had gone by in a flash. While the flames of World War I engulfed Europe and its colonies, Sherwani Sahib was running a campaign to recruit young men to go to the front. He had offered his own son's services to show his loyalty to the government of His Majesty in England. As Khansab was preparing to leave for Mesopotamia, Sherwani Sahib suddenly died of a heart attack and Khansab was excused from army duty. He had to take over the affairs of his land while his peers were still boys. Khanum was still in charge at home. At eighty-two, she showed no sign of cognitive decline. Although she had gained some weight over the years, being a tall woman, she did not appear fat. No one noticed the wrinkles on her face since they could not see beyond her piercing blue eyes. Even when she reprimanded her servants, her lips seemed to smile. Her face reminded Khansab of a serene lake, with still waters, and he looked at her with affection, listening to her words of wisdom.

Bhagwan Das grew up to be a proud man. Khansab always treated him like a brother. Whenever he tried to persuade him to come and work with him, Bhagwan Das declined the offer with a smile. "I am just a poor woodchopper, and know nothing about crops and harvests," said Bhagwan Das. He spent the day in the forest, cutting down trees and chopping them into pieces. In the evening, he loaded wood on the donkey and brought it to his little hut, where he and his wife, Parvati, lived. He piled the stock at the hut's back, leaving it to dry under the sun for several days. There was not much sun in those days, as the monsoon season had started. Whenever Parvati saw the first raindrop, she rushed outside to cover her firewood stock with a tarp sheet. No matter how careful she was, water seeped down through holes in the old tarp. Women tried to light damp firewood in their kitchens, but all they got was a cloud of black smoke in their eyes. They cursed Bhagwan Das as they wiped their watery eyes. "Why can't he supply dry wood?" they complained to one another.

"But then, what can the poor woodchopper do?" someone would ask. "Everything is wet these days."

 Everyone praised Bhagwan Das for his humility, honesty, and good humour. It was not his fault if the firewood was damp. He had been chopping wood since he was a little boy and had started accompanying his father into the forest. After his father died, he had to work hard since he was the only one supplying firewood to the homes of wealthy families who did not burn cow dung in their kitchens. Even though he had been married for only a year, the women in the village had started talking about him not becoming a father. They speculated that Parvati was barren, but those sympathetic to her were confident that her husband was impotent. Older women, experienced in those matters, never missed an opportunity to pass a word or two of advice to her.

"Why don't you grind some turmeric with an equal weight of cinnamon and take a pinch every night before you go to bed?"

"Try approaching your man on a night when a new moon falls on a Thursday!"

"Maybe the fault is with your man. Give him a glass of goat's milk with seven almonds every day!"

Parvati was tired of their advice and sarcasm. Was it any of their business if she was not getting pregnant? If they had their way, they would want a bride to deliver the moment she stepped into her in-laws' home.

Then came the day when she realized that she was expecting her first baby. It was the happiest day of her life. She conveyed the news to Bhagwan Das as he was preparing to leave for the forest. He hugged her passionately. "If it is a boy, we will name him *Phagna*," he said. "You know, I had an uncle, whose name was Phagna. He was the wisest man in Birehra."

Parvati looked at him affectionately, softly saying his name, as she always did, since he was like a god to her. "Bhagwan."

She said good-bye to him as he left, not realizing that it would be the last time she would see him.

***

It was a foggy day, and water was still trickling down the trees. Every gust of wind brought down more water, as leaves quivered in the breeze. Bhagwan Das looked at the log left from the tree he had cut down the previous day. It would take him until the evening to finish it.

As the day passed, he kept thinking about what Parvati had told him in the morning. Bhagwan Das was the only child of his parents. He had no memory of his mother since she had died when he was only two years old. His father, who had raised him like a mother, died when Bhagwan Das was thirteen. That was the first time he had taken his father's axe and gone alone into the woods. He never had a younger brother or sister to care for. Now a child was coming into his life. *When he grows up, I will bring him into the forest and show him how to get a tree down.*

He was thrilled that day. The thought of becoming a father thrilled him. He wanted to run back to his hut and embrace Parvati. As he threw a piece of wood on the pile, he put his axe down and lifted a corner of his dhoti to wipe his face. Streaks of sweat flowed all over his body. He sat down under a tree to catch his breath. He smiled when his thoughts carried him forward in time to when he would be holding his baby. *What if Parvati dies during childbirth?* Suddenly his smile vanished, and he felt pressure in his throat as he swallowed. Feeling that he was not fair to himself, he shrugged off the thought. *Is it a sin to be happy?* The smile came back. He noticed a continuous whirring sound all around him. He looked up to spot the birds singing in unison, but he could not see any of them. There must have been thousands of tiny birds in those thick trees, and they had managed to camouflage themselves too well. As they stopped singing, the birds in the neighbouring trees picked up and whirred. Then the birds in trees farther from them started. It was as if waves of bird-calls were passing over him. *How do they know when to start and stop? Are they competing with each other?* He picked up his axe and got back to work. The recess was over.

It was mid-afternoon when he decided to quit work and go home. It was getting foggier, and he would find it difficult to get out of the forest if the visibility got worse. He wanted to get back soon and surprise Parvati. As he chopped the last log and threw its pieces on the pile of wood he had gathered that day, he heard a growling noise and looked back. He was shocked to see that a wild boar was chasing his donkey. As he ran to scare the boar away, making noise and holding his axe high in the air, the boar turned back and attacked him. Before he could hit the animal, it tore off a piece of flesh from his thigh. He dropped the axe and tried to fight with his bare hands but to no avail. The boar kept attacking him and tearing the flesh off his body until he fell to the ground and lost consciousness. His eyes were closed, and his body was motionless. *We will call him Phagna!* Did he say that, or was he hallucinating? No, that was not a hallucination. He could see Parvati standing in front of him, and he was talking to her. *Why does she not reply?* She just stood there staring at him. *Parvati, why don't you say something? Parvati, is that you?* The vision was gone, and it was dark all around. Then suddenly, another flash came. *She is not Parvati. Who is she? I have seen her somewhere. I know. That is my mother. She has always visited me in my dreams. Mataji, we will call him Phagna.*

He lay there bleeding for several hours. He kept getting flashes of visions while the pool of blood around him congealed slowly, and then the images faded until there was total darkness around him. Several vultures encircled overhead, and their number grew as he lay motionless on the ground, devoid of pain.

***

As the sun started to set behind distant fields, Parvati stood at the door, waiting for her husband. He was usually back long before it got dark in the forest. She kept staring into the distance. She would soon be able to spot Bhagwan Das and his donkey entering the village. Suddenly she heard the call for evening prayer in the mosque, which meant that the sun had already set. *That is odd; Bhagwan has never been this late,* she said to herself. As she stood there, Kareem, the blacksmith, passed by. He felt that it was not proper for a young woman to stand at the door aimlessly. "Who are you waiting for, Parvati? Where is Bhagwan Das?"

"I don't know, Chacha. He is not back from the forest yet." She felt stiffness in her throat as she spoke. She called him *Chacha* since he was like an uncle to her.

"What do you mean he is not back?" Kareem asked impatiently. "He should have been back before sunset."

"I am not sure. Bhagwan has never been this late."

"I hope he didn't lose his way in the fog."

The news spread fast. Soon the entire village knew that Bhagwan Das was missing. People started gathering in front of his hut.

Parvati watched them quietly. Everyone offered a possible explanation and a suggestion. Finally, they agreed that some men should go into the forest. Nobody had ever dared enter the woods at night. There was no problem confronting wild animals, but who would risk facing ghosts and witches! There were stories of strange happenings in the woods, passed down from generation to generation. "When my father was still a boy," said Kaalia, the potter, "he saw a headless man on the edge of the forest one evening as he was returning from a trip to the city!" They all turned their faces to him.

"He called my father's name and asked him for a cigarette! My father looked at him, and every hair on his body stood up! He ran into the village as fast as a bull! My grandmother tells us that, by the time he entered the house, he was burning with fever." They listened to his story with their mouths wide open. "My father was unconscious for three days, and his body was so hot that you could roast chickpeas on it! He kept mumbling only one word: *Sarkataa! Sarkataa!* Finally, my mother called a pundit from the temple to exorcise the evil spirit."

"You are right!" someone said. "Sarkataas exist. They are headless men who cast an evil spell on you!"

"Many people have seen a Sarkataa on the edge of the forest. He always asks for a cigarette!" Mitthu, the sweeper, confirmed Kaalia's story.

"Ghosts or no ghosts," said Kareem. "Bhagwan Das is missing, and we must go look for him."

Someone remarked, "But why don't we wait until the morning?"

"We have to go now. I need some courageous boys. Prove to me that you were fed on your mother's milk; otherwise, I will know that you ere raised on the milk of a donkey's mother!"

Soon he had a dozen volunteers who wanted to prove to Kareem that, indeed, they were raised on their mothers' milk. They took several bamboo stalks, wrapped old rags at one end and soaked them with slow-burning oil to serve as torches. They took sticks, spears, and swords in case they encountered any wild animals. As they departed, Kareem looked back and told Parvati not to worry. "Wherever he is hiding, we will find him," he assured her. Parvati stood there without uttering a word. Several women had gathered to console her. Kareem and his team disappeared in the thick fog as they left.

When they reached the outskirts of the forest, they lit their torches. Kareem gathered them at one spot. There were twelve men in all, and there were five torches. He instructed those who did not have light to stay close to those who carried torches. The fog was so thick that one hand could not see the other. As they moved on, the level of their frustration grew. It was no use. They knew that, even on a clear day in the jungle, the daylight is always subdued and shadowy, but then it vanishes in an instant, as the sun comes down, being replaced by pitch darkness. It seemed as if the night of the jungle had penetrated every artery of the universe. Jungle noises from unseen bugs, lizards, and birds filled the air. The fog had made it worse, and even their torches did not help. They heard voices and felt motion all around them but could not see even their feet. The occasional hiss of a snake or the hoot of an owl, punctuated by the continuous chirping of crickets and croaking of frogs, sent chills down everyone's spine. It was too dangerous. They knew that the forest was full of snakes and scorpions. Kareem decided to abandon the search and return to the village. It would be wise to wait until the morning after all, as someone had suggested earlier.

When they reached the village, Kareem saw that Parvati still stood at the door. He assured her that Bhagwan Das must be okay. "We know that he is a good man, and no harm can come to him."

"I know that, Chacha, but I can't get rid of evil thoughts."

"Why don't you go in and get some sleep?"

"How can I sleep when I know that Bhagwan is out there, somewhere in the woods, and I don't know what has happened to him?"

"Don't worry. I'll send your aunt to sleep here so that you don't feel lonely."

Kareem left, but Parvati kept standing at the door. She kept staring at the ever-thickening fog, hoping that Bhagwan Das would suddenly appear out of it.

***

Kareem woke up as usual with the first crow of the rooster at dawn. He got up from his rope bed and noticed that the fog had lifted during the night. The few stars left in the sky were struggling to keep shining but to no avail. Soon, they would extinguish one by one, as the sky prepared itself for sunrise. He looked at the colossal neem tree, just outside the wall, which had crept upon his courtyard. He could spot several early birds chirping as they moved between branches. The morning would pass, and the day would get warmer until everything was baking under the blazing sun by midday. The cool shade of the neem tree would provide relief from the heat at that time. Kareem and his wife, Kareeman - children in the neighbourhood were not sure if that was her real name or called her by that name because she was Kareem's wife - used to move their cots under the tree for their afternoon nap.

He reached the wooden stand that held the earthen water pitcher. The stand was always wet and had developed mildew around the circular hole on which the pitcher rested. An old enamel plate served as a lid on the pitcher's mouth, and a brass tumbler kept upside down on top of the cover. A garland of jasmine flowers, which Kareeman had put around the pitcher several days ago, was still there. Water always tasted fresh and fragrant if the pitcher was decorated with jasmine. Even though the flowers were dead, the moisture around them still maintained a faint fragrance. He held the tumbler in his fingers and picked up the lid with the other hand. He dipped the tumbler into the pitcher up to his wrist to fill it with water and replaced the cover after he pulled the tumbler out. He rinsed his mouth, massaged his teeth with his index finger, splashed several handfuls on his face, and drank the rest of it. He took another tumblerful and drank some more water. According to an old saying, a tumbler of water in the morning was a cure for a thousand ailments. He poured the remaining water back into the pitcher before replacing the lid. He was now ready to go out.

Even though Kareem knew very little about religion or things other than moulding iron, he was nevertheless religious. He usually went to the mosque as soon as he woke up at dawn and prayed with the other men; he used to stand up and bow and prostrate with everyone but did not know what to say while praying. Kareem just moved his lips as the others did. By the time he returned from the mosque, Kareeman would have a bowl of buttermilk with a big loaf of cornbread ready for him. That was his usual breakfast. This morning though, Kareeman was not there. She had stayed with Parvati for the night. He had no time to go to the mosque or to have breakfast.

As Kareem approached Bhagwan Das' hut, he saw a silhouette at the door. It was still dark, and he could not see it very well; as he came nearer, he knew that it was Parvati. "Were you standing here all night?" he asked her. Parvati did not reply. She kept staring into the darkness with empty eyes. Just then, Kareeman appeared from behind her and approached the door. "I had sent you here to take care of this poor girl, but you slept like a log all night while she stood here at the door!" Kareem yelled at his wife.

With sleep still in her eyes, she put her hand on Parvati's shoulder. "I can swear that I had tucked her in, but I don't know when she got up."

"How could she sleep? You snore so loud that even the angels in heaven thrust their fingers in their ears while you are sleeping."

As volunteers gathered, Kareem talked about the strategy to go into the woods and resume their search. While they waited for the rest of the volunteers, people stopped there to find out if Bhagwan Das was back. Kareem told them that he was still missing and said they were about to go looking for him. Some of them stayed to help and assured Parvati that everything would be fine. It was a clear morning, and it had already started getting hot as the sun came up. They decided to get started before it was too hot.

They spread themselves through the forest as they made their way through thick bush. They called Bhagwan Das' name, hoping that he would respond, but all they heard was the fluttering of birds in the trees as they flew away or the rustling sound in the grass as animals ran for refuge. Almost three-quarters of the morning had passed, and there was still no sign of Bhagwan Das anywhere. Then someone called out to Kareem. He stood still to establish the direction and heard his name again. He sped through the bush with the others around him. Everyone was running toward that voice. He arrived at an empty spot, with no trees, and saw some men who had already gathered there. They spoke in whispers that sounded like bees. He could not understand what they were looking at. He pushed them aside as he came to the front. It was a horrible sight. He saw a carcass lying there in a pool of dried blood and shreds of clothing scattered all over the area. There was hardly any flesh left on the body. Flies and maggots churned inside the skeleton to devour whatever flesh was left sticking to the bones. Kareem took a corner of his shoulder cloth and put it on his nose as he felt like vomiting. It was Bhagwan Das for sure. They recognized his watch, still wrapped around the bones of his wrist. He had bought it a few years back when he had gone to the city. He was one of the few people in Birehra who could tell time. His axe lay nearby, and they could see his donkey standing quietly under a tree, with his head hanging low as if he were mourning the death of his master. A pile of firewood was neatly placed near the huge log, which he could still chop into many more piles. Several vultures sat in a row on the hill nearby. They flew away when someone picked up a stone and threw it at them. There was a hush in the air as people stared at the carcass without saying a word. "Bhagwan Das was a good man," Kareem said, finally breaking the silence.

"At least I never saw him being angry at anyone," someone remarked.

"It was only yesterday or was it the day before, that he was joking about my fat belly. He always called me *Ganesh* and asked me where my mouse was!" said Ram. He was referring to Ganesh, the Hindu elephant god of good fortune, who rode a mouse.

"They say that the good die young, but why do they have to die such a painful death?"

"Who knows? Only He understands His secrets," said Kareem, pointing his finger upward. "We have to go back and start making arrangements."

People had already started returning to the village to convey the news. Kareem asked some of them to stay there until he came back to prepare for the funeral. As he arrived, Parvati still stood at the door, staring far, far away. Her eyes were dry, and there was no expression on her face. Kareeman stood with her arm clenched around Parvati's waist. Kareem came forward and put his hand on Parvati's head. "May you have the strength to spend your life with courage!" He wanted to say something more, but the words were caught in his throat.

Khansab was overcome with grief at the death of Bhagwan Das and wept like a child. Considering the circumstances in which Bhagwan Das had died, no one was allowed to see his face. What was there to see, except cheekbones and empty eye-sockets? The body was wrapped from head to toe in a white shroud and carried directly from the forest to the cremation ground. It was all over by the time the sun started descending on the horizon. No ploughs moved in the fields, and no buffaloes were bathed that day.

By the time the men returned from the cremation, it was dark. They gathered for the evening meal and sat on the ground, in circles, according to their castes and creeds. Banana leaves were spread in front of them; volunteers put down rice mounds and poured curried lentils on the top. There was so much food that no one in the village was left half-fed that evening. They talked about Bhagwan Das in low voices for a while and remembered what a good man he was until someone mentioned his wit and good humour. The mood became jubilant again. After all, he was a good man, and he must be happy wherever he was!

***

Parvati spent the rest of her pregnancy without shedding a tear. She welcomed all the attention she received from women in the neighbourhood, but her lips were sealed. Kareeman prodded her to answer some questions but did not get much response from her.

"Does the baby kick inside your tummy?"

"You don't feel sick in the morning anymore. Do you?"

"Do you want me to make some pickles for you?"

All Kareeman got was a nod or an occasional yes or no. Eventually, she started getting agitated. "I know that Bhagwan Das was like a god to you," she said. "But this is life. When the time comes for one to go, you cannot stop him, but life must go on. You have to take care of yourself so that you can take care of your baby.”

“Yes, Kareeman Khala,” was the brief response from Parvati.

Finally, the day came when Kareeman laid a thick layer of dirt under the cot to collect blood droppings and brought in a bag of rags, which she had been collecting all those days. Parvati’s labour was getting intense, and she tightened her jaws with every contraction. Several older women entered the hut to help with the delivery, as men gathered in front of the hut. They talked about the hard times that Parvati had gone through after her husband’s death. “Bhagwan Das was a good man,” someone remarked.

“I wish he were alive today to raise his child.”

“They say that good men have short lives.”

“I am sure he must be happy and comfortable wherever he is.”

Parvati went through the childbirth without a scream or a whimper. Her lips were shut, and her jaws were tight as she slipped into unconsciousness until Kareeman awakened her. “Here! It’s a boy,” she said, as she lowered the bundle in front of Parvati, who kept staring at it in a daze and then broke into sobs that grew into wails. An ocean of tears gushed through her eyes. It seemed that she had been saving all her tears for that day.

“He looks just like his father,” said Kareeman.

Parvati looked at the baby, with its dark, shiny skin, high forehead, bushy eyebrows, and charcoal black hair. She thought she was looking at Bhagwan Das. Tears started flowing again as Kareeman put the baby close to Parvati. “What will you call your son?” asked Kareeman.

“We will call him Phagna,” she replied as she closed her eyes and fell asleep.

Khansab made sure that Parvati received her provisions regularly.

He could have easily found someone from her caste to marry her and take care of the baby, but she had refused to remarry. She preferred to raise the only gift that her husband had left for her alone. It was not easy for her to live on her own and raise her child. She was still young, and the drooling eyes of men chased her whenever she went out to get water from the well, but they stayed away from her due to the fear of Khansab's wrath!

At first, she felt uncomfortable about getting undeserved attention from Khansab. She knew that he did not have any ill intentions. No one had ever questioned his integrity, but you never knew when a decent man could succumb to temptation. *No, the question does not arise;* she argued with herself. *Khansab is of noble caste, and I am nobody.*

But then, one could not stop foul mouths from spreading rumours.

She would not have tolerated it if people had started casting doubts on Khansab's integrity. Finally, she decided to take a bold step and block every trail leading to suspicion.

The Hindu festival of *Raksha Bandhan* was a week away. That was the event when a sister tied a *rakhi*-a holy thread-around the wrist of her brother to show her love to him, and in return, he showered her with gifts and took a vow to take care of her. It was unnecessary for a man and a woman to be siblings by birth; a woman could adopt any male as a brother by tying a rakhi around his wrist. The adopted brother didn't need to be a Hindu, either. It is said that when the Nawab of Gujrat threatened the Rani of Chittorgarh in the sixteenth century, she had sent a rakhi to the Mughal emperor Humayun, who was a Muslim. The emperor came with his armies immediately to rescue her from the invader, a fellow Muslim.

Parvati came to Khansab's place and told his wife that she intended to tie a rakhi around Khansab's wrist. "So why are you telling me that, Parvati," she asked with a smile. "Are you looking for my approval?”

“No, it is just that I am scared of Khansab,” replied Parvati.

“Why are you scared? You are only making him your brother!”

“It is just that I have never talked to him before. I don’t know how he will treat me.”

“I am sure he will appreciate it.”

The following week, Parvati bought a secure future for herself and her son by tying a string around Khansab’s wrist. In return, he gave her a new sari and fifty-one rupees as a gift.

The Rainmaker

An aeroplane used to fly over Birehra every Thursday afternoon when the length of one's shadow was exactly twice his height. The peasants called it *cheel gaadi*-the eagle cart. They could not believe it when Irshad, who worked in Khansab's stables, pointed to the little thing high up in the sky and told them that people were sitting in it. "How can people sit in such a small thing?" asked old Sharfu, the shoemaker.

"They must be very tiny people," someone laughed.

"No, it just looks small," explained Irshad. "But it becomes big as it comes down."

Everyone was perplexed. There was no doubt that Irshad was an educated boy. He had read four Urdu primer books and coached by his uncle, who lived in the city and regularly visited the village. But no matter how intelligent Irshad was, it did not give him the right to consider other people stupid. Old Sharfu was especially offended. He showed his displeasure by taking his cap off and pointing to his hair.

"Do you think this hair has turned grey in the sunshine?"

"What did I say, Chacha?" Irshad asked him apologetically.

"How can something so small suddenly become big when it comes down?"

"I meant that it just looks small since it is so far. Things always look small when they are at a distance."

"Oh, yes! You think you are a wise man?" Sharfu pointed to his grey hair again. "Wisdom does not come from reading books. Wisdom comes through age."

"But Chacha ... God forbid, I am not claiming that I am wiser than you."

Nobody in the crowd believed Irshad. They all thought he was making fools of them. When Irshad apologized to Sharfu, someone suggested ignoring the whole conversation. Sharfu should not have been so upset, anyway. But then, he was always rash.

After that day, Irshad showed extra courtesy to Sharfu whenever he came face to face with him, but Sharfu always gave him the cold shoulder. It continued until the day a farmer working in the field yelled, "*Cheel gaadi aarahi hai!*" Farmers used to announce approaching hurricanes, and other farmers in neighbouring fields repeated the announcement until the word reached the village minutes before the storm approached. It gave them enough time to call the children home, escort the chickens to their coops, tie up the cattle in cowsheds, and close their doors. But this announcement was puzzling. Why was someone announcing that an aeroplane was approaching? Even though the farmers in neighbouring fields could not interpret the message, they repeated it anyway, and other farmers followed suit until the news reached the village. People were confused and started talking about it. What was the big deal if an aeroplane was coming? It passed through the village every Thursday. "Ah! But today is only Wednesday," someone said.

"Still ... who cares if an aeroplane is coming?"

Confusion grew as they each offered their explanation. There were as many explanations as there were mouths until a loud roaring noise was heard, and a massive object appeared in the sky. It was gigantic, compared to those tiny objects flying high in the sky. One could even see windows on the two sides of its belly. "So that is where the passengers are sitting, and probably looking down at the village," someone said.

People were scared. Everyone thought that it was about to fall. Farmers working in the fields started running back and forth for cover; children who were still playing outside ran into their homes, and their mothers closed the doors. The cattle tore off their leashes and started running amok through the streets. Old Sharfu looked at it with awe, and his cap fell as he staggered to maintain his balance. People took a sigh of relief when the plane left and disappeared on the horizon. It took them a while before they could round up all the cows and buffaloes and tie them back to their posts. Sharfu confessed that Irshad had been right all along when he said that the eagle cart is much larger than it looks from the ground.

For many months, people talked about their experience of seeing the giant aeroplane. Whenever a visitor came from a neighbouring town, people told him about the eagle cart, which had almost fallen upon the village.

***

Khansab had built his current *haveli* after giving away his previous "mansion" to one of his cousins, Noor Khan, who had returned to the village after working for several years in the city. He was a matriculant from Aligarh and did not have any interest in farming. As such, he had gone to the city and took a job as a clerk, but eventually missed the village's fresh air and returned to rural life.

Many of Khansab's relatives, who abhorred western ways and considered the English to be filthy people, who did not even take water into the lavatory, believed that everything from the West was un-Islamic. They did not want to pollute the minds of their children by teaching them English.

"Today you start teaching them English, and tomorrow they will start saying 'good morning' and 'good evening' instead of '*Salaam Alekum*' and '*Adab Arz.*'"

Those families acquired the services of renowned scholars and poets to educate their children. They came to the village and lived with the family for several years, teaching calligraphy, language, and poetry to boys, who learned Urdu and Persian and studied philosophy and poetry of great Islamic thinkers and poets. Brahmin teachers, who were good with numbers, were also hired to teach arithmetic and accounting. Those were important for understanding the matters of revenues and taxes.

Education was important for girls, too. After they had learned to read the Qur'an, their mothers gave them a copy of *The Heavenly Ornament*. It was a ten-volume encyclopedia for women, which covered everything a woman was supposed to learn to be an obedient wife and a good mother. There was hardly any topic relevant to women's issues that were not covered by the book. It had chapters on cooking, sewing, soap-making, letter writing, home remedies for common ailments, theological matters, gynaecological problems, and stories of pious women like Hagar and the Virgin Mary. What else would a woman need to know? It was the prime source for educating a girl about adult matters and explained everything in detail.

When a girl started her monthly periods, her mother knew that the daughter would have several questions on her mind; but mothers were too shy to talk about adult matters. Instead, they quietly handed their daughters a copy of *The Heavenly Ornament*. Growing boys did not miss any opportunity to lay their hands on the book when no one looked. Those were the days when the boys of Birehra lost their adolescence while sneaking through the pages of *The Heavenly Ornament*.

There was no school in Birehra for children of Muslims or Hindus of the working class. There was no need for one. Why would someone send his children to school anyway? Who could be a better teacher for the son of a blacksmith than his father, who took the son as an apprentice at an early age and taught him the art of flattening, bending, and moulding red-hot iron? The son would grow up to be a blacksmith. Education was supposed to be for city folk, who had to become postmen, policemen, bookkeepers, and teachers.

Khansab's cousin Noor Khan was in favour of providing western education to his children. He sent his two sons and a daughter to Aligarh, where they lived in the boarding school and eventually got into the university. He agreed with Sir Syed that the only way Indian Muslims could drive the British out of India was to learn their ways and understand their language. When Sir Syed set up the university in Aligarh to provide modern education to Muslims, Noor Khan's father, who owned some land in Aligarh, donated it for building the campus. Following in his father's footsteps, Noor Khan persuaded other relatives to support the Aligarh movement, and some of them joined him. Boys who graduated from Aligarh found jobs in cities and never came back to live in the village.

Khansab was not a prominent landowner, but he was still very influential in the area and known for his generosity and flamboyance. He was a friend of friends, as the expression went. It was understood that any visitor in the village would be his guest. Everyone called him Khan Sahib out of respect, but most people had abbreviated *Khan Sahib* to *Khansab* with the nasal "en" for pronunciation ease. Whenever there was a quarrel among people, they came to him to settle the issue, and he rebuked the party at fault.

There were scores of servants who worked on his land and around the house. Their allegiance had been with the family for several generations since their fathers and grandfathers had also toiled in those fields. Although they were not paid in cash, their families were looked after at harvest time. When the crop was cut and thrashed, the grain was loaded on bullock carts, taken to Aligarh and sold in the market. The carriages came back loaded with cloth, which was dumped in piles in Khansab's courtyard. All the tailors in Birehra came with their sewing machines and spent a whole month measuring, cutting, sewing, and stitching. The village people gathered there every day to deliver their clothes: orange and red skirts and *dupattas* for women and white dhotis and kurtas for men. There were enough clothes for members of every family for the whole year.

As the land passed from generation to generation, the Sherwanis ensured that the wealth stayed within the family, and one way to do so was to marry strictly from within the tribe. A significant factor in choosing a bride was how much land her family-owned. The first choice was always a first cousin, and they would look outside only if they could not find a match, suitable or not so suitable, among close relatives.

It was said that Khansab was the most eligible bachelor in his youth and was eyed by the father of every girl of a marriageable age among his relatives. A distant relative who wanted Khansab to marry his daughter dropped hints to other relatives that they persuade Khansab's grandmother to send the proposal. When he could not arrange the marriage, he turned against Khansab's family and hired a fakir who practised black magic! The fakir pronounced a curse on Khansab and condemned him to remain childless.

After his father's death, Khansab was responsible for making his own decisions and did not succumb to his coaxing relatives. When he turned twenty, his grandmother chose a distant cousin to be his wife, but she died during her sixth baby's birth. None of her earlier children had survived. By the time they were a year old, they had developed *sookha*, a disease that stunted their growth. No matter how much they were fed, they suffered from malnutrition until they were reduced to mere skeletons, and their bodies could no longer support life.

Khanum believed that her grandson was under the influence of the curse and would never have an heir. The women in Birehra advised her to pray to Sufi saints to break the spell. She told Khansab that she planned to visit the shrine of Khwaja Baba in Ajmer. He did not believe in curses and spells but did not argue with his grandmother. When she returned from her pilgrimage, she was convinced that her grandson had been cured and started looking for another girl for him.

Unaware that history was about to repeat itself, Khansab was thirty years old when his grandmother persuaded him to remarry. As soon as Khanum declared that she was looking for a bride for her grandson, the news spread like forest fire among the Sherwanis, and she started receiving referrals from relatives. She went from village to village, visiting the homes of prospective girls, but kept rejecting every girl she interviewed; some were too short, some too tall, some lacked etiquette, and some did not possess adequate culinary skills; every girl had some flaw. Finally, she met a girl who delighted her. When Khanum looked at her, she thought of the full moon: a shining face, majestic looks, and bright eyes bubbling with life. Khanum looked at her with a smile on her lips as the young woman bowed gently, touching her forehead with the tips of her long fingers to greet her guest. Her mother gestured to her to sit in the chair on the right side of Khanum.

"So, which flower are you?" Khanum asked her, and the girl was taken aback. Khanum could read a question in her eyes. "Your name is *Gulrukh*, which means flower face. So you must have a favourite flower."

"I have always found it difficult to make a choice," she answered hesitantly. "For beauty, I choose rose, and for fragrance, my choice is jasmine; then, I can choose lilies for innocence and marigold for being mischievous."

"Good answer," Khanum said, impressed by her boldness, wit and intellect. "You are all those, my dear."

Gulrukh blinked as she bowed gently. It was a subtle expression of her gratitude. Khanum had already made her decision to go ahead with the proposal.

***

The gentle flow of time seems to turn into a waterfall when one grows old. Khanum thought that ten years had gone past in a flash. She had spent the entire decade in a state of lingering hope, punctuated by disappointments. She learned soon that the curse was still looming over her grandson. None of his children from the second wife survived beyond the age of a few months. At last, when Khanum learned that Gulrukh was pregnant for the sixth time, she was extra careful and asked her to stay away from the kitchen. "You just take rest and take care of the baby and yourself," she told her.

At first, Gulrukh was bored of sitting in bed all day with her back resting against a large bolster, but then she found a project for herself. She decided to sew fitted covers for fifty rattan chairs, which Khansab had brought from the city. Each chair had a cylindrical base made of slanted columns of rattan. A large curved back clasped the occupant at the back and on the sides. She measured a chair carefully and estimated the yardage for all the fifty chairs. Once the fabric was brought, she started measuring, cutting, and sewing. She had used a brilliantly iridescent greenish-blue velvet, with eye-like spots that looked like peacock feathers. Each cover was hand-stitched with such perfection that the stitches followed one another like pearls in a necklace.

Khanum was satisfied. At least her granddaughter-in-law was not moving around, lifting heavy things, or sitting in the kitchen, where it was hot and uncomfortable. As the days passed, Gulrukh covered each chair until her pregnancy came to full term. She wanted to finish the job before the baby was born, but as her labour pains started, she was just finishing her last but one cover. The last chair stayed bare since she did not survive the childbirth, and neither did the baby. She was buried next to Khansab's first wife.

When Khansab returned from the graveyard, those who had been to the funeral came back with him and gathered on the patio. All the fifty chairs had been placed in a circle-all but one looking like peacocks with their feathers stretched. Khansab sat on the one without the cover, and it became his personal chair for all times to come. While the guests seated, reading chapters from the Qur'an to bless the departed soul, he sat quietly without shedding a tear. His heart was bleeding, but his eyes were dry. The mourners finished the entire Qur'an three times that evening.

***

Even though many years had passed, Khansab never sat in any chair with the peacock cover. His late wife's memory was too painful, and the wound in his heart was still raw. He decided to spend the rest of his life as a widower. His grandmother had passed away quietly in her sleep, and no one was left to influence his decisions. Eventually, the elders in the family persuaded him to get married for the third time. He offered many excuses but finally gave in to their pressure.

The women decided to call the new bride *Chhoti Begum* or "Junior Lady" since she was the youngest wife of Khansab. When she left her home to go with Khansab, he requested that her mother accompany them since no one else took care of his new mother-in-law. At first, she hesitated; it was beneath her dignity to be supported by her son-in-law, but Khansab insisted. "I have never experienced the love of my mother since she gave her life to bring me into this world," said Khansab. "If you agree to come with us, I will give you the same love and respect that I would have given to my mother."

Khansab pleaded with her until she agreed to spend the rest of her life at his home. He was true to his word and never raised his voice in front of her.

Although Chhoti Begum was related to Khansab, she had never met his previous wives; however, she was sensitive to the pain that he had gone through. She wanted to make him realize that she was there to share his sorrow. Every year, during the month of Ramzan, she reserved one day to commemorate the memory of Khansab's departed wives by preparing a special meal and inviting two hungry beggars to break their fast with Khansab. After meals, they prayed that the reward for feeding the poor should go to his late wives' souls. That little gesture from Chhoti Begum touched Khansab tremendously, and he reserved a special place for her in his heart.

When Chhoti Begum announced that she was expecting a child, Khansab swore that he would break the spell. He went to Aligarh and looked for a doctor who could come to Birehra to take care of the baby. No one was willing to leave his practice and move to a village. He went from city to city, talking to many doctors, until he found an old doctor in Lucknow who had decided to retire and hardly saw any patients. Khansab offered him a full-time job to take charge of the baby at birth and keep it alive. That is how Doctor Ali Hussain and his wife came to live in Birehra. They did not have any children, and neither did they need much money; they were contented as long as their needs were met.

Finally, the moment came. It was a boy. He was taken to the doctor right away. After examining the newborn, the doctor took a small bottle out of his medicine bag and put a drop on the baby's tongue. After that day, he came every morning to examine the baby and administer the "drop." A servant used to go to the door to announce that the doctor was there to give the baby drop, and a maid took him outside. People thought it was the city doctor's miracle that little Azad became Khansab's first surviving child.

***

When the sun descended after flaming all day, and the air-cooled down, Karmoo Bhishti, the water carrier, splashed water all over Khansab's patio, which was so big, he had to make four rounds to the well to cover the entire area. It used to be so hot in the day that every grain of corn would pop as soon as it fell on the ground. The earth absorbed every drop of water and emitted a refreshing fragrance: the breath of Mother Earth. Servants started putting peacock chairs in a large circle long before it was time for the guests to arrive. Azad would stand in the centre, and whirl like a dervish stretched out from his sides with his arms. He felt as if he were in the midst of an assembly of dancing peacocks. He imagined himself to be the centre of a universe that revolved around him. He could hear faint warnings from servants, who called him to stop before he threw up or fell awkwardly, hurting himself, but he did not pay any attention to them. He could not stop even if he tried until he lost his balance and let himself fall gently to the ground. He lay there with his eyes closed, enjoying the trance, and still feeling the universe circling him until his ecstasy subsided.

Khansab used to receive many visitors in the evening. They sat there until late at night, talking about politics and everyday affairs. As guests arrived, women were ushered into the house while the men stayed outside. Azad could always tell with whom he could interact. If someone was invited to sit in the chair, Azad could safely approach him if he was called. He was allowed even to sit in their laps as they hugged him. They were upper-caste Hindus, government officials, relatives, or Muslims of high status. Others sat on the floor. There were separate smoking water pipes, one for guests sitting in chairs, and one for people on the floor. Khansab talked to them until late at night. They spoke about the village's problems, the war's progress, the British's departure, and India's independence plans.

Among the many men who worked for Khansab, there was Fattu, the son of carpenter Bilal. His job was to go to Aligarh every day and buy the newspaper. Fattu was one of the few people in the village who could read and write. He started early in the morning and bicycled all the way to Aligarh. By the time he reached there, it was the afternoon. He listened to the one o'clock news on the radio, bought the newspaper, and returned to the village. By the time he was back, it was already after sunset. As he stepped on the patio, he found that Khansab and his guests were waiting for him. He related to them the latest news from the radio and handed over the newspaper. Khansab read the paper and told everyone what was written in it. They discussed the news for hours and exchanged their comments. "It appears that the war is over," Noor Khan commented.

"You can't say for sure," said Zakaria Khan. "This could be just the British propaganda."

"They say that Hitler is dead, but where is the body?" asked Khansab.

"Who knows? He might still be alive," replied Noor Khan.

"He must be sitting somewhere, planning the next strategy. You will see that he will come out any day and descend upon the Allies like a hawk." Silence fell upon them as they thought about the news. What would happen if the British were telling the truth?

"Who cares if Hitler is dead? What has it to do with us? It is *their* war anyway, and doesn't affect us, whether they win or lose," said Khansab.

"As long as they get out of India," Zakaria Khan remarked.

The family of Zakaria Khan, a distant cousin of Khansab, lived in the *Central Haveli*. Khansab's great grandfather had taken a second wife from outside the tribe, and his descendants from that marriage were outcast. They lived in a huge estate called the *Neem Haveli* since it had a tall neem tree within its courtyard. Other relatives took care of the *Neem Haveli* people and gave them all the respect their elders' seed deserved. However, they did not give their daughters in marriage to that family, and neither did they accept any girl from *Neem Haveli*.

Khansab's house was called the *Outer Haveli* since it was located outside the compound, which had an imaginary wall around it. At one time, there was a real wall to protect the dwellers from intruders, and there were still remnants of it in places, but it was never rebuilt when portions of it fell over the years.

Just then, all eyes turned toward the stairs when they heard a loud cough. It was Pundit Ram Kishan, the astrologer. He must have been visiting one of the Brahmin families in Nagla. Most of them believed in his knowledge and consulted him before making major decisions. He named babies, calculated blessed days for engagements and weddings, and drew horoscopes. Whenever he visited his clients in the area, he met with Khansab, who did not believe in astrology and ridiculed him openly. Somehow, the pundit enjoyed being teased by Khansab. He was a renowned astrologer and psychic who travelled across the country, calling upon Nawabs and Rajas, drawing their horoscopes, and writing birth charts. From those charts, he could extract detailed diaries of their future, listing significant events, sicknesses, accomplishments, and failures, all the way until the end of life. He was a short, bulky man, wearing a pair of glasses with a wireframe that hung low over his nose. His iodine-deficient, bulging eyes watched the world from above his glasses. His lips had turned crimson due to his habit of chewing betel leaves.

"Adab Arz," he greeted everyone and joined his palms as he approached them. They all stood up to welcome him.

"What brings you this way, Punditji?" asked Khansab, pointing to the chair next to him.

The pundit sat down, picked up a corner of his dhoti, and wiped the sweat from his clean-shaven head. "I was in the area, so I thought of dropping in here to convert a non-believer," he said and gestured to Khansab. Everyone laughed.

"Punditji, my future is not in my stars; it is in my fists." Khansab smiled as he raised his fists.

"Why don't you close your eyes, Punditji," said Noor Khan, "and tell us what you see for Khansab."

"Well, we will do it another day. Right now, I am here just to find out how my cynical disciple is doing."

"I have not seen anything yet, Punditji, to persuade me to change my belief," said Khansab.

"Okay, Punditji," said Zakaria Khan. "Let us convert Khansab today."

"Yes, Punditji. You have my permission." Khansab decided to join the game.

"Let us see. I will close my eyes, and you do that too so that I can borrow some psychic energy from you."

Khansab smiled as he closed his eyes. Noor Khan and Zakaria Khan seemed to be serious, and they followed the instruction too. However, they did not know that Khansab was cheating, opening his eyes slightly from time to time to watch them. An eerie silence fell over the surroundings, and he started feeling uncomfortable. To him, it was a silly game.

"I have seen it," the pundit finally declared as he opened his eyes.

"What did you see?" asked Zakaria Khan.

"I saw a tree, a large tree," said the pundit. He did not seem to add anything else to his statement.

"Is that all? All you saw was a tree?"

"No. This tree was huge. Its top reached the sky. It was a strong tree. I think it was *sheesham*."

"So?" Khansab interjected. He got interested in Pundit's account.

"This tree stood like a rock. Not a single branch swayed. Not a single leaf fluttered."

"And?" Noor Khan asked. He knew that the pundit was an expert in dramatization and punctuated his conversation at proper spots to arouse his listeners' curiosity.

"Then a gust of wind came! Then another one! Then another one! The branches swayed from side to side, and the leaves fluttered restlessly!" The pundit stopped again, waiting for someone to prompt him, but no one did. They kept looking at him, waiting for him to continue.

"Then I saw the ground around the tree crack! The roots were coming out-hundreds of them, moving like the arms of an octopus!"

He was quiet again and took the time to wipe his head with a corner of his dhoti. Perhaps it was a habit that he could not control.

"Suddenly, I saw that the tree started leaving the ground! It moved on hundreds of legs that were its roots! It moved farther and farther! I kept watching it until it disappeared on the horizon!"

When they realized that it was the end of the story, they all laughed. It was an exciting story.

"Punditji, are you saying that Khansab is that tree in your vision?" asked Zakaria Khan.

"I am not saying that," replied the pundit. "All I say is what I see. I do not pass judgement, nor do I decipher my visions."

"It was an interesting vision, though," said Khansab, but despite not being superstitious, he started pondering this. Was it prophesy?

***

There were days when the hot wind blew all day, and the sun blazed like a ball of fire. Farmers looked up toward the sky for traces of clouds through the canopy of their palms over their foreheads. Unfortunately. their gaze returned to earth with disappointment. The dry weather had continued for weeks and months until a rainmaker dropped in from somewhere. Children looked with fascination at the naked *sadhu*, a Hindu holy man, whose body was covered with ash.

Disappointment gave way to a ray of hope when the sadhu sat down in the centre of an open field, and people started lighting up a circle of fire around him. Dark-skinned, shirtless crowds gathered to watch the spectacle, as lines of sweat and dirt flowed on their bare backs. Trees were motionless-not a leaf stirred. As he chanted his mantras, they kept piling wood to keep the fire going. Impatience grew as time passed, but the rainmaker was not going to give up. The chant became louder, and the fire grew higher until a finger was pointed to a piece of cloud in the sky! More eyes looked up, and more fingers were pointed. As dark clouds started gathering, and the first clap of thunder was heard, the first drops of rain touched faces and sighs of relief were heard. Within no time, water was falling in sheets, and the wet pile of firewood could not sustain the flames. The rainmaker put his palms together and touched his forehead to show his gratitude to Indra, the god of thunder and rain. He received a generous reward as he left in the pouring rain.

It was the first monsoon rain of the season, and it poured continuously for two weeks. People got up on rooftops of their mud houses to fix leaks. They covered their heads with hoods, made by tucking one corner of a gunnysack's closed-end into the other corner. Roofs developed large holes, mud walls started being washed away, and the central alley turned into a stream, with water running knee-high. There was as much water inside the houses as there was outside. Beds were wet, firewood was soaked, matches were damp, dung cakes turned into paste, and armies of ants marched through the houses, looking for dry holes. Dhobis stopped coming to pick up the laundry since they could not dry it anywhere. While life stood still, people started cursing the rainmaker. If they had known that he was so holy, they would have asked him not to be so fervent in his chant.

The mullah in the mosque announced, after the night prayer, that one of the signs of the coming of the Judgement Day was that there would be growing incidents of floods, storms, and earthquakes. "It is about time that we repent for our sins and follow the straight path!" he advised the congregation and followed it with a special prayer to stop the rain. When people returned from the mosque, they got on their knees and thrust their fingers in their ears while chanting the call for prayer, as the mullah advised them. The village was filled with the eerie sound of *Allaho-Akbar* all night.

Eventually, it seemed to pay off, and by the late hours of the night, the downpour was reduced to a mere drizzle. Everyone congratulated the mullah as the sun came up.

Look Up! There's a Bird!

When Azad was born, the Second World War was raging in Europe, and the *Quit India Movement* was at its peak. The Indian leaders had given an ultimatum to the British to leave India. It led to a popular revolt, and people came out into the streets. The Indians rejoiced whenever they got the news of Hitler's victories or Japanese attacks. They followed Chanakya, from the first century AD India, who had written *Arthashastra*, a treatise on statecraft. According to him, "the enemy of my enemy is my friend." Freedom for India was in the air, and Khansab celebrated the revolt by naming his son Azad or *free*. His family name, Khan, pointed to his Pathan heritage.

Nobody remembered the exact date of Azad's birth since there were no calendars in those days. The only measures of the time were harvests and monsoons. The elders in the community kept track of happenings by connecting them to major events. For instance, one of Azad's cousins was born on the day an assassin killed Mahatma Gandhi. Azad's great uncle could not recollect which date his gallstone was removed, but he clearly remembered that he was recovering from the operation when he heard the news that the Japanese had just bombed Calcutta. He had spent a month in a hospital in Aligarh recovering from his surgery. When he left the hospital, they gave the gallstone to him as a souvenir. He kept it in a jar filled with alcohol for many years and showed it to everyone. Those who had seen it claimed that it was the size of a pigeon's egg.

It was the same hospital where Chhoti Begum had once gone for her chest x-ray. That was before Azad was born. She used to tell him that they had started early in the morning, well before sunrise and rode all day in a bullock cart. They reached the city after sunset and spent the night at the home of a relative. Getting the x-ray done was the most chilling experience of her life. The room was filled with strange machines that whirred as the technicians worked on them. They assured her that it would not hurt her a bit, but she was still terrified. They made her lie down in a narrow bed; then, a machine came descending upon her from the ceiling, and she started reciting a prayer. An uncle of hers was in the room with her. She clenched his hand firmly, fearing that the machine was about to crush her!

Nevertheless, it stopped a few inches away from her, and she let her uncle's hand go. The next day, they told her that the x-ray was clear and gave her the film. She folded it like a scroll and wrapped it in a piece of cloth. It stayed in her old rusted trunk for many years. When Azad was old enough, she gave it to him to play with and asked him to take good care of it. He used to show it to the boys in the village and told them that it was the picture of his mother's rib cage. Eventually, it became so brittle that it started cracking as he unfolded it. Many years later, when burglars came one night and stole all their valuables as the family slept, that x-ray film was gone too.

***

Since there were no midwives in Birehra, Azad was delivered by an experienced *sweeperess*, named *Mitthua's Bride,* who was too old to keep cleaning toilets and had started helping to deliver babies. Her daughters cleaned toilets in Khansab's home and performed other chores. Khansab had told Azad that he should respect her just as he respected his own mother since she was the one who had brought him into this world. Azad did respect her and called her *Amman,* but he could not understand why he was not allowed to touch her.

Mitthua's Bride came every day to sweep the floor. She was a very gentle and quiet woman and told Azad softly not to do this or that when he misbehaved. Whenever Khansab entered the house, she lowered the edge of her shawl slightly over her face. "You do not have to cover your face in front of me," he told her with a smile. "You are of my mother's age, and I have seen you enough since I was a child."

"It is just out of respect, Khansab," she replied, as she swept the floor. "I don't dare to come in front of you with a bare face."

Chhoti Begum also respected Mitthua's Bride. She asked her at times to take a break for lunch before finishing the job. There was an aluminum plate and a brass tumbler that Mitthua's Bride kept in a cabinet. As she held her plate, Chhoti Begum placed a few loaves of bread and a full ladle of curry on the plate and poured some water into her tumbler. After she finished eating, she washed the plate while Chhoti Begum poured water over it. Nobody except Mitthua's Bride herself was supposed to touch those utensils.

Azad did not understand why he could not touch her or her belongings. After all, Mitthua's Bride was like a mother to him and loved him so much. One day, while she was sweeping the floor, he went running to her from behind and wrapped himself around her leg as he lost his balance. She looked back at him with shock and pulled her skirt out of his hands. "You should not touch me, Master. Go wash your hands," she said, sounding angry while looking around her to make sure that no one was watching.

"Why can't I touch you?" Azad asked her angrily. "You are like a mother to me, and I call you Amman."

"We do dirty work. Your hands will get dirty if you touch me."

"But your clothes are not dirty. You take a bath, don't you?"

"You don't understand these matters. What will people say if they see you touching me?" she tried to explain to him. "You will know these things when you grow up." Azad still could not understand what the fuss was.

***

On the left side of the veranda in Khansab's home, there was a *chowki*. It was a large rectangular wooden seat, on which several people could sit at a time. Azad's grandmother had spread a prayer mat on it for her daily prayers. Women from the village visited Chhoti Begum every night after dinner, while men gathered outside for their daily chat. The relatives sat on a cot while women from the working class were seated on the floor between the cot and the chowki. Chhoti Begum brought her gramophone and a box of records from inside. It was a new toy, which her husband had bought for her. When she played it for the first time, her visitors were taken aback! Where was the sound coming from? She told them that there were tiny singers and musicians inside the box. Some women pretended that they believed her and came forward to take a closer look at the singing machine.

It had become a nightly routine. Azad sat on the chowki next to his mother. He handed her the records, which were black circular discs with spiral grooves all over them. There was a circular label in the centre. It had a picture of a gramophone and a little dog sitting in front of the horn. It was said that he was listening to his master's voice. Azad's mother put the disc on the turntable and turned the crank on the box's side to wind the spring. Then she took out a new gramophone needle from a little box and fitted it into the soundbox by tightening the screw. When she released the brake that held the turntable in place, it started rotating. She placed the soundbox gently on the edge of the record. Women watched with interest as the music started coming out of the big horn.

It was a used machine, with a collection of two hundred records. There were recordings of classical songs, romantic songs, religious songs, dramas, and comedy skits. Listeners felt that they were hearing every record for the first time.

***

Nobody could understand why Azad was terrified at the sight of Chokha, the barber, who was perhaps the most gentle and loving man in Birehra. He was the official barber of the Sherwani families and made regular house calls to Khansab. Chokha carried a small samovar of water, with a built-in base that contained burning coal to keep the water hot. As he took out his shaving paraphernalia from his bag, Khansab sat in front of him and took off his cap. Chokha dipped his hand in hot water and massaged Khansab's scalp several times. When the hair was entirely wet and washed, he dipped a bar of soap in water and rubbed it on the head in front of him until thick lather covered the entire area. He wiped his hands with his shoulder cloth, which had been white at one time but had now turned grey. "You should bring a new towel when you come to my place," complained Khansab as usual.

"I have almost run out of the towels you provided at the last harvest."

"I am sure you will get the new supply next month. Wheat is now ready to be taken down. But you can, at least, wash these towels regularly. I don't want other people's lice to infest me!"

Chokha could not find proper words of apology. After he reached into his bag and selected a clean razor knife, he took out a strop of leather from his pack; he held one end between his toes and the other in his left hand. He dipped the razor in hot water and rubbed it back and forth several times over the leather strop to sharpen it. As he held the razor in his right hand to scrape Khansab's head, he wiped the razor from time to time and collected the lather on the back of his left hand. He wiped the scalp dry with his shoulder cloth to remove any remaining lather. He had a unique tool to remove dandruff - a sliced kidney-shaped mango seed hollowed and dried. As he rubbed it on the scalp, it gave Khansab a soothing massage and cleaned off all dandruff. Finally, he poured a little oil on his palm, rubbed the two palms together and massaged the scalp. The job was done! Khansab asked Fattu to bring Azad, who had already seen Chokha and was hiding inside. He did not like Chokha at all!

Khansab had the "nasty" habit of rounding up his relatives' children and getting their heads shaved. While they played around the house, they made sure to run away as soon as they saw Chokha stepping on Khansab's patio. If any boy was caught, he was sure to get his head shaved. Azad was no exception. Khansab believed that hair collected lice and sweat in hot weather and must be shaved regularly. He did not even spare little girls. If they were routinely shaved, their hair would grow long and beautiful. Some mothers protested that their daughters were already too old to get their heads shaved, but they had too much respect for Khansab and did not dare to complain loudly.

Chokha was a street barber. He did not need to maintain any shop because he made house calls. He shaved beards and trimmed moustaches. Every moustache was like a fingerprint, as unique as the people of Birehra. No two pairs were alike. There were sharp sword-cut moustaches, drooping moustaches hanging over the mouth, long bushy moustaches pointing upward to show the wearer's male character, a single Charlie Chaplin moustache that looked like a fly sitting under the nose, and countless other styles. Chokha trimmed them and combed them with such expertise that one side was a mirror image of the other. As he shaved a beard, he gestured for his client to tilt his mouth away from the cheek he was working on. It tightened the cheek and made it easier for Chokha's razor to flow smoothly. Azad watched with interest when Chokha shaved someone's beard. He thought that it was funny when two adults made faces at each other. He and the other children mimicked their facial expressions and giggled when they saw their funny faces! There was no question that Chokha had mastered the art of shaving. After all, he had learned the skill from his father.

Notwithstanding his mastery, accidents did happen that resulted in cuts during shaving, but that was not a problem. When he had finished the job, he took out a piece of alum, dipped it in hot water and rubbed it on the cut. Even though it stung a bit, it managed to stop the bleeding instantly and acted as the aftershave lotion.

Chokha served everyone: Hindus and Muslims, rich and poor. People stopped him on the street to get a haircut or a shave, and he obliged everyone without any excuse. He never charged anyone since he got enough provisions from landowners at the harvest time.

Besides giving haircuts and shaving heads, Chokha performed circumcisions; he circumcised all Sherwani boys. When Azad turned three, his mother told him that he would have his *musalmani*, an event that would make him a Muslim.

"What is musalmani?" he asked.

"Oh, all your cousins will gather, and you will be dressed up," replied Chhoti Begum.

"You mean just like Eid?"

"Yes, just like Eid."

After that day, Azad told everyone that he was going to have his musalmani. Finally, the day came when close relatives gathered for the celebration. A cartload of sweetmeats was brought from Aligarh; there were enough laddoos for the whole village. Little Azad, dressed like a bridegroom, sat on top of a large dome made of twigs and dried branches as cousins and uncles gathered around. Boys who had already been circumcised were there too. Other boys were too scared to be in sight if someone would pick them up and put them on the dome! They usually hid away from the scene until they were sure that it was all over and that Chokha had left. Azad was too preoccupied with the ceremony to understand what was about to happen to him. They took off his pyjamas, and he sat there, watching Chokha curiously as he collected the foreskin and clamped it. Uncle Noor Khan reached for the bag of sweets and picked up a big laddoo. He held it hidden in his fist and waited until Chokha looked up and pointed to an imaginary bird in the sky. *"O-oh, chirya urh gai!"* As Azad looked up, it was all over in a flash. As he opened his mouth to scream, the laddoo was thrust in his mouth. Chokha worked with the speed of light to sprinkle the soothing antiseptic powder and bandaged the cut. Azad was too confused to know whether he should finish his scream or start chewing the sweet laddoo. Greetings were exchanged, and sweets were served, as Azad was picked up and taken inside.

Women gathered around Azad and garlanded him amid hugs and kisses. They came forward one by one, holding a one-rupee coin between their fingers, swirled their hand three times around Azad's head to ward off evil and put the money in a plate. It was to be given in charity. Chokha received a new suit that consisted of a pair of pyjamas, a long kurta, a new shoulder cloth, and a turban, together with eleven rupees for his service. By the time he finished gathering all his gifts, the plate had come from inside and was given to him. He was happy to see that it must have contained a large sum of money, perhaps sixty or seventy rupees. He thanked the family for their generosity and prayed for their health. As he left, someone asked him to open his mouth and put another laddoo in it. It was a bad omen for the circumciser to go home with an empty mouth.

As Azad grew up, he had forgotten all about his circumcision, but the fear of Chokha stayed with him, even though Chokha was the gentlest fellow in Birehra!

How to Count Stars

Azad was taught by his mother to address his grandmother as *Nanijan*. From then on, she became Nanijan for the entire village. Even the servants in the house called her Nanijan. People said that Chhoti Begum, with her fair skin, blonde hair, and blue eyes, had inherited her beauty from her mother. Even though Nanijan's hair was snow-white, she still had fair skin, though wrinkled, and blue eyes with the sparkle of life. No one had ever seen her laugh. She said that it was unwomanly to burst into uncontrollable laughter, but she did smile whenever appropriate. She maintained a decorum of majesty around her, which reminded Khansab of his grandmother. The people of Birehra considered her the wisest and the most respectable woman in the village.

Nanijan had never gone to school, but she was highly educated. She quoted from the Qur'an frequently during conversation and had memorized the Persian poetry of Rumi and Hafiz. Her father, who was a renowned scholar in his village, had taught her everything she knew. He had also told her to be soft-spoken and never let her anger be out of control. Therefore, she grew up to be mild-mannered but assertive. When she gave servants instructions, she always addressed them with respect, and they did not dare to disobey her.

There was no doubt that Nanijan was afraid of the dark; otherwise, why would she show such urgency to make sure that every room in the house was lit at sunset? She supervised the maid who collected all the lanterns in the place, well before the sun came down, and put them in a row as she sat down on the floor to prepare them for the night. It was a daily ritual. Azad watched the maid with fascination as she gathered the necessary material: a canister of kerosene, a pair of scissors, a dark green bottle containing some oil left from the day before, and a kerosene pump. She dipped one end of the pump into the canister and held the bottle in place under the spout. As the maid moved the wire passing through the pump up and down, a continuous stream of kerosene flowed into the bottle. She was careful not to spill even a drop of oil. Nanijan did not like to see oil spills on the floor! When the bottle was full, she put it aside and worked on the lanterns one by one.

Nanijan was busy around the house, moving charpoys and making sure that the beddings were in place. "Hurry up, Munni!" Every time she passed through the veranda, she stopped to give instructions to the maid. "You are becoming lazier day by day. I have told you so many times to light all lanterns before dark. Look at the sun. It will be dark soon."

"Yes, Nanijan." Munni did not mind the criticism. She respected Nanijan for her age and loving nature.

"Remember that evil spirits gather in dark corners of the house and plot to harm those who live there!"

"Yes, Nanijan."

Munni picked up a lantern and pulled up the cover until there was enough space above the chimney. It had collected a lot of black soot from the night before and needed a thorough cleaning. She wiped the inside of the chimney with a rag until there was not a speck of soot left on the glass. Azad sat in front of her, with his chin resting on his palms, watching every action with interest. Munni rotated a knob that raised the wick slightly. She trimmed it with a pair of scissors, making sure that the charred portion on the top was clipped away, and the wick had been cut in a perfect arc so that she could get a wide, smooth flame. When satisfied, she adjusted the wick and closed the chimney. All she had to do was fill the container with kerosene and touch the wick with a burning matchstick.

Azad counted the lanterns as they were lit one by one. There were more than twelve of them. He had learned to count only up to twelve, and there were three more lanterns to be counted. They reminded him of the night of Diwali, the festival of lights when he went with the servant into Hindu neighbourhoods to watch rows upon rows of oil lamps resting on walls. Nanijan passed through the veranda again and decided to sit down on the cot nearby to make sure that Munni finished in time.

"Why don't you wash up and get ready for the mosque," she advised Azad. "Your father will call you any time now."

"Yes, Nanijan."

Azad knew that Nanijan was very particular about evening prayers. "You know that the world will eventually come to an end, and it will happen at sunset!" She had told him that story many times. "When the last day approaches, God will instruct Israfel to blow his horn to declare the beginning of the end of the universe."

"Who is Israfel, Nanijan?" Azad got up and sat down closer to her.

"Israfel is an angel whose heart-strings are a lute and who has the sweetest voice of all God's creatures."

"What will happen when Israfel blows his horn?"

"The sun will start rising back from the west and will get closer and closer to the earth until it will rest at a distance of one and a quarter spears. Oceans will evaporate in an instant, stars will fall, the earth will tremble to spill out its contents, mountains will fly like flakes of cotton in a ginning factory, graves will open, and souls will start rising to the skies!"

Azad never liked that story because it always scared him, but he still wanted his grandmother to continue.

"It will be the Day of Resurrection when everything will be finished, and we will be in front of God to give an accurate account of our life on earth. After that, we will be sent to heaven or hell, depending on how good or bad we were while we lived on earth."

"Nanijan, I don't like the Day of Resurrection."

"Everything has to end one day," his grandmother replied. "You should not be afraid if you are good at heart and wish good for everyone around you."

***

Azad got up as Munni took the lanterns, two at a time, and started putting them in strategic locations so that no dark corner remained in the house. Meanwhile, Nanijan began securing the home for nightfall. She stood in front of the kitchen in the far left corner of the courtyard. Azad could see her lips quiver as she recited a prayer. Then she blew into the air around her to spread the blessing and walked to the far right corner to bless that area in front of the toilet. He knew that Nanijan would go to the two rooms at the back corners to recite her prayer. Once she had completed the ritual, the house was safe from thieves and evil spirits.

Nanijan had a prayer for every occasion. There was a prayer to recite as she sat down to eat, an after-dinner prayer, a prayer while going to the washroom, and a blessing while coming out of the toilet. She prayed before falling asleep and after waking up in the morning. When Azad lay with her before going to sleep, she gently talked to him and taught him those prayers. "If a snake comes in your path," she said, "recite this prayer and blow on it."

"What will it do to the snake, Nanijan?" asked Azad with curiosity.

"The snake will become blind and will get out of your way!"

"Even if it is a cobra?"

"It doesn't matter what kind of snake it is."

"But what if the snake knows this prayer too and blows on you before you blow on it!"

"Don't be silly, *Baytaa.*" She smiled and touched his cheek with the tips of her fingers as if she was slapping him. "Snakes don't know this prayer!"

"What if the snake bites you before you blow on it?"

"Then, we have another prayer. You recite it three times and blow on the snakebite. It will neutralize the venom instantly!"

Nanijan taught him the prayer for snakebites too. By the time Azad was four years old, he knew many prayers. Most of them were verses from the Qur'an that were supposed to have special healing powers. When he felt cramps in his stomach, he approached Nanijan and told her where it was hurting. She asked him to lie down and lift the edge of his shirt. She recited a prayer, blew upon her palm, and massaged his tummy until the pain was gone. She had another prayer to bring the fever down. Whenever he was sick, and his eyes burned with fever, Nanijan sat in his bed and murmured a prayer, as she dipped a towel in a bowl of cold water and put it on his forehead. She blew upon him, pointing her breath all over his body. God always listened to Nanijan and brought his fever down!

Nanijan was scared of thunder and lightning too. When the monsoon season approached, and the clouds started arching and rumbling, she went into the courtyard and blew her prayers into the sky. "Why do we have lightning, Nanijan?" Azad asked her as he wrapped himself around her leg.

"Satan is trying to get back into heaven! You know that he was kicked out of heaven when he confronted God. Since then, he always tries to sneak back, and the angels whip him back to the earth. You see, their whips in the sky appear as lightning, and the roar of those whips comes out like thunder."

Even though Azad did not like thunderstorms, he watched with interest as Satan ran all over the sky, trying to enter heaven. "What a sneaky fellow!" He cursed Satan and appreciated the hard work that angels were doing to keep him away. The rain would continue for several days. Heavy downpours brought floods and made roofs leak. Nanijan waited until she felt that the fields had received enough water. She stood on the veranda, reciting a prayer to stop the rain and blew into the sky. Azad knew that the rain would stop since Nanijan had started praying. Eventually, the lightning subsided, and the sun started peeking through the clouds. He was happy that the battle was over, and the heavens had been secured from Satan one more time!

The family started sleeping in the courtyard, under the open sky, as the nights got warmer. Chhoti Begum's cot was next to Azad's bed, and Khansab slept on a bed beside her on the left side. Nanijan slept on the right side of Azad's bed, mostly empty since he liked to curl up with Nanijan. He used to watch the sky every night before falling asleep. It was full of stars, and every one of them twinkled. He knew that they were talking to each other. People think that stars twinkle. They do not twinkle at all. They just appear to twinkle as they open and close their lips to talk! "Nanijan, what are the stars talking about?" he asked his grandmother.

"Of course they are talking about us-about the people on the earth!" she replied. "They are making fun of those who keep yawning and cannot fall asleep."

Then there was the Milky Way, a road in the sky shimmering with jewels. Azad could see it as far as the human eye possibly could. His grandmother had told him that the Milky Way was a highway in the sky, reserved for the Prophet's carriage. Whenever Azad saw a shooting star, he pointed at it and yelled with excitement. "Look, Nanijan, there goes another one." She told him that we see a shooting star when Satan tries to sneak into heaven! An angel takes his bow and shoots an arrow at him to scare him away. We see these arrows as shooting stars. "But Nanijan ...?" he said, remembering what she had told him earlier, about angels whipping Satan with the whip of lightning. He was hesitant to ask her why she had changed her story.

"But if he gets too close, the angels start using their whips!" she explained.

Azad was satisfied. *These angels have many weapons!* He thought.

Nanijan was a very wise and knowledgeable woman, and Azad wondered how she had learned all those things. Sometimes he started counting stars-one, two, three-and she told him that nobody could count stars that way.

"How can you possibly count stars anyway?" he asked her. "There are so many of them."

"There is one way that you can count all the stars in the sky," she replied. "You never say, 'One, two, three.' You always count them as '*One* twinkling star, *two* twinkling stars, *three* twinkling stars!'"

"Why don't you go to sleep?" Azad's mother, half-asleep, interrupted the conversation. "It's almost midnight."

God always answered Nanijan's prayers since she had a special relationship with Him. Sometimes, Azad thought that God had His ears tuned to her all the time to make sure that He did not miss any of her wishes! *Why not?* He thought. *Nanijan is such a nice person. She treats everyone with love and helps everybody. No wonder God cares so much for her!* She always spoke to him in whispers while teaching him a new prayer or telling him a bedtime story. He lay with his eyes closed and his head on her shoulder as she combed his hair gently with her fingers. He wanted to keep listening to her but could not keep his eyes open. Her words seemed to be coming from far away.

Nanijan will not let that day ever, ever come, he thought. *When God orders the angel Israfel to blow his horn, Nanijan will start praying, and God will have to take His orders back.* He was satisfied for a moment and closed his eyes, hoping that he would fall asleep, but a new fear crept in. *What will happen if Nanijan dies before that day? I hope it does not occur. I hope she lives forever.* He felt like choking with grief as he flung his arm around her neck and moved closer to her.

By that time, his father was usually fast asleep, and Nanijan could hardly keep herself awake. "Look, Nanijan, the angels shot another arrow at Satan!" Azad whispered. She mumbled something, and he knew that she had fallen asleep.

"One twinkling star ... *two* twinkling stars ... *three* twinkling stars ..."

He usually succumbed to deep sleep before reaching the twelfth twinkling star.

The Miracle Worker

Even though Khansab had hired Doctor Ali Hussain to look after Azad on a full-time basis, there was not much to do since Azad was a healthy boy. So the doctor spent most of his time seeing other patients but did not charge them any fee since that was a part of his contract. Adjacent to the house that Khansab had built for him, there was a room where he had set up his clinic. He put a rack on a wall with bottles containing *mixtures* of different colours. The red *mixture* was for indigestion and the brown *mixture* for cough. There was a counter under the rack, on which he ground various ingredients in a mortar and dispensed the powder in small wrappers. A thick copy of the pharmacopeia was placed on the counter in one corner. He received visitors all day. They came there mostly to spend their time chatting with him and watching him as he worked, but some of them came with genuine complaints of upset stomach or constipation. "Have you brought your bottle?" he asked everyone who wanted medicine.

"I don't have a bottle."

"What did you do with the bottle I gave you last time?"

"It must be lying somewhere. My wife tried to look for it but couldn't find it."

"That is bad." The doctor was always angry when people did not bring their bottles.

He got a clean bottle from the bottom shelf and reached the medicine rack to select the patient's appropriate mixture. After pouring the medicine into the bottle and putting a cork on it, he cut a strip of paper of the right size with his scissors and folded it three times. He cut notches on both sides of the strip, and when he unfolded it, it showed eight evenly divided doses. He glued the strip onto the bottle and handed it to the patient. People were fascinated when they saw the old doctor cutting strips of paper and dividing them into doses.

"Here, take one dose every morning, and next time don't forget to bring the bottle back!"

As the doctor handed over the bottle, he asked the patients to take one dose right away. They put their thumb under the first dose, removed the cork and poured some medicine into their mouth. It tasted awful, and they made faces as they swallowed. "Doctor Sahib, why can't you give me a medicine that tastes good," they complained.

"Don't be foolish. Good medicine always tastes bad."

When Azad was old enough to run around the house, Doctor Ali Hussain felt adequate to examine him weekly instead of paying daily visits. The doctor spent his day at his clinic, chatting with visitors and enjoying his retirement since he had to see only a patient or two now and then.

***

It was a hot sunny day, and the crop had just been harvested. As they threshed wheat, a fight broke out between Sukhdev and Chunnu, two of the workers in Khansab's fields. They were both hot-tempered and used to fight over petty things, but it went too far this time. No one working with them remembered who had started the fight. It was nothing new, and everyone knew that they would calm down eventually when they were tired of wrestling. They watched from a distance as the two of them exchanged blows and bites until Chunnu wrestled Sukhdev down and sat on his chest. When they saw Chunnu raise his sickle in the air, the people started running toward them. By the time they reached the scene, it was too late. Sukhdev's throat had been slashed. He lay there with his body twitching and his hands on his throat. They pushed Chunnu aside and started beating him. As blood kept oozing from Sukhdev's throat, they picked him up and carried him, running to the doctor's house.

By the time they reached the doctor, Sukhdev was not moving. As they lay him on the cot in front of the house, Doctor Ali Hussain approached the patient quietly and examined him. He was unconscious but was still breathing. "At least the trachea is intact," the doctor mumbled as he opened the wound. He asked two volunteers to come forward and hold the wound's flaps until he brought his instruments.

As people got the news, they came running and gathered around. They talked in whispers while the doctor prepared an injection and pierced Sukhdev's arm with the needle. "This will keep him unconscious for a while," Doctor Ali Hussain said in a low voice.

"Is he going to live?" someone murmured.

"Hmm," was the old doctor's only comment on that.

He got to work, talking to himself, it seemed. "We have to close the wound first."

He went in again and came out holding a little tray in his hand. As he sat on the cot next to Sukhdev, he pulled the cover from the tray. The crowd moved a little closer to see what was in the tray. There were tweezers, tongs, clips, and all kinds of strange-looking instruments. The doctor started putting clips along the wound as he asked the volunteers to move back. They were surprised when they saw him putting a thread in a needle. "What is he doing?" someone whispered.

"Looks like he is going to operate." They moved even closer and watched the doctor with their mouths open as he started sewing up the wound.

It was a hot, dusty day, and the spectators felt the grit of dirt on their teeth as they watched the doctor operate in the open air. Just then, Khansab arrived. Someone had told him that Sukhdev had been murdered. The crowd moved aside to make way for him. The doctor had finished closing the wound as he approached and had his fingers on Sukhdev's pulse.

"Is he going to live, Doctor Sahib?" Khansab asked him.

"It's hard to say," replied the doctor. "He has lost a lot of blood; plus, this is not the proper environment for surgery. I am afraid that, if he survives now, the infection may kill him later."

"You must do everything to save him. He is the only son of his parents and has been just married. We cannot afford to let such a young man die."

"Well, there is a new drug in the market," replied the doctor after some hesitation. "They say that it can instill life into a dead body. It is called penicillin. Why don't we try that?"

"Try anything, but don't let him die." People could sense impatience in Khansab's voice.

"Khansab, I am only a doctor. My job is to treat, not to heal," the doctor looked up and pointed his finger to the sky. "Only He is the healer. I will provide medicine, and He will heal."

The doctor took his prescription pad and wrote down the name of the medicine. "Here, send someone to the city right away! I have ordered seven injections." Khansab looked back at the crowd and asked for Irshad, who worked in the stables. People moved aside as

Irshad came forward. Khansab gave him the prescription. "Go home and ask Chhoti Begum to give you some money for the medicine." Irshad nodded as he took the piece of paper.

"Take Raja from the stable otherwise, Sukhdev will die by the time you come back." Raja was the fastest thoroughbred in Khansab's stable. The doctor called Irshad back as he prepared to leave. "Take a thermos with you with some ice in it," he told him. "The medicine has to be kept cool." He asked the people to pick up Sukhdev's cot and take it inside the dispensary. It was too hot and dusty outside.

They waited impatiently as some volunteers waved hand fans over Sukhdev to keep the flies away. He had regained consciousness but did not open his eyes. Doctor Ali Hussain watched him with concern and poured a spoonful of water between his lips as he moaned. He touched his forehead. His temperature was rising. He asked the volunteers to fan more briskly to keep him cool. Some people sat outside and contemplated the events of the day. Someone asked about Chunnu and found out that he had run away. "It is entirely his father's fault," one of them grumbled. "He always gets angry when anyone complains about his son."

"If my son were like Chunnu, I would take my shoe and beat him with it twice in the morning and twice in the evening."

"That would certainly keep him in line."

"Boys these days are so rash and disrespectful that they don't listen to their elders."

"These are the signs of the last days," advised an old bearded man. "One of these days, we will find that Christ has returned. They say that when he comes back, he will find the world in turmoil. People will be killing people for no reason."

They talked as they waited for Irshad. The sun had started dipping to the west, and shadows were lengthening. Occasionally, one of them went out and stood in the street to see if Irshad was anywhere in sight. Finally, someone pointed to the dust flying in the distance. Suddenly there was a stir among them, and a few more came out to see if it was Irshad. In a few moments, he was there. He jumped off the saddle and rushed inside with the thermos in his hand. Several people came in with him. Those who were already sitting on the floor inched forward to make room for the newcomers. They watched quietly as the doctor opened the thermos. He took out a little brown bottle and held it between his fingers. He moved his glasses up with the other hand so that he could see the label. "In this bottle, we have one million units of antibiotic," he said to Khansab as he read the label. Khansab nodded but did not say anything.

"Did he say that the bottle costs one million rupees?" someone in the back whispered.

"I think so." Everyone thought that a unit was equivalent to a rupee.

"How much is one million?"

"It's a lot of money. Khansab can buy a herd of thousands of cows for that much money!"

"Is that right?" asked someone else. "Is Khansab going to spend that much money?"

"That is true. Each bottle costs one million rupees, and there are seven bottles in the thermos." They could not believe that Khansab was going to spend so much to save Sukhdev's life! While the doctor prepared the injection, they talked about Khansab's generosity.

As time passed, Sukhdev felt better. He was brought in every morning for injection until he could walk, and his wound healed. People asked him from time to time to take off his muffler and show them the scar. There was a long scar from side to side. They wondered how Sukhdev had come back to life. The old doctor had performed a sheer miracle. His clientele increased suddenly. They came to him even if they sneezed once or gas moved in their stomach more than usual. As far as Khansab's generosity was concerned, they felt that they owed a great deal to him. He could have bought thousands of cows for the money he had spent on one of his workers!

Chunnu disappeared from the scene for months but returned eventually to the village and went straight to Sukhdev. He took off his turban and put it on Sukhdev's feet. "I will owe you my life if you forgive me," he pleaded to him. At first, Sukhdev was angry, but then he thought for a moment and came forward to embrace him. Tears flowed from Chunnu's eyes as he promised that he would be the best friend Sukhdev could ever have and that he would be respectful to his elders. People were angry at him and did not want him back in the village. Chunnu's father, too, refused to let him enter the house. Then they asked themselves who they were to disown Chunnu if Sukhdev himself had forgiven him!

Bless the Dead!

Azad believed that mullah was a nice man. Even when boys played pranks on each other while they prayed, he advised them gently-not like other elders, who yelled at them. Boys were always lined up in the back row, and they pinched and tickled one another as the congregation went into prostration. It was not long ago when little Yakub had disrupted the prayer! He was at one end of the row, and no one knew what came over him. Right in the middle of prostration, he decided to knock his neighbour with the side of his buttock. Boys fell on each other like dominoes, and the whole row was toppled to the other side! They tried hard to stop their giggles, but everyone knew that something had gone wrong in the boys' row. As soon as the prayer was over, the elders turned back and started scolding them.

"Don't you have manners?"

"Don't you feel ashamed, being naughty inside the mosque?"

"Don't you know that you are in God's house?"

The mullah came forward to calm them down and told them that boys are boys. Every boy pointed his finger at Yakub; he was asked by the mullah to repeat his prayer to show his repentance.

Located under the mosque's boundary wall was a well, with one half inside the mosque and the other half outside. Each side had a pair of slanted beams, fitted with a pulley, and contained a leather bucket with a long rope. Inside the mosque, the bucket was for the mullah's exclusive use, who spent several hours every day filling the water tank in the mosque. A long pipe, fitted with taps, ran from the tank. When people came to the mosque, they sat on stools in front of the water taps and performed their ablutions.

The mullah was busy all day, performing his duties with diligence. He washed the cement floor of the entire courtyard every day. The daytime prayers were held inside the hall. People avoided stepping into the courtyard since it was baked in the sun all day, and walking barefoot on the floor could cause blisters under their feet. When the sun came down, they preferred to pray outside, as a cool breeze started blowing gently. The mullah never missed washing the floor before sunset.

Nobody knew his real name, nor did anyone know where he had come from. When he first arrived in Birehra, he had just dropped in, but then he decided to spend the rest of his life there. Everyone called him *Mullanji* out of respect. People thought they could use him as an Imam to lead prayers, but he said that he did not know much about religion. They were impressed by his honesty; otherwise, he could have posed himself as a great scholar and could have taken over the mosque. Therefore, they asked him to be a caretaker of the mosque and keep it clean. His primary duty was to climb the stairs to the top of the minaret and say *Azaan* to call worshippers to prayers five times a day. Every woman raised the edge of her *dupatta* to cover her head when she heard the Azaan.

As time passed, the mullah gained confidence in religious matters and offered help in simple rituals; he spent most of his day chasing the squirrels that ran all over the mosque floor, nibbling on dried dates falling from the trees around the mosque. The mullah could not tolerate that the little animals were leaving tracks of their activity on the clean cement floor, on which people prayed under the open sky. He made sure that the floor had been well washed ahead of time to get rid of the mess that the squirrels had left. He kept the entire courtyard under his watchful eye, and as soon as he spotted a squirrel approaching, he ran after it like a puppy, chasing it away! The squirrels were too fast for him and climbed the nearest tree before he could reach them.

One of the mullah's duties was to go into homes to bless the food prepared to feed the poor. It was done to remember the dead grandparents and other close relatives. He was invited to pray for the departed souls. He recited verses from the Qur'an while sitting on the floor in front of a tray containing a full meal for one person - every course in separate plates, ranging from pulao, qorma, and naans to yellow rice or pudding for dessert. When he finished reciting his prayers, the family requested that he eat the meal himself. After all, who was more deserving than he was? He was not only poor but also a pious man, and God loves those who are righteous. At times, he had already taken his dinner but had to eat another meal if the host got offended.

It was not a busy mosque. There were only a few men and boys who came regularly. Others occasionally joined when they could not withstand the pressure of guilt any longer. When some wealthy landowners were seen in the mosque, it was a sure sign that a court hearing was approaching. They were under pressure for a loan payment to Lala Ishvari Lal, the local moneylender, who would undoubtedly take over their land if payments were not made in time. At those times, it was essential to please God and ask for His forgiveness before He decided to punish them for their sins! Only God could instill mercy in the hearts of the judge and Lala Ishvari Lal!

When the mullah came to the village, he caught people's attention like a magnet. He was not attractive, as far as his physical appearance was concerned. He was a short, dark man, with thick curly hair and a narrow forehead. Part of his face, which was not covered with his bushy beard, was pockmarked with the scars of smallpox. The most prominent feature of his face was a pair of fat lips. Nobody cared what the mullah looked like. They just loved his company. When he was not filling water tanks in the mosque or chasing squirrels, he sat on a charpoy under the fig tree with a group of villagers, telling stories of the lands he had visited. He had seen every corner of the country, from Assam to Kashmir. He imitated the shrill sound of a siren that announced an air raid in Calcutta, spoke of walking, talking, and singing pictures in a cinema, and told them about his trip to a zoo where he had seen strange animals. The villagers listened to his stories with their mouths open as they took turns on the hookah. They did not want to believe some of the stuff. How could pictures walk, talk, and sing? However, since he was a pious man, he must be telling the truth!

The mullah hesitated whenever people invited him to lead prayers in the mosque. He said that he had committed too many sins in life and did not consider himself worthy of leading prayers. Even though he occasionally volunteered when people insisted, it was usually the responsibility of Hasan Khan, a very knowledgeable man. However, when Hasan Khan was away, it was difficult to decide who would lead the prayers. Whenever people held someone by the shoulder and asked him to take the Imam's place, he hesitated. "How can I dare to lead you in prayer? You are more knowledgeable and much more pious than I am. You should lead the prayer." After much resistance, the mullah eventually volunteered.

Now and then, a sick bird or some other animal fell into the well, and the water was considered unusable. As soon as the problem was discovered, people gathered to clean the well. The mullah supervised the operation personally. There were clear rules in theology about cleaning a well. "If it is a small animal, like a sparrow or a lizard, twenty buckets of water must be drawn and discarded," said the mullah.

"What about a bigger animal?" someone asked.

"If it is the size of a pigeon or a crow, you need to draw forty buckets."

However, if the body had bloated and exploded, or if it was a larger animal, the entire well had to be emptied. The mullah offered a complicated formula to define the *entire* well. It was measured in arm-lengths of water. The level of the well had to be reduced by so many arm-lengths. After a few calculations, it was agreed that it translated to three hundred buckets of water. A new controversy started when someone asked about the definition of a bucket. "What is the acceptable size of a bucket?"

"Any bucket that is used regularly on a well is acceptable for that well," said the mullah.

"But this is a new bucket," said Murad Khan, who claimed that he was well-read and knew a lot about religion. "The regular bucket was replaced only last week. So will this bucket be considered *regular?* If it is smaller than the old bucket, we will have to draw more buckets of water."

The mullah was stumped at that point; he said that his knowledge of religion ended there. The controversy grew. They offered arguments and counter-arguments. Finally, someone suggested consulting *The Heavenly Ornament.* Even though it was primarily a book for women, it talked about everything. A copy of the book was brought from the nearest house, and the mullah started looking for the subject. It was an old copy, and the paper had turned brown and brittle. Several pages were torn and kept carefully folded in places. He found the chapter on cleaning wells, but it did not explain the situation at hand.

Meanwhile, Hasan Khan passed by. People gathered around him

and presented the problem to him. He decided that, since the old bucket had been discarded, the current bucket would be considered *regular,* even if it were put on the well at that instant. The explanation was logical and acceptable to everyone, so the task of cleaning the well resumed.

Someone had to keep score. Sometimes, there was disagreement about how many buckets had been drawn; the lowest number was accepted to be on the safe side. In the meantime, news got back to homes, and women started emptying their pots until the well was cleaned, and Karmoo had brought a freshwater supply. He became swamped at those times. Whenever they had to clean the well, the mullah reminded people that all ablutions performed from the time they discovered that the well was polluted were invalid. So were all prayers offered during that period!

The mullah's favourite pastime was to sit under the old fig tree, smoking a hookah and telling the story of his life to the people around him. Whenever someone saw a group of little boys and girls gathered under the tree, he knew that the mullah must be there. Kids were his biggest fans. He put his fat lips on their cheek and blew on it. As his lips vibrated, they got a funny tickle on their cheek and could not help but giggle as the *phurrr* sound came out! Every child wanted to get a phurr from the mullah. They lined up and fought for their turn.

"Mullanji, please, phurr me!"

"No, phurr me first!"

"You get out of here. It's my turn!"

"You already got a phurr. Now it's my turn!"

Every boy or girl was allowed only one turn, but Azad could get several. After all, he was the son of Khansab. While the mullah sat there *phurring,* the people sitting with him laughed as the children giggled. After every child had received his phurr, the mullah asked the kids to play and started his story from where he left it off.

The Divine Watch

Hasan Khan, who was a distant cousin of Khansab, was the richest man in Birehra. His great-grandmother, who was the only child of her parents, had come from Nawabs's family and had received a massive estate in inheritance. She used her family connections with the British aristocracy to send her son to England after his matriculation. He was supposed to study law and return to India as a barrister, but he returned without a diploma after spending a whole year partying and travelling through Europe. Not only did he speak English like an Englishman, but he was also fluent in French and German. His mother wanted him to settle down with her side of the family, but he followed his father and decided to settle in Birehra. He hired an Italian architect to design a colossal mansion for his family. It was built like a palace, fit for a king.

There was a huge, milk-white marble courtyard behind the mansion's main gate, so big that one had to shout to be heard on the other side. With tall and sweeping arches, an arcade ran around the courtyard, behind which was a deep veranda with rooms at its back. The columns of arches were ornamented with hexagonal pieces of sky-blue lead crystal. The light from Petromax lamps, hanging around the courtyard at night, was reflected individually from each crystal, and the entire square glittered like the star-studded sky. In the daytime, when the sun blazed, the courtyard assumed a bluish tint, softening the sunlight's intensity.

There was a fountain in the middle of the courtyard. It had a large alabaster basin, with swirling bands of brown and cream colours, and sat on the heads of twelve marble lions sitting around the basin. The entire structure came from Italy. The architect had told Hasan Khan's grandfather that it was the duplicate of the famous Fountain of Lions in the Alhambra Gardens in Granada. The mansion was known as *mahal* or the palace, which it certainly was.

Behind one of the mahal's side walls was a well that was fitted with a Persian wheel, driven by a pair of oxen, going round and round all day, rotating the wheel, which was connected to a vertical belt containing a chain of leather bags. As the wheel turned, the bags picked up water from the well and carried it up to a tank, from which it was supplied to the fountain through a pipe. The bulls encircled the well all day without any supervision as if they were programmed just for that.

The mahal was surrounded by a thirty-foot-high wall with two gates on opposite sides. When the gates were open, two elephants walking side by side could easily pass through each gate. The four walls were spread over several acres with men's quarters, servants' barracks, and the village mosque within the perimeter. It was a village within a village, with scores of servants going about their business.

Adjacent to the main building was an annex, which was built as a library. Hasan Khan's grandfather was a lover of books and had collected thousands of volumes over the years. After his death, his son continued to gather books. Every publisher in the country ensured that two copies of new publications were promptly sent to the library in Birehra. By the time Hasan Khan took over after his father's death, the library had contained over ten thousand volumes on philosophy, religion, and history.

As the library in Birehra gained fame, seekers of knowledge came from all over the country and stayed there as long as needed. Hasan Khan had persuaded an old librarian, who had retired from the university in Aligarh, to come and live in Birehra. Nobody knew his real name. So people simply called him *Mudeer Sahib*, or "the manager." His passion was books, and he treated them with love and care as if they were his children. Most of his day was spent cataloguing them, moving them around, and answering letters from those who inquired about a particular book. Chances were that it was in the library, but he did not allow anyone to take a book outside the reading room.

Nobody asked the names of people who came looking for a book. They were simply called *readers* and could stay in the mahal as long as they wished. They were given a bed and were fed from the kitchen. Some of them who were engaged in research or were writing a book stayed there for months.

Pundit Uday Lal, a Brahmin from Nagla, spent his day in the library and had become a permanent member of Hasan Khan's household. He acted as a host to the readers and engaged them while Hasan Khan was away. Uday Lal was a voracious reader; it was said that he had read every book on philosophy and history that was available in the library. He could talk for hours about Greek, Islamic, and western philosophers from Thales to Aristotle, from al-Rawandi to al-Bihari, and from Karl Marx to Alan Turing.

***

There was no doubt about the piety and scholarship of Hasan Khan, who had even been to Mecca for Hajj several times. On one of his trips, he had received a gold watch from King Saud! What happened was that he was coming out of the Grand Mosque after completing his seven circles around the Kaaba; he was stopped at the gate while a huge crowd tried to get in. As he made his way out, he suddenly found himself face to face with the king, who was entering the mosque, surrounded by security guards who were pushing people aside to make way for the king. Hasan Khan extended his arm to the king, and the king shook it! A servant, who was carrying a bag, pulled out a gold watch from it and presented it to Hasan Khan, who accepted it graciously. The king moved on.

When Hasan Khan came back from the pilgrimage, his encounter with the king became the major story in Birehra. When people came to greet him on his safe return from the trip, he showed them the watch, and they all kissed it. After all, it had come from a holy place. "Hasan Khan must be a very important person, otherwise why would the king present him a watch?" They also appreciated the fact that he had brought gifts for them. Everyone got a can of water from the Zamzam well and a packet of dates from Medina. Selected friends also received sandalwood rosaries that he had bought for them just outside the Grand Mosque. At the head of each rosary was a piece of sandalwood, fitted with a cylindrical piece of glass. When he asked his friends to bring the glass close to their eye and peek into it, they were amazed to see the life-size picture of the Kaaba in it. The scene was so realistic that they felt as if they were standing in front of the Kaaba. The inscription under the picture said, "Made in Japan."

People always consulted Hasan Khan on religious matters, and even though he said that he was not qualified to issue a fatwa, he always gave them proper advice. He was, therefore, the right choice to lead prayers in the mosque. The problem, however, was that he was seldom in the village.

The people of Birehra, Hindus and Muslims, lived strictly by religion. From the time they got up in the morning until they went to sleep, every activity was guided by their religion. It was a "Made in India" religion, based on legends and folklore, passed from generation to generation. Hasan Khan felt that every moment he spent in Birehra replaced a portion of his intellect with ignorance.

Whenever his intellectual constipation hit its peak, he got out of the village, travelled through the country, met great Islam scholars, and engaged in discussions with them. Those discourses fed his intellectual appetite.

***

Ammanji was the only one in Birehra who despised Hasan Khan to the extent of outright hatred. Whenever his name came up in conversation, she referred to him as Satan and covered her nose with her dupatta. At ninety-five, she had outlived her children. She was a great-aunt of Khansab and Noor Khan and lived alone in her ancestral haveli. They had tried their utmost to persuade her to move in with them to be cared for properly, but she refused, saying that she was the custodian of her property, and her job was to guard it. Finally, they convinced her to let a live-in maid stay with her, even though she insisted that she did not need one. Despite her old age, her eyesight was perfect, all her teeth were intact, and she could hear things that others could not. The reason for her hatred for Hasan Khan was that, according to her, he was polluting the minds of his relatives with wrong ideas when it came to religion. It all started when he invited a cleric from the seminary in Deoband to stay with him for a few days.

The Sherwanis were not very particular about religion. They did fast during the month of Ramzan, prayed occasionally, and followed the Islamic code of conduct, but that was the extent of their religiosity. Whenever a wandering preacher passed through Birehra, he was invited to stay for a few days and enlighten people with his message. The more they listened to those preachers, the more confused they became since every preacher contradicted the others. Some of them talked about Sufis and saints, while others came and negated them. Khansab believed that most of them were just making a living and did not know much about religion. Whenever someone asked the mullah for his comment, he just shrugged his shoulders and said, "If you believe in it, it is everything; otherwise, it is nothing!"

Ammanji had a strong faith in the great saint Gilani, who had lived in Iran in the twelfth century, and was known as the Master of All Saints. Many years ago, when she was desperate to find a suitable match for her son, she had promised God that she would cook every year on the saint's birthday if she were successful. She would invite everyone around her, regardless of religion or caste, to share the meal blessed by the saint. It so happened that the very same day, someone mentioned the name of a distant relative in another village, and Ammanji decided to go and take a look at the girl. It was undoubtedly a miracle of the saint that she had found the perfect match for her son. The new daughter-in-law brightened her home, but fate had other plans. It was only a month after the wedding that her son was shot dead by a new bride's distant cousin on a hunting trip. The police concluded that it was an accident. Ammanji was heartbroken when she had to take the bangles off her daughter-in-law's still henna-covered hands and put a white dupatta on her head, which was how widows were supposed to dress.

No sooner had the mourning period of four months and ten days ended than the young man who had shot her son showed up at her door. He was overcome with grief and guilt.

"I feel personally responsible for what happened," he said. "Especially because I was the one who invited him to go hunting."

"What can one do?" she said. "Where, when, and how one will die is all predestined. That is God's will, and we are helpless."

"I promise you, Ammanji, that I will be the son you have lost."

"You are a good man, my son, but you have your parents to take care of."

"I am willing to marry your daughter-in-law because I feel that she is now my responsibility."

"I respect you for your sacrifice," Ammanji replied, "but now that the mourning period is over, she is free to go back to her parents. I suggest that you approach them."

So the wedding took place. No one ever knew that the new couple had held a soft corner in their hearts for each other for many years already, but knew that it was not their job to choose their mate. When the girl's parents had accepted Ammanji's proposal that she marry Ammanji's son, the young lovers were heartbroken, but destiny had somehow brought them together anyway. God does work in mysterious ways!

Ammanji kept her word. Every year on the great saint's birthday, she baked and cooked all day and was ready to receive her guests. The mullah was asked to come and bless the food, after which the feast began and continued until late at night as people kept dropping in. For many years, it had continued until Hasan Khan invited the cleric from Deoband, who told the mosque men that there was no place for saints in Islam.

"You have a direct connection with God," he preached. "He listens to you without any need for a middle man."

He also told them it was forbidden to worship graves or eat any food that was blessed in the name of anyone other than God because it negated monotheism, which is the pillar of Islam. Ammanji was furious when none of her relatives showed up for her feast. Not even women and children! They had been told by their men to stay away from forbidden food.

"It's all Hasan Khan's doing," she told Khansab when he visited her the next day to calm her down. "We are simple Muslims, and he is turning you into Wahhabis."

"Don't say that, Ammanji. Hasan Khan has nothing to do with it."

"I knew that he was a changed man when he came back from Hajj. He must have been misguided by the Wahhabis there."

The cleric was gone. People went back to their old ways and kept coming to Ammanji' s feast every year, but her contempt for Hasan Khan stayed with her until she died.

Thakur Baldev Singh

The elders of Birehra knew why Khansab and Thakur Baldev Singh were thirsty for each other's blood. Baldev used every opportunity to outsmart Khansab and burned with rage at every defeat. Khansab never retaliated. He just smiled whenever someone told him that Baldev cursed him furiously. It seemed that he took pleasure in tormenting Baldev with his indifference, and this game had gone on for most of their lives. Their enmity had started when they were teenagers, and it was all because of a wrestling match.

Baldev's father, Thakur Amar Singh, was a famous landowner of his time, whose lands stretched as far as the eye could see on the far side of Nagla. He maintained good relations with the Sherwanis of Birehra, who also respected him as their equal; they knew that Rajput blood flowed through his veins and recognized that Rajputs were a match for Pathans' courage and bravery. Amar Singh had a special relationship with Khansab's father, whom everyone addressed as Sherwani Sahib. They sat for hours, relating to each other the stories of their ancestors' valour, but it was not certain how much truth was left in those tales after having been passed from generation to generation.

It was unfortunate that the Thakur and Sherwani Sahib's friendship led to a bitter rivalry between their sons. One day, Sherwani Sahib decided to take young Khansab with him when he went to Nagla to introduce him to his friend's son, who was about the same age. As the two boys looked at each other with reservation, they immediately decided that they would be adversaries for the rest of their lives.

The Thakur was known for his quirks, one of which was his obsession with wrestling. He had built a wrestling pit on the grounds in front of his courtyard and invited young men of Nagla to show their wrestling skill. People gathered around the pit as the tournament started. Every team had its drummers, who fiercely beat their dhols as contenders leapt into the pit, slapping their thighs. Their fans burst into roaring cheers as the wrestlers tangled with each other, wrapping their arms around their adversary's waists. The Thakur stood up with excitement as the wrestlers fell upon each other, and the referee declared the winner!

When the Thakur saw his friend's son, the first thought that came into his mind was to have him wrestle with his own. "Tell you what," he said to his guest. "Why don't we get the boys to have a wrestling match?"

"Be serious, Thakurji," Sherwani Sahib said, thinking that his friend was childish.

"Why, Sherwani? Are you afraid that your son will lose?" the Thakur chuckled.

"No, I am not afraid. If your son is a Rajput, my son is a Pathan too."

The Thakur took it as an open challenge. He called a servant and asked him to bring a pair of shorts for each boy. Sherwani Sahib kept smiling, even though he felt a bad taste in his mouth over Thakur's childish behaviour. Khansab was nervous too. He had never wrestled anyone, except in a play fight. He hoped that the servant would come back empty-handed to tell the Thakur that he could not find any shorts, but he was disappointed to see him coming back with two pairs of shorts in his hand. He knew that he had to prepare himself for a fight since it was too late to run away.

As they faced each other in the wrestling pit, Khansab looked at Baldev and saw disgust in his eyes. He stepped back a few steps to give himself enough manoeuvring room and waited for his opponent. As Baldev came charging at him, Khansab flung his arms and wrapped them around his waist while lodging the back of his foot behind Baldev's calf. As he pulled his foot, Baldev lost his balance and fell in the dirt with a thud. He landed on his back, and Khansab dropped himself with full force on top of his opponent. The fight was over in a flash! The Thakur stood up from his chair with his mouth open. Two servants ran into the pit, but before they could separate the boys, Baldev opened his mouth and dug deep into Khansab's upper arm, leaving a circle of teeth marks, which were left permanently on his bicep. "Thakurji, it looks like you have not yet taught your son to lose gracefully!" Sherwani Sahib smiled as he looked at the Thakur.

"You are right. My son needs to have a sportsman spirit." The Thakur was noticeably embarrassed.

That was the first and last encounter for many years to come between Baldev and Khansab. As they grew up, Khansab got busy with his horses, guns, and hunting dogs. He pushed the memory of that wrestling match somewhere to the back of his mind, except when he took his shirt off and looked at the circular scar on his arm- then he would smile at the recollection of his victory. Baldev, on the other hand, remained a sore loser for the rest of his life and wished for one last chance to revenge his defeat.

***

Sherwani Sahib's flesh and bones had been consumed by his grave long ago, and the River Ganges had absorbed Thakur Amar Singh's ashes.

Baldev Singh grew up to be a rough, tough, ruthless landowner who

93

stood at six foot five. His face was painted with eternal anger, and no one had ever seen even a slight tinge of a smile under his well-buttered, long moustaches, which stood straight up. When he shouted at his workers, they urinated in their dhotis! If he coughed while a pregnant woman walked by, she was sure to drop her fetus out of fear! The people of Nagla were terrified when they faced him. Not even a fly could dare to land on his moustache! Everyone hated Baldev for his arrogance and egocentricity. His obsession with defeating Khansab grew into extreme revulsion for everyone living in Birehra. Unfortunately, he had to pass through Birehra whenever he travelled since that was the only way out of Nagla. He kept looking straight in front of him as he rode his horse on the dirt road through Birehra, especially when he passed Khansab's home on his left. He did not know how he would react if he came face to face with Khansab; it was just chance that their paths had never crossed.

Anger was Baldev's major weakness. He beat his servants for even minor mistakes. When he wanted to punish a servant, he took off his shoe and hit him on the head. However, despite that ferocious exterior, he was not a bad man. No one could say that he had ever hurt anyone. When his anger subsided, he called his victims back and gave them money. They received one rupee for each strike and thanked him for his generosity. He kept an accurate count of the number of times he had hit a servant, and none of them had ever complained that he had been short-changed. They even looked forward to being beaten up by their master to raise some spending money.

Baldev threw parties and invited neighbouring villages. The village crier went from village to village, announcing that Baldev had invited the entire village to celebrate a pony's birth in his stable or to commemorate his father's death anniversary. People in Birehra watched with curiosity as his guests walked in hundreds along the dirt road leading to Nagla, raising clouds of dust under their feet. Khansab watched the crowds with amusement, knowing that Baldev had thrown the party just to tease him. He enjoyed playing the cat-and-mouse game with Baldev and smiled at the thought of his agony. The village crier did not make any announcement in Birehra, and the people assumed that they were not invited. Baldev never came out to meet his guests. They came, ate, and left, everyone carrying a platter of sweets-expressing their gratitude for the generosity of their host.

Baldev had such a sweet tooth that he had retained Nathu Halwai-a famous *mithai* maker from Mathura-in his employment. Nathu claimed that his family had been preparing sweetmeats for seven generations, and no mithai maker in India could match the taste of his preparations. After eating just one Gulab Jaman, one felt for hours as if he had gargled with honey and rose water. Nathu and his staff were always busy in the kitchen. People dropped in every day to pick up sweets, and they were served with Baldev's compliments, regardless of their caste or religion. Whenever there was a party, Nathu started several days earlier to collect enough ingredients to ensure that no one left the party without sweetness in his mouth. As Baldev watched from his terrace, while his guests left after the party, his loneliness grew, and so did his anger, because no one had cared to thank him personally.

Baldev looked for opportunities to provoke his foe and gnashed his teeth with rage every time Khansab ignored him. One evening, while Khansab sat with his friends, sharing that day's newspaper, one of his workers came up the stairs. He was accompanied by another young man, whom Khansab had never seen before. They came and stood there to wait until Khansab addressed them. "Yes, Sharif, who do you have with you?"

"Khansab, this is Ram Prasad," Sharif said and pointed to the man beside him. Khansab nodded his head to greet him. Ram Prasad raised his hands and joined them to show his respect.

"He works for Baldev Singh in Nagla."

"Yes?" Khansab wanted Sharif to tell the whole story without being prompted.

"The Thakur has beaten Ram Prasad and kicked him out of his service."

"What happened, Ram Prasad?" Khansab addressed him directly.

Ram Prasad raised his hands again and joined his palms. "It was not my fault, Khansab. But Thakurji thinks that I am responsible for the death of one of his buffaloes."

"And how did the buffalo die?"

"It took a fall somewhere and broke a leg. Thakurji had to shoot it."

"Okay, Sharif, give Ram Prasad some work." He returned to the newspaper as the two men left. Everyone in the gathering looked at one another, but no one said anything.

Someone finally broke the silence. "You should not have taken the man into your service."

"What did I do wrong?" Khansab looked at him with curiosity.

"Isn't there a rule that no landowner will accept anyone in his service if another landowner has fired the person?"

"Baldev has a bad temper, and it will not sit well with him," someone else remarked.

"He has grown old, but not grown up," replied Khansab. "He still thinks that he is ten years old and has not forgotten when I threw him down in the wrestling pit."

"I hear that his teeth marks are still on your arm," someone else said, and everyone laughed. Khansab rolled up his sleeve and showed them the scar.

People were right. Baldev did not take the news politely. He stood up from his chair and closed his fingers into fists when someone told him that Khansab had accepted Ram Prasad into his service. "How dare he! How dare he do that?" he screamed as he threw his fist in the air. "If my father did not have so much regard for his father, I would teach him a lesson that he would not forget for the rest of his life!"

Ram Prasad was assigned to sleep in the field to ensure that no prowlers could steal the vegetables at night. He had hardly spent a week there before his decapitated body was found on his charpoy. His head lay among the watermelons that were ready to be picked. Khansab sent a servant to call the police, who did not get there until the evening. Ram Prasad's corpse stayed there untouched until the police had registered the case. Khansab was asked if he could point the finger at someone, but he declined to express his suspicion. It was not until late at night that the police left, after a sumptuous dinner with Khansab, and he instructed his workers to arrange for Ram Prasad's cremation.

***

Baldev did not share his life even with his wife. His father had brought the daughter of a Rajput for his son, just a year before his soul departed for the journey of reincarnation, as destined by his karma. The girl was a piece of the moon and brought light into the Thakur family's home, but Baldev could not drop his guard even in front of her. *Thukra'in*, as everyone in the household addressed her, was the first woman in his life. He had no sister and had never known his mother since she had died while he was still on her milk. His father had spent the remainder of his life as a widower and left his estate to his only son. Thukra'in did not care much about the lack of her husband's attention since she was too busy supervising the servants and taking care of the house. The only grief in her life was that her bosom was still barren. As time passed, her longing to embrace a child grew. Older women coming into the house kept reminding her constantly. "May Bhagwan turn your bosom green," they said, expressing their wish for her to bear a child.

Baldev and Thukra'in had been married for ten years. Baldev had never mentioned to his wife that he wished for her to bear a male child for him, but even so, her pain grew with time. She felt that it was somehow her fault that she could not fulfil the demand of womanhood. One day, while Baldev sat in his chair listening to his record keeper, who was giving him the tally for grain sale, an old servant came from inside the house and stood quietly in front of him.

He looked up. "What is it?"

"I just found out that Thukra'in sits in the courtyard every morning and vomits!"

Baldev reached his pocket and pulled out a five rupee note. The servant came forward and bowed to accept the reward for communicating the news.

"Congratulations, master," said the record keeper.

"So, what were you saying about the crop?" Baldev did not respond to the greeting.

Thukra'in was sparkling with joy. The old maid had told her that three days of morning sickness confirmed that *she was with hope!* She knew that the news had been sent to Baldev and expected that he would come into the house any minute, and she would fling her arms around him. She kept looking at the door from time to time, but he did not enter until his usual lunchtime. She was disappointed to see that he kept a stiff upper lip and did not say a word. It would be shameful for her if she mentioned herself that she was pregnant.

While her pregnancy progressed, she wanted to talk to Baldev about the baby, but he never brought up the subject. He did not even ask her why her belly was bulging day by day. Her disappointment gave way to anger and eventually to indifference. *What difference does it make if he is not interested in his child?* she argued with herself. *After all, it is my baby, and it will be dearer to me than anything in the world.* Finally, the day came when the village crier went around the neighbouring villages, announcing that Baldev was blessed with a daughter, and he wanted everyone to share his joy. The people of Birehra were excluded from the invitation once again.

***

Thukra'in had just returned from a trip to the temple of Lord Krishna. She took this trip every year on her daughter's birthday, and it was the fifth year that she had taken little Preeti to the temple. As soon as the cart stopped at the door, the girl rushed to the toilet; she had been holding all day and had refused to go to the temple's dirty washroom. Thukra'in followed her daughter to the lavatory if she needed help, but she stopped suddenly upon entering the toilet. Her eyes were fixed on a row of ants lined up on a streak of urine. She looked back and called the old maid. "Do you know who has visited the toilet last?"

"Why do you ask that, Thukra'in?" The maid was confused as she approached.

"Do you see this streak of urine?"

"Oh! Thakurji had just come in to visit the lavatory."

"Are you sure?"

"Why would I lie, Thukra'in?"

Therefore, it was Baldev who had sweet urine. "Don't let Baldev know that," she said, as she turned her head to the maid.

"No, you must tell him! Otherwise, he will continue eating mithai, and it will eat him instead."

"Baldev will start worrying unnecessarily. I will ask Nathu not to give any sweets to him."

"Do you think you can stop Nathu? I think you should tell the Thakur."

That evening, when Baldev came in for supper, Thukra'in gave him the bad news. Ants had started coming to his urine. He ignored her warning, but she insisted that he should not touch any sweetmeats.

"If you take away sweetness from my life, what else do I have left to live for?"

"You have a lot to live for. Your daughter has just turned five. Tomorrow she will be ready to get married, and before you know, you will have grandchildren playing around you, and you say you don't have anything to live for?"

She picked up a corner of her dupatta to wipe her tears. Baldev listened to her quietly. He knew that, no matter how much he resisted, his heart melted whenever he saw tears in her eyes.

"Don't worry, I will call the Vaidhraj tomorrow, and he will take care of my sweet urine."

Everyone in Nagla came to know that ants were coming to Baldev's urine. No wonder. He had been eating tons of sweetmeat, and now he would have to spend the rest of his life with diabetes. Only time would tell if he would fight it well or be consumed by it.

***

Pratap Singh of Jaunpur preferred to be addressed as *Rai Bahadur*, or only RB, a title conferred on him by His Majesty's Government, in recognition of his family's services to the British Empire over three generations. His grandfather was a small landowner, but his land holdings had increased markedly because of exemplary service to the government. The expansion continued during his father's time. Pratap followed in his elders' footsteps until he owned so much land that it would take a horseman an entire day to encircle his lands at gallop speed. He had a fun-loving, flamboyant personality. He loved to throw parties and go on hunting trips with friends. As a Rajput, he was supposed to be a tall man with long, handlebar moustaches, duly waxed, and a traditional turban on his head, but he was relatively short, with a slim body and a clean-shaven lip. Pratap admired the British, dressed like Englishmen, and mimicked their body language. He had a permanent smile on his lips, and nobody had ever seen him in anger. They said that he probably smiled even in his sleep. His subjects in all his fifty-three villages loved him for his caring persona.

Among Pratap's friends were Khansab and Baldev, who were eternal foes, and ready to pounce upon each other. He was always sad that he could never invite two of his best friends together. "What is wrong with you?" he asked Khansab.

"What is wrong with me?" Khansab replied. "Why don't you ask Baldev what is wrong with him?"

"Baldev is a hot-headed bum. But you claim to be sensible."

"I do not have any problem with Baldev," Khansab defended himself. "I am willing to meet him anytime, anywhere."

"It is ridiculous," Pratap conceded. "Whenever I mention your name, he starts gnashing his teeth."

Khansab laughed as if he enjoyed Baldev's helplessness.

Eventually, Pratap accepted that he could never bring his two friends together; he decided to stay out of their dispute. Baldev was his relative besides being a fellow Rajput. He could not figure out how they were related, but there was some distant connection several generations earlier. When Baldev's daughter was born, Pratap had visited him and held little Preeti in his arms. "You know, Baldev," he said thoughtfully. "Would it not be great if your daughter was married to my son?"

Pratap's son, Anand, was only two years old at that time. Baldev did not respond immediately. He thought for a while. "It is a match," he finally said. "This will solidify our friendship and renew our relationship." Preeti was thus engaged to Anand at birth.

***

The common bond between Khansab and Pratap was their love for hunting. Khansab was obsessed with hunting dogs and owned a pack of twelve dogs of different breeds. He would talk for hours about each breed and its characteristics. Whenever Pratap arranged a hunting expedition, he sent a messenger to Khansab, asking him to come with his gun and bring Tiger with him. "If you cannot come, send Tiger," said the note. Tiger was a white sighthound with black patches; Khansab had specially trained him to hunt *nilgai* or blue cows. Tiger could spot a nilgai from miles away and dash for the kill. He interacted with Pratap's dogs as if he were part of the pack and acted as the lead dog. Herds of blue cows were the worst enemy of farmers and roamed through northern India, destroying crops and trampling over sugarcane plantations. Villagers looked forward to the hunt and feasted on blue cows' meat whenever Pratap's hunting party arrived in their area. The hunt was stopped when some influential orthodox Hindus objected that a cow was a sacred animal, and it was sacrilegious to kill it. When they realized that the animal did not differentiate between the fields of Hindus and Muslims, they withdrew their objections reluctantly but insisted that it should be called a *nilghora* or a blue horse instead of a blue cow, even though it was neither a horse nor a cow; it was classified as an antelope.

***

Baldev had not visited Pratap for many years. Not only was he slowly consumed by diabetes, but his arteries were also clogged, and his kidneys were quitting. Whenever he was about to fall asleep, his legs jumped; he woke up screaming and throwing his legs in the air as his body convulsed. It had driven him so insane that he had developed a fear of sleeping. He spent the night sitting in his chair, with his eyes closed and his mind occupied. If he managed to doze off, he had a recurring nightmare, in which he was face to face with Kali Devi, the Hindu goddess of death and darkness, with bulging eyes and long, bloody tongue, and wearing a garland of skulls. The sight terrified him, and he woke up drenched in sweat. Chronic insomnia had turned him into one of the walking dead. Whenever he wanted to go upstairs to sit on the terrace, he climbed slowly, one stair at a time, and stopped after every few steps, until his angina pain subsided. Thukra'in helped him as he went up. "If you had taken care of yourself, it would not have come to this," she said, blaming Baldev for his disease.

"What else do you want me to do?" he replied with resentment in his voice as he settled in his chair. "I do not even say a word anymore when all you feed me is chickpea bread and bitter melons."

"The Vaidhraj has been telling you from the beginning that diet alone will not help you. You should-"

"Don't talk about the Vaidhraj," Baldev interrupted her. "He wants me to run around like a horse. The truth is that I cannot even put my feet on the ground. They burn as if I am walking on fire."

"You should at least follow his instructions. What is stopping you from spending an hour every day doing yoga?"

Baldev did not answer. He was not interested in anything anymore; he had no desires, no plans and no motivation to live. Self-pity took over his arrogance, feelings of guilt replaced his anger, and loss of his appetite had turned him into a skeleton. Even his moustaches, which once had pointed upward to show his manliness, had drooped to tell the world that he was a defeated man. The man with towering personality, who was once a living terror to his peasants, had been reduced to a mere shadow of himself.

Baldev closed his eyes as he reclined in his chair; He thought about his condition and felt angry at himself. His wife was right. If he had followed the instructions of the Vaidhraj, he would not be in the shape that he was in. *I will send a messenger for him tomorrow*, he thought. *I will make him my mentor from now on and will get back on my feet.* He heard his wife's voice as she walked up the stairs.

"Here, you have received a letter from Rana Pratap Singh," she said as she handed the postcard to him. "I wonder why he has thought about you after so long."

Baldev took the postcard and brought it closer to his eyes. He could barely see the words. "Why don't you read it aloud?" Thukra'in was impatient. "What does it say?"

"He says that we should consider getting Preeti married because she is old enough."

Thukra'in did not like the idea. "She has just turned sixteen. How can we get her married off today when she was playing with dolls just yesterday?"

"I think Pratap is fair. Preeti is old enough to be married."

"But she has not even learned to cook. Her in-laws will blame me for raising a girl who knows nothing about the kitchen."

"We are not sending her to join Pratap's household tomorrow," said Baldev. "By the time she is married, she can learn cooking. You can start teaching her from today."

"Your daughter in the kitchen?" Thukra'in sneered. "You must be joking!"

"What is wrong with my daughter being in the kitchen?" Baldev asked.

"Because it is too hot for her in the kitchen," responded Thukra'in sarcastically.

"It is up to you to teach her cooking and sewing or be labelled as a bad mother by her in-laws."

"I don't understand why she should learn to cook and sew anyway?" asked Thukra'in. "She is going to the home of someone who calls himself Rai Bahadur. Does he not have servants and maids who cook and sew?'

"Still, I think you should educate your daughter in good manners and teach her how to behave like a married woman."

"Whatever you say," Thukra'in conceded. "I still think that she is too young, but she is your daughter, and it will be your decision."

"I think I will write back to Pratap that we are ready. Let us get Punditji to find an auspicious date for the wedding."

As Thukra'in left the terrace, she had wedding plans in mind. Bridal dresses had to be tailored, jewellery had to be made, and Preeti had to be trained for married life. There were a thousand and one things to be done. It was not a child's play.

Baldev also had wedding plans on his mind. He suddenly felt that he was back in the driver's seat. There was no other way for him except getting better and retaking the charge of his life.

***

Pundit Ram Kishan, the astrologer, was led by a servant into Baldev's living quarters and was greeted by Thukra'in.

"We are thankful to you, Punditji, that you responded to our request on such short notice," she said.

"No trouble, sister. I was in the neighbourhood and did not have any problem getting here," the pundit replied.

"We called you to get us an auspicious date for our daughter's wedding," she said.

"Yes, I got the message. Do you have *Janam Patris* of the couple?" the pundit asked, referring to the horoscopes of the bride and groom.

"I will get you the Janam Patri of Preeti, but you will have to draw one for Anand."

Thukra'in got up and left the room. The pundit moved the writing desk closer to him, took out a bundle of old books from his bag, and placed them on one side of the desk. The books were worn out, and the paper had turned brown. Thukra'in returned with a scroll, folded into a cylinder and tied together with a red ribbon. It was Preeti's horoscope, which had been drawn when she was born. She handed it to the pundit, who unfurled the scroll and studied it.

"Hmm," he mumbled, "Preeti is a Virgo! She is a passionate girl who will be loyal to her husband."

The pundit pulled out a stack of paper and drew three concentric circles with a pencil. Then he drew twelve equidistant lines from the outermost circle to the innermost. Thukra'in was impressed that they were perfect circles, drawn without a pair of compasses. "What is the groom's name, and where was he born?" the pundit raised his eyes and looked at her.

"His name is Anand; he was born in Jaunpur." He wrote the name and the place of birth on top of the sheet on the left side.

"Do you know his date and time of birth?"

"No, but he will be eighteen in two weeks."

The pundit calculated the date of birth and wrote it down under the first two entries.

"Do you know the time of his birth, Thukra'in?"

"Not exactly, but Anand's mother once told me that he was born in the morning; when she heard Anand's first cry, the rooster was crowing."

The pundit wanted the time to be as accurate as possible. He consulted the table in a book to find the time of sunrise in Jaunpur on the date of Anand's birth. Then he subtracted two hours from the time. "He was born at a quarter past four in the morning," he muttered under his breath, as he wrote the time next to the date of birth. Thukra'in watched him with interest while he quickly labelled the twelve sections in the outer circle with the zodiac signs. Then he consulted several books, looking at charts and tables to determine the ascendant sign of Anand and the positions of the moon, sun, and planets at the time of his birth. Then he quickly drew in the houses, each signifying an aspect of Anand's life, and the horoscope was ready. He put down his pencil, took his glasses off and wiped his eyes with a corner of his dhoti. Then he put his glasses back on and picked up the horoscope.

The pundit gave his verdict. "Anand is a Pisces, which is the natural opposite of a Virgo." "Is that good or bad?" asked Thukra'in.

"It means that he is an ideal husband for Preeti. He has every quality that she does not have, and she has every quality that he does not have. They complement each other, and there is no problem in this marriage that they cannot resolve. It will be a good marriage."

"That is good news, Punditji," Thukra'in smiled.

"Let us now find out the best dates for their wedding." The pundit put the two charts side by side. "We all know that there are days when a person is in an easy mood, and there are days when he is under stress. I will choose dates when they are both relaxed."

He consulted another book and moved his pencil across a chart. "Let me choose a period when Venus is in easy aspect to Neptune. That will support compassion and spiritual growth."

Thukra'in kept watching him without interrupting his concentration.

"I have some dates here," he said and wrote down some numbers on a sheet of paper. "Do you want Hindi dates or Engrazi dates?"

"Give me Engrazi dates."

"The best period is between the fourth and the tenth of February next year."

Just then, Baldev walked in; the pundit stood up to greet him. Baldev joined his palms, and the pundit responded.

"Forgive me, Punditji," said Baldev. "I would have been here earlier, but I am not well these days."

"Bhagwan will make you well."

Baldev sat down in front of the pundit.

"Punditji has come up with a period between the fourth and the tenth of February," said Thukra'in.

"That is good," replied Baldev. "I will write to Pratap tomorrow."

"But that is only nine months away. How can we arrange a wedding in nine months?"

"If you can produce her in nine months, why can't you arrange her wedding in nine months?"

The pundit smiled at Baldev's sense of humour as he folded the horoscopes and handed them over to Thukra'in. He started collecting his books and putting them in his bag. Baldev reached into his pocket and counted several large bills. It was impolite to ask the pundit his fee. He was sure that the pundit would be satisfied with the amount. As he got up to leave, Baldev came forwarded and slid the money into his pocket.

"Here is a token of our appreciation, Punditji."

"There is no need for such formalities," the pundit said and put his hand in his pocket to return the money to Baldev.

"No, no. It is not a fee. It is just to show our appreciation to you."

"As you wish." The pundit hailed him as he left.

***

Vaidhraj Ramachandra, who was an Ayurvedic doctor, claimed that he was ninety years old. Most people thought that he exaggerated his age to impress his patients, but no one could refute his claim. *Vaidhraj* was his title, to show that he was a senior doctor, but it had become part of his name. That day, he had started at dawn and walked ten miles from his village to respond to Baldev's request. He was a fair-skinned Brahmin, with a lean, wiry body frame and a mostly clean-shaven head on which some hair was left to form a ponytail. Clad in white dhoti and shirt, it seemed that he floated in the air while he walked; men much younger than him could not keep pace with him. He attributed his strength to yoga and a healthy lifestyle.

Baldev's servant escorted him into a carpeted sitting room. There were large bolster pillows, lined against the walls, for guests to sit with their backs resting against them. The Vaidhraj chose to sit in the centre of the room. "Open the windows to let the sun in," he instructed the servant.

"Yes, Vaidhraj," the servant responded.

The room was lit brightly with sunlight as the servant opened the windows. The Vaidhraj looked around and noticed Trimurti's brass statue, a Hindu god with three faces, signifying Brahma the Creator, Vishnu the Preserver, and Shiva the Destroyer. The statue was placed along the centre of the wall facing him. He reminded himself that those were the three forces maintaining the balance of nature. A small table with a ceramic incense holder stood on each of the four corners of the room. The walls were decorated with pictures of different Hindu gods. As he shifted his gaze from one image to the next, Baldev entered the room and stood facing the Vaidhraj with his palms joined to greet him. He returned the salutation and made a gesture with his hand for Baldev to come and sit in front of him. "What have you done to yourself, Baldev?" he said in a soft voice. "I think we are meeting after ten years."

"You are right, Vaidhraj," replied Baldev, as he made himself comfortable. "My condition has been worsening all these years."

"Despite following my advice?"

"No, I confess that I have been a bad boy."

"Now, you know what happens when you do not watch your health."

"Yes, Vaidhraj. I was stupid to ignore your directions."

"Well, nothing is lost if a boy who has gone astray in the morning returns home in the evening. We should be worried only if he decides not to return at all."

"I have decided to return, Vaidhraj," Baldev pleaded. "I have surely decided to return."

"I am glad you made that decision. Let us start where we had left off, and I am sure you will come back to life."

The Vaidhraj told Baldev that he would send one of his interns to live at Baldev's house and help him with his exercise, yoga, and meditation; he would also supervise his diet for two weeks. After that, he would visit him once a week to check the progress. Vaidhraj would pay monthly visits to examine him personally.

"How long do you think it will take for me to be cured?" Baldev asked.

"You will never be cured," answered the Vaidhraj. "Once you have diabetes, it stays with you for the rest of your life. But if you take care of it, you will forget that you even have it."

Baldev listened to his soft voice and was impressed by his relaxed disposition. He spoke in a monotone, with each word pronounced elegantly. *He must be a very educated man,* thought Baldev.

"Do you know what your worst enemies are?" the Vaidhraj asked him with a smile on his lips.

Baldev shook his head from side to side.

"Your worst enemies are anger, hatred, and jealousy. When you are angry, your blood thickens, and your blood vessels cannot carry it to the heart. That can even cause heart attacks."

"But what can you do when people make you angry?"

"People do not make you angry. You make yourself angry. I am not saying that you should never get angry. Just treat anger like a wave in the ocean. Let it rise, let it hit the coast, and let it retreat. Stay in control as it passes through you."

Baldev kept listening to the Vaidhraj quietly.

"Remember, Baldev, that hatred and jealousy do not harm the person you hate, or you are jealous of," he said. "Hatred and jealousy hurt you alone. Get rid of them and learn to forgive people."

Baldev was in deep thought; he kept staring at the Vaidhraj with a blank look on his face. "Smile," said the Vaidhraj. Baldev smiled back.

"Remember that a smile brings serenity to you. Your entire body smiles with you."

"You are so right, Vaidhraj," said Baldev. "You have shown me a new path, and I promise you that I will follow your advice."

"Good, let us do a little exercise before I leave. Let me see if you can sit the way I am sitting."

Baldev sat with his legs extended in front of him. He folded his right leg and brought his foot under his left shin. Then he tried to fold his left leg to get his foot under the right shin, but the leg snapped back.

"Your muscles are tight due to years of a sedentary lifestyle," said the Vaidhraj. "Just hold your foot with your right hand and pull it gently to bring it into position."

Baldev succeeded after several attempts.

"You will feel a bit uncomfortable in the beginning, but when your muscles get used to it, you will find it the most comfortable position," the Vaidhraj said, satisfied. "Now, raise your hands and join your palms in front of you, then close your eyes and smile."

Baldev complied with instructions; he sat in front of the Vaidhraj, his eyes closed and a smile on his lips.

"Relax, and think of something good in your life." Baldev thought of Preeti. She had grown up to be a beautiful and well-behaved woman, and she would bring happiness to her husband and her in-laws.

"Now think of someone you hate or are angry at," said the Vaidhraj.

Suddenly, Khansab's face came in front of him; his smile gave way to a frown. His eyebrows moved closer together, and his forehead was wrinkled.

"No, no, no. Keep smiling."

Baldev's eyebrows moved back; the wrinkles on his forehead disappeared, and he smiled again.

"Now forgive this person, no matter how much wrong he has done to you," the Vaidhraj said in a commanding voice. "Look, he is smiling back. He is inviting you to be his friend. So accept his invitation."

Baldev kept smiling. He felt light as if he was floating in the air. He was on his way to taking charge of his life once again.

"Bring your hands down slowly, and open your eyes."

Baldev took a deep breath and looked at the Vaidhraj.

"How do you feel?"

"I feel good ... after many years, Vaidhraj."

"Just remember that happy people are healthy people, and the happiest ones are those who stay away from anger, hatred, and jealousy."

"I agree with you."

"Practise this exercise every day until you have conquered your demons."

Baldev nodded in agreement.

"My assistant will be here tomorrow, and you should make arrangements for him to stay with you so that he can help you with your exercises and prescribe a good diet for you."

"You are staying with us tonight, are you not?" asked Baldev.

"No, I have to get back before sunset."

"You should have at least stayed for dinner; we could drop you off tomorrow morning."

"Maybe some other time."

The Vaidhraj stood up, raised his palms in salutation, and left. Baldev followed him to say goodbye.

That afternoon, Baldev was ecstatic and filled with vitality. So much had happened in one day. He felt on top of the world and did not even notice that he had climbed the stairs to the terrace without having to stop in the middle to catch his breath. He sat down in his chair, and when Thukra'in brought him a cup of tea, he smiled at her. She smiled back, wondering if there was something wrong with him. He looked at the sun setting behind a row of mango trees on the far side of his fields. It was an ordinary day and a typical sunset. A thin cloud cover, high in the sky, appeared as if someone had splattered thick molten gold all over the sky. A yellowish-orange hue had filled the horizon as far as the eye could see. As the bright orange disc descended behind the mango trees, Baldev thought that the trees were on fire. He had never before seen such a beautiful sunset.

***

When Baldev Singh handed over his daughter to Pratap Singh, his eyes were moist. "I am giving you a piece of my heart," he told his old friend. "So take good care of her."

"Just think that, from this day on, your daughter is not your only child," replied Pratap. "You have a son too."

When Preeti entered the home of Pratap Singh, as the bride of his youngest son, Anand, she found out soon that her new home was not a rose garden. Pratap had three other sons, who lived in the same house with their wives and children. Pratap's wife, addressed as *Rani*, was known for her arrogance and bad temper. There was an army of male and female servants in the house, and Rani screamed at them, day and night, at the top of her lungs. Even while Preeti was alone with Anand in her bridal chamber, she heard Rani scolding someone:

"Why didn't you mop this dirty spot?"

"Are you blind?"

"You are becoming careless day by day."

"Do you want me to kick you out of this house?"

Her shrill voice pierced through everyone's ears. She criticized every move of her daughters-in-law, who had eventually become indifferent to her. They spent their day decorating themselves with jewellery, makeup, and dresses. Whenever they were together, they referred to their mother-in-law as the *barking bitch.*

Anand had a younger sister, whose nickname was Nini. Since she was the youngest in the family, everyone had spoiled her. Even though Nini was the same age as Preeti, she behaved like a child. Whenever there was a dish at the dinner table that was not to her liking, she left the dining room in anger, and Rani asked one of her daughters-in-law to go and bring her back. When Preeti entered the house as the new member of the family, Nini felt threatened to see someone else in the family compete with her for attention. Therefore, she was hostile to Preeti from the start.

Being a newcomer in the family, Preeti was shy at the dining table; she did not participate in the conversation because she was supposed to behave as a bride. Nini looked at her occasionally with disgust but kept eating quietly. Eventually, she burst out in rage. "This is the woman who has stolen my brother from me!" She pointed her finger at Preeti and walked out of the room. Rani's daughters-in-law exchanged glances, wondering why their mother-in-law had not reprimanded Nini.

"She is still a child," said Rani, after some thought. She knew that everyone was expecting a reaction from her.

Pratap and his sons spent the day in the men's section of the house, outside the four walls. They were busy taking care of their land affairs, settling quarrels among peasants, and entertaining guests. They entered the house late at night and went straight to their living quarters, where their wives complained to them regularly about their mother-in-law. The husbands always ignored them.

Preeti's honeymoon lasted for seven days and ended abruptly when her mother-in-law told her that she was supposed to take over the kitchen. "The youngest daughter-in-law runs the kitchen in our home," she said to Preeti. "You should make *Royal Toasts* tomorrow. The new bride always starts with a dessert."

Preeti had never stepped inside a kitchen and had no idea how to cook. She went into her room and started crying. How could she tell her mother-in-law that she did not know how to cook? Lying in her bed, she sobbed and wept until her eyes turned red, and her nose was puffy. Finally, she decided to face her mother-in-law and tell her that she did not know how to make Royal Toasts.

"Have you been crying because you don't know how to make Royal Toasts?" Rani noticed Preeti's swollen eyes.

Preeti nodded while still looking down.

"That is not a problem. You can make some other dessert. How about carrot pudding? You can make carrot pudding. Can you not?"

Preeti shook her head from side to side. Rani was starting to lose her temper. "What can you cook?" she asked Preeti.

"I don't know how to cook. I have never been in a kitchen," replied Preeti while still looking at the ground.

"Then you must be good at sewing. Are you not?

Preeti did not respond. Rani did not like that. "Your mother did not teach you how to cook, she did not teach you how to sew, and she got you married. What are you good for in our home?" Preeti stood there, tears flowing from her eyes like a stream, and listened to her mother-in-law's rebuke without looking at her.

After that day, Preeti was declared by Rani to be a useless member of her home. She faced her mother-in-law's scorn day after day. When Preeti could not take it anymore, she decided to complain to her husband.

Anand entered the room later than usual that night. He was acting strange, staggering as he walked in, and his speech was slurred. She had never seen anyone intoxicated and could not figure out that her husband was drunk. As he settled himself in a chair, Preeti sat down next to him and told him how his mother mistreated her. He kept listening to her with his eyes closed. Suddenly he opened his eyes and got up from the chair. "How dare you insult my mother?" he said and slapped her on the cheek. Preeti stood up from the chair, with her hand covering her cheek. By the time she could understand what had happened, Anand had slapped her again on the other cheek.

A month had passed since Preeti's marriage. She faced a mother-in-law who was a bully, an abusive husband, and sisters-in-law, who were arrogant. Her father-in-law was the only one who treated her with compassion, but she did not get much opportunity to interact with him. Whenever he entered the house, she came forward and touched his feet. He put his hand on her head to bless her and moved on.

One night, when Pratap entered the house, Anand walked in with him. Preeti came forward and touched his feet as usual. He blessed her as usual and then turned to Anand. "Why don't you take Preeti to visit her parents? Leave her there for a week or so and let her spend some time with them."

***

Baldev and his wife were happy to see Preeti. Anand stayed overnight, and Baldev invited all his friends for dinner to meet his son-in-law, who was the son of Rai Bahadur Pratap Singh. Most of the guests already knew that, but Baldev emphasized *Rai Bahadur* to ensure that his guests recognized that his son-in-law was from noble lineage. They stayed up chatting until late at night, but Baldev asked Anand to go to bed since he had to leave early in the morning.

Thukra'in noticed that Preeti was not the girl she had raised. Before her marriage, she was a happy girl, playing with dolls and enjoying life. After marriage, she was a different woman. She had a gloomy look on her face and did not talk much. Suddenly, she had grown old. Thukra'in asked her what was bothering her. "You don't talk, you don't laugh, and you don't play anymore. What is wrong with you?"

"Nothing is wrong with me," Preeti answered. "You have seen me after too long; that is why you feel that something is different."

"No, something is bothering you. Are you treated well by your in-laws?"

"Believe me, Mother, there is nothing wrong, and nothing is bothering me. They treat me very well."

Preeti did not open her mouth because her father had once advised her never to complain to her parents about her in-laws. "Good girls always protect the secrets of their homes," he had reminded her just before she got married.

"Let me massage and oil your hair," said Thukra'in. "That will relax you."

As Thukra'in massaged Preeti's hair, she noticed a blue mark on her neck and closely looked at it. "What is that blue mark on your neck, Preeti?" she asked.

"I don't know," Preeti said and tried to cover it with her palm.

Thukra'in did not respond for a while. Then she whispered in Preeti's ear, "Does your husband beat you?"

"There is nothing of the sort. What makes you think that?"

"Tell me the truth. Does your husband beat you? How do they treat you?"

Preeti was silent at first, but then it seemed as if floodgates had been opened. She cried bitterly. "Yes, Anand beats me, and I have no respect in that house. My mother-in-law curses me all day, and they treat me like a maid."

Baldev was furious when Thukra'in told him the whole story. He could not believe that his daughter would be mistreated in the home of a lifelong friend. "Preeti is not going back to that house," he finally declared.

Anand returned after two weeks to pick up Preeti. He was surprised to find out that his in-laws gave him the cold shoulder, even though only two weeks earlier, Baldev and his wife had given him a warm welcome. What had changed in those two weeks? Finally, he told his in-laws at the dinner table that he had come to take Preeti back. They did not respond. Anand's curiosity grew until his father-in-law spoke: "Preeti is not going back."

"Sorry?"

"I said Preeti is not going back."

Preeti got up from the dinner table and left the room. Anand could not understand what was going on.

"Is anything wrong?" asked Anand.

"Is anything wrong?" Thukra'in responded. "You ask if anything is wrong. We gave you our daughter, whom we raised with love and compassion; your mother turned her into a maid, and you ask me if anything is wrong! Is that how you expect your sister's in-laws to treat her?"

Anand listened to her quietly. He could not think how he should respond to Thukra'in.

"I have seen blue marks on her neck and her back. Now, don't tell me that you have not been beating her. Is that how women are treated in your home?" Anand was still quiet.

"He asks me if anything is wrong." It appeared that Thukra'in was talking to herself. Anand got up and left without saying goodbye.

When the word reached Pratap that Baldev had refused to send Preeti back, his Rajput blood started boiling. He did not know about how Preeti had been treated in his home. Rani blamed Baldev and Thukra'in for insulting her son without any reason.

"I will teach Baldev a lesson that he will never forget." Pratap trembled with anger as he spoke. "He has seen my friendship; now, he will see my hatred."

***

Khansab took care of his *lathi* as if it were one of his favourite hunting dogs. It was a six-foot-long, heavy bamboo stick, tipped with a bronze cap; a lathi was customarily used as a weapon. He oiled it regularly, wiped it clean with a rag, and polished the metal. Unused for several years, it stood in a corner in Khansab's bedroom. He was a well-known lathi fighter in his youth. In a real fight, he could face dozens of fighters, their weapons swinging in the air, and the fight was over in a flash when his opponents lay on the ground with bleeding skulls. Lathi fights often settled disputes among peasants. As a martial art, though, lathi fights seldom caused injuries. The competition was based on mastery in handling the stick and defensive moves to stop the opponent's stick from touching one's body.

Khansab was oiling his lathi when Fattu came running. "Khansab, the village is under attack." He was out of breath.

"What are you saying?" It did not make sense to Khansab.

"The village is under attack," Fattu repeated himself. "Pratap Singh is coming with five hundred men to attack us."

"Why would Pratap attack Birehra?"

"No, he is coming to attack Nagla." Fattu was relatively relaxed by that time. "Baldev Singh has refused to send his daughter back to her in-laws, and Pratap is coming to take her back by force. People are running in fear and shutting themselves in their homes."

"How do you know all that?"

"Chaita Dhobi was coming back from a visit to his relatives and met them on the way. There are at least 500 Rajputs with Pratap, and he is swearing to restore his honour. They will be here soon."

Khansab got up and asked Fattu to follow him. He came outside with his lathi and stood in front of his house. The street was deserted; there were people on every rooftop; women peeped from behind half-open doors. Even the children, who usually played in the street, had disappeared. Khansab looked back and saw a man coming toward him at a fast pace. He held a young woman by the arm, almost dragging her with him.

"Who is that man?" asked Khansab.

"He is Baldev Singh," replied Fattu.

"Baldev Singh? What is he doing here?"

By the time Khansab could get an answer, Baldev stood in front of him.

"Are you not going to ask me what I am doing here?" said Baldev.

"Yes, Baldev," replied Khansab.

"I am here to invoke the friendship between your father and my father."

"You don't have to do that. Even I can be your friend."

"I want you to protect my honour. Pratap is coming to snatch my daughter from me."

"Well, you have already given your daughter's hand in marriage to Pratap's son. He has every right to take her by force if you do not let her go unless you have a genuine reason."

"You don't understand," explained Baldev. "My daughter has been treated like dirt in his home. She has been mistreated, ridiculed, harassed, beaten, and turned into a maid."

"If it is true, then I will truly be your friend," Khansab replied. He asked Fattu to escort Preeti into the house.

"You go home, Baldev, and leave it to me."

"Remember that my honour is in your hand."

"Your honour is my honour," replied Khansab as Baldev left.

Khansab walked through the street until he was on the edge of the village. The afternoon sun blazed in the sky, and he stood alone, holding his lathi firmly in his right hand. There was a cloud of dust floating in the air at a distance. He could not see anything behind the dust but knew that men were walking toward the village, and there must be many of them. When the dust cloud thinned, he could see Pratap and his four sons approaching swiftly. They were all armed with lathis. Behind them was a huge crowd of people, equipped with spears and lathis. Fattu was right. They did not seem to have peaceful intentions.

Pratap stopped a few feet from where Khansab was standing. "What are you doing here, my friend?" said Pratap.

Khansab moved forward a few steps and drew a line in the dirt with his lathi. "If you cross this line, Pratap, we will not be friends anymore."

"I do not have any quarrel with you," Pratap replied. "We are on our way to Nagla and intend to pass through Birehra in peace unless you want otherwise."

"You don't have to go to Nagla. Your daughter-in-law is in my home, under my protection. So you will have to deal with me."

Pratap was perplexed. He could not understand why Khansab was protecting Baldev. After all, they had been bitter enemies. The people of Birehra were dumbfounded as they watched from their rooftops. Khansab was all alone, protecting them. Only time could tell if they would have to come down with their lathis and join the fight. Seconds ticked into minutes, and time slowed down. Birehra was at a standstill, waiting for the first lathi to rise.

"Why are you protecting Baldev's daughter?" asked Pratap.

"Because Baldev has asked me for protection," Khansab replied. "I cannot refuse anyone who seeks protection."

"That sly, dirty dog," Pratap cursed Baldev. "I knew that he would do something like that. He does not dare to face me himself."

"Whatever! The matter is now between you and me."

"I cannot go back without my daughter-in-law. Baldev has insulted me and violated my honour. Now you are taking his side."

"Your honour is as dear to me as my honour. I promise you that your honour will be restored, and you will return with your daughter-in-law. It is your choice whether you want to do it like a Rajput or like a bully."

"I have no intention to fight if we can settle the matter peacefully."

"Then tell your men to go back. You and your sons will be my guests tonight, and you can take your daughter-in-law with you tomorrow morning."

Pratap was hesitant at first, but then he told his sons to ask the men to go back. As they started retreating, Khansab stepped forward and embraced Pratap. People on the rooftops took a sigh of relief. Khansab had confronted the enemy single-handedly and had averted bloodshed. They started coming out into the street. Pratap's fighters turned back, and he walked with Khansab-his sons following them-to Khansab's home.

***

As the sun descended, the air-cooled down. Karmoo had sprinkled several *mashak* loads of water onto Khansab's patio. Chairs had been laid as usual, and Khansab had settled himself for the company. Pratap sat next to him, and his sons occupied the chairs facing them.

"I am still unable to understand why Baldev is acting this way," said Pratap.

"You know that he is your friend, and I am your friend, too," replied Khansab. "I do not want to pass judgement. Baldev is on his way, and he will tell you his reasons."

Just then, Baldev walked in. Khansab realized that it was the first time that Baldev had stepped into his home.

Baldev sat down next to Khansab on the other side, without any formal greeting. There was a long silence, which made everyone uncomfortable. Eventually, Khansab broke the ice. "Baldev, why don't you tell Pratap what the issue is?"

"Why don't you ask Pratap?" replied Baldev. "He knows very well what the issue is."

"If I knew, I would not have come this way," Pratap interjected.

"Does he know how my daughter is being treated in his home?"

Baldev was referring to Pratap as a third person to show his anger.

"As far as I know, she is happy. She is a good girl and always touches my feet when I enter my home."

"Does he know that his wife mistreats her? Does he know that my daughter is being used as a maid in his home?"

"What are you talking about, Baldev?" Pratap addressed him directly.

"So, you don't know what is going on in your home," replied Baldev. "Don't tell me that you don't even know that your son beats my daughter."

"What?"

"Ask your son, and let us see if he will deny it."

Pratap's patience was running out. "What am I hearing?" he said and looked at Anand.

Anand kept on staring at the ground without saying a word; it proved that Baldev was right. Pratap got angrier at every passing moment of his son's silence.

"What am I hearing? I asked," Pratap shouted.

Still, there was no response from Anand. Suddenly, Pratap took off his shoe and headed for Anand, who raised his hands to protect his head, but Pratap's aim was precise. Anand covered his head, and his father kept hitting him with the shoe. Anand's older brother got up to protect him and stood between him and their father. Pratap started hitting him too, and he retreated. Finally, Khansab got up.

"That is enough, Pratap," he said. "I am sure the boy has learned his lesson."

"We Rajputs do not lift a finger at a woman. I am ashamed of my son." Pratap's anger seemed to have subsided. He turned back to

Baldev.

"I owe you an apology and am embarrassed that I could not take care of your daughter." Baldev did not respond. Pratap put his hand on Baldev's shoulder. "I beg you to forgive me and promise you that your daughter will be treated like a flower in my home."

Baldev got up and embraced Pratap. Everything was forgiven and forgotten.

The next morning, Preeti was ready to go back to her in-laws. She had stayed at Khansab's home overnight because he insisted that she depart from his home. Thukra'in had already arrived there with Preeti's belongings and met Chhoti Begum for the first time. They liked each other, and Chhoti Begum expressed her regret that they did not have an opportunity to meet earlier. Khansab had instructed Wafati, the bullock cart driver, to prepare his cart for the travel.

Wafati and his wife had worked on decorating the cart all night to make it fit for a bride. He had chosen two of his youngest bulls, each as tall as a pony. Their horns had been painted green, with red ribbons tied around them. There were chains of tiny bells around their necks, and a shawl with rainbow colours was hanging on the back of each bull. The cart had been decorated with a parrot-green curtain on all four sides, resting on a yellow canopy.

The people of Birehra were curious to know how the situation was developing. They talked about the way Khansab had handled the tense situation on the previous day. The news of reconciliation spread fast, and people came out to witness Preeti's send-off. Men, women, and children were lined up on both sides of the street. Many women stood on their rooftops and watched as Preeti's bridal carriage started moving. Pratap and his sons walked behind the cart. They were accompanied by Khansab and Baldev, who escorted them to the edge of the village. The crowd followed them. When they stopped to say goodbye, Khansab stood for some time, and when Pratap's party was at some distance, he shouted: "Rai Bahadur Pratap Singh!" His voice boomed throughout the village. Pratap turned his face to listen to Khansab.

"Just remember that if anyone touches even Preeti's hair, I will descend on your village like a hawk with 5000 Pathans, and when I am finished, not even a dog in your village will breathe!"

A hush fell over the spectators, and it seemed as if they had stopped breathing! A Pathan had challenged a Rajput, and they waited silently for the consequence. The air stood still. Not a leaf moved in a tree nor a bird chirped. The world came to a halt as people waited in suspense! Pratap walked back slowly until he stood in front of Khansab. He looked straight into Khansab's eyes and smiled. "I have already apologized," he said in almost a whisper. "What do you want me to do, put my turban on your feet?" he took off his turban, and as he bent forward, Khansab put his hands under Pratap's arms and pulled him up.

"No, I just wanted to remind you," Khansab replied as he took Pratap's turban and put it back on his head.

"I assure you that Preeti will sleep on nothing but a bed of roses in my home."

As Pratap walked back to the carriage, people sighed relief and praised Khansab's wisdom. Someone shouted: *"Khansab ki!"* and the crowd responded with, *"Jai ho!"* It was a prayer for Khansab to be always victorious. The sound of Jai ho filled the air; They could hear it in the entire village. Khansab ki, Jai ho! Khansab ki, Jai ho!

The story of Khansab's bravery and his confrontation with an army of 500 lathi fighters single-handedly was going to be told generation after generation, with a bit more spice and a bit more exaggeration each time, until it would become part of the folklore of Birehra!

The One-Eyed Water Carrier

Karmoo, the water carrier, was a short, dark man, with thin legs and a built-in sneaky smile on his lips. Even though his real name was Karamat Ali, most people called him *Karmoo* or *Kaana* Karmoo, because he had lost his left eye to smallpox in his childhood. Once, when Azad had referred to him as Kaana Karmoo in front of his grandmother, she reprimanded him. "God does not like those who make fun of someone's handicap," she said to him in a soft voice. "Karmoo is a good man, and you should respect him."

"But Nanijan, everyone calls him Kaana Karmoo. That's his name."

"Nooo, Baytaaaa ... his name is Karamat Ali. Only those who are cruel call him Kaana Karmoo." She always addressed Azad as *Baytaa* with affection and stretched it when she wanted to emphasize her point. From that day, Azad always called him Karamat.

Even though Karmoo did not have moustaches or a beard like most men in the village, he was not clean-shaven either. He was just too lazy to be bothered with shaving. Once in a while, while he was returning to the well after dropping off a load of water in someone's house, he met Chokha the Barber on the way and asked him for a shave right there. They sat down facing each other in the shadow of a wall, and Chokha unpacked his gear. Karmoo was a complicated case since smallpox had left permanent scars on his face. Despite that, Chokha moved his long sharp razor through the pits and crevices of Karmoo's face with such expertise that not one hair was left.

Karmoo had to change his water bag whenever the old one had developed so many holes that water leaked out in streams in all directions as he made his deliveries. He knew that it would almost be empty if he did not change it soon when he reached his destination. Whenever Khansab noticed the leaks, he stopped Karmoo. "Do you use your mashak as a dartboard?" he asked him.

"No, Khansab, I have been using this mashak for over six months now. I think the stitches are worn out."

"Don't forget to collect the hide when we slaughter a goat next time," Khansab replied.

It was always Sharfu, the shoemaker, who processed the goat hide and sewed the leather to make a water bag for Karmoo. It took him a whole month to dry the hide and tan it. He sewed the front legs together, then the hind legs, and connected them with a leather strap. The neck was used as the spout, while the rear end was stitched shut. The new mashak was now ready to be delivered to Karmoo. When he put the strap on one shoulder and rested the mashak on his back, it appeared as if he was carrying a goat hanging upside down. He always tied a string around the spout to keep water in and held the mashak in place by taking his arms behind and holding it.

Azad could never understand why Karmoo bent forward and ran while carrying a full mashak on his back. Karmoo always stooped while walking, even when he was not carrying a mashak. Perhaps it had become a habit for him. He always wore a pair of khaki shorts and an undershirt that must have been white when new but had turned grey due to the accumulation of dirt on it. Khansab had taken it upon himself to supply a new pair of shorts for Karmoo when the old pair was worn out. He sent a servant to the city to buy cloth, and

Chhoti Begum sewed it herself. Karmoo's clothes were always wet due to leaks from his mashak. As some wise man had once said, a Bhishti cannot stay dry just as a coal seller cannot help but get his face blackened.

When it was time for prayers, and Karmoo saw people coming to the mosque, he left his mashak on the well and went into the mosque. After he had performed ablutions, he reached the cabinet in the ablutions area, where his loincloth was kept. People knew that it was Karmoo's cabinet, and no one ever opened it. Karmoo wrapped the cloth around his waist on top of his shorts and made sure that it reached his ankles because he was not supposed to pray with his knees exposed. After prayers, he folded the cloth and put it back in the cabinet.

Nobody had any doubt about the character of Karmoo, but he had a disgusting habit that caused a great deal of aversion among the Sherwani women. His only weakness was that he could not keep his eyes off them! Whenever he entered Khansab's home, he just came in without any announcement; that was highly impolite. Men did not enter women's quarters unnecessarily or without permission. It would be okay for a man to enter his house if only his wife were there. Still, there were usually daughters, sisters, daughters-in-law, maids, or other women from the neighbourhood who had dropped in. When Khansab entered his house, he stopped in the doorway and announced with a loud cough that he was coming in, as was the custom for honourable men. He stood there to give women enough time to be dressed appropriately and ensure that everyone had put her dupatta on her head. He stepped in only when someone inside gave him a word that it was proper for him to enter. Karmoo, however, was another story. He did announce that he was coming in, but he was already halfway inside the house by that time. Women rushed to pick up their dupattas and cursed him! Chhoti Begum always shouted at him. She had complained to Khansab several times, but he still ignored her with a laugh. "Poor Karmoo! He is helpless at the hands of his habit," he laughed. "The poor fellow has only one eye; how much of you can he see?"

Karmoo walked past with his mashak along the wall and kept his gaze down, as gentlemen should. It was impolite to stare at women. They also knew that his blind eye was toward them, and he could not see anything in their direction. However, even though he was looking down on his way back, he tilted his head and peeked. Women kept an eye on him, as if they were waiting for the moment, and cursed him again. "You miserable Karmoo, you haven't learned any lesson after losing one eye. May God take away your other eye too!"

Karmoo just smiled and pretended that he had seen nothing. He was not innocent, though. He told stories to everyone as he sat at night in the gathering to smoke a hookah and exchange local gossip. "You know, Khansab's sister-in-law is visiting these days. I have never seen anything so beautiful. She looked like a fairy in her pink suit." His friends reminded him that it was rude to look at women with unclean intentions, but he never admitted that he had any impurity in his heart.

***

Karmoo could never say that there was any major problem in his life. His family was well fed and well clothed. The Sherwanis were always generous to give him his share of the harvest. They all cared for him, despite his nasty habit of staring at their women. Whenever he entered a home at lunchtime, he was always asked if he had taken his lunch. He reciprocated their favours by providing them with the best service. He never grumbled if any of them were extravagant in using water and supplied them with as many mashaks as they asked for.

Karmoo's mother had started looking for a bride for him as soon as he had turned eighteen, but she failed. Who was going to give his daughter to a one-eyed bhishti with dark skin and a scarred face, unless the girl was blind or deaf? Her younger son, named Juma, because he was born on a Friday, was only three years younger than Karmoo. He was also waiting to be married, but how could she look for a bride for him while the older brother was still unmarried? *What will people say?* When Karmoo turned twenty-five, she lost all hope. Women in the neighbourhood convinced her that she should not punish Juma, who would soon go downhill. That was when she declared reluctantly that she was ready to get Juma married. Many parents whose daughters were ready to be married were waiting for this announcement; they whispered in the ear of *Shareefan*, the matchmaker. Her full-time job was to peep into every home in Birehra, and the neighbouring villages, where there were boys and girls. She was an authority on the financial and moral data of every family. Karmoo's mother had never mentioned to Shareefan that she was looking for a younger son's match. Still, the mothers of several eligible girls prompted her to pay a discreet visit to Karmoo's mother and present their daughters' names to her.

When Karmoo's mother saw Shareefan, she knew right away that the word had reached the matchmaker, but she did not mention anything about her plans. Shareefan, on the other hand, hesitated to initiate the conversation from her side in case Karmoo's mother thought that she had an ulterior motive behind the visit. She talked about a marriage that she had arranged a year ago and mentioned that the couple recently had a beautiful baby boy. "The groom's mother was so impatient for a grandson that she expected to hear the news of her daughter-in-law getting hopeful the day after the wedding," she said as she took off her slippers and put her feet on the charpoy. "I get swollen feet if I sit for long with my legs hanging down."

"You know you are getting old, Shareefan khala," replied Karmoo's mother. "How long do you think your feet will be with you?"

"You are right, dear. There was a time when I used to walk all day from village to village without getting tired."

"Here, let me get a glass of sharbat for you. It's a hot day."

"May He reward you for that!" Shareefan said, looking up and pointing a finger to the sky.

Karmoo's mother reached the water-pot and dipped an aluminum tumbler into it. She mixed in a spoonful of sugar and offered it to Shareefan, who emptied it in one breath and acknowledged that it was cold and sweet. She was waiting for her host to give her a hint, but Karmoo's mother was tight-lipped about the matter.

"As I was telling you, the groom's mother expected the news of her daughter-in-law being hopeful right away."

"I can imagine that," replied Karmoo's mother. "Some mothers-in-law don't have patience."

"Almost two months passed, and nothing had happened. When I visited the groom's mother, she started blaming me. She said that I had tied a barren girl to her son."

"*Toba Toba*, how appalling!" Karmoo's mother touched her right cheek with her index finger and then the left cheek as well as if she were slapping herself when she heard such blasphemy. "How can one interfere with God's work?"

"That's what I told her. You will not believe me, but she was all smiles when I visited her the next time. She asked me to open my mouth and put a whole laddoo in it as she told me that her daughter-in-law was *hopeful!*"

"You must have been relieved."

"I was, and it was just last Thursday when the girl gave birth to a moon-faced boy."

Shareefan could have continued with the story, but she wanted Karmoo's mother to come to the point. Finally, she gave up. "I see that Juma has reached the age. Do you have any plans for him?"

"You know, Shareefan khala, Karmoo is older than him and has to get married first." A ray of hope shone in her eyes. She made another effort to sell her older son to the matchmaker. Maybe she could provide a two-for-one service. Maybe there was a girl somewhere for Karmoo.

"They say that every child is born with the spouse's name written on its forehead," replied Shareefan. "You should not get impatient. If God has already chosen a mate for Karmoo, she will come."

"You are right, but he is already past the age of marriage, and I am worried."

"You should not worry."

"I can't help it. I am Karmoo's mother." She cleared her throat to overcome the heaviness on her chest.

"The time for marriage is predestined. When the time comes, Karmoo will get married, too," answered Shareefan.

"But when will that time come?"

"You know what the wise have said: *Haste is the act of Satan, and the fruit of patience is sweet!*"

"Can't disagree with that, but what would you suggest, Shareefan khala?"

"You should not wait any longer for your other son."

"But what will people say? *There must be something wrong with Karmoo; otherwise, why would his parents get the younger son married first?*"

"Why do you care what people say, as long as you have

grandchildren playing around you?"

"I will leave the matter in your hands. I call you *khala* because you are like an aunt to me, and I am sure you are a better judge of our circumstances."

"By the way, what is Juma doing?"

"He works in Khansab's fields. You do not have to worry about our living. You can see yourself that God has given us everything."

Shareefan looked around and nodded in approval as she had a sigh of relief. She had initiated the matter, and the machine was in motion. She talked about several girls, starting with the ones harder to sell, but Karmoo's mother kept hesitating until she mentioned the right girl's name. She was the daughter of another water carrier in the neighbouring village; Karmoo's mother knew the family well. As far as beauty was concerned, the girl was part-moon, part-sun, as they say, and would bring great joy into their home. Deep down, Shareefan was confident that it was a done deal. She had already received approval from the girl's family, and it was only a matter of time before she would be in a position to initiate the proposal. She expected to be rewarded handsomely for her effort.

"I will mention it to Karmoo's abba and will let you know as soon as I get his approval," said Karmoo's mother.

"Of course. How can you decide anything without consulting your husband?"

"I am satisfied, and I am sure Karmoo's abba will agree too."

She always addressed her husband as Karmoo's abba. It was impolite for a woman to take the name of her husband. Before Karmoo was born, she referred to her husband simply as *he*, and women understood to whom she was referring. Some women in those days believed that, if the name of their husbands came even on the tip of their tongue, their marriage would be void. Of course, there was no truth in it because there was no mention of it in *The Heavenly Ornament*; it was merely out of respect that husbands and wives did not take the names of each other. Her husband's real name was Ibrahim, but people in the village called him Ibrahim Chacha, out of respect since he was old enough to be their uncle.

***

When Karmoo's brother got married, Khansab took good care of the family and contributed extravagantly to the wedding expenses. The bride received several heavily embroidered suits, silver jewellery from head to toe, a full set of kitchen utensils, pots and pans, a generous supply of winter bedding, and a sewing machine. For what else could a bride wish! A year later, she had twin boys, and Chhoti Begum sewed many clothes for them.

Life was good for Karmoo and his family. While his parents played with the twins all day, his sister-in-law was busy in the kitchen. Juma worked in Khansab's fields, and Karmoo went from house to house, delivering water. Karmoo's mother was always cheerful and counted her blessings. Whenever a woman in the neighbourhood complimented her for her good fortune, she ensured that the compliment included *Masha-Allah*! One never knew when an evil eye would spoil everything. Juma's boys, Chandan and Madan, were two years old and had started running around the house, chasing each other. They were identical twins; not even their parents or grandparents could differentiate between them easily. They were still breastfed, and it frequently happened that, after Chandan had been fed and left to run around, his mother would go and pick him up to feed him again, thinking that it was Madan. It was only after he refused to accept any more feed that she realized her mistake.

Confusion continued until Karmoo told the mullah at the mosque that the boys were always catching the evil eye from women in the neighbourhood, who gave compliments to the children without mentioning God's name. As a result, they caught cold and fever regularly. The mullah wrote a verse from the Qur'an on two pieces of paper and folded them several times to make them into small talismans.

"One *taweez* is for Chandan and the other for Madan." Karmoo wiped his hand over his shirt as he accepted the talismans. He kissed the pieces of paper and touched them to his forehead to show respect.

"They contain verses from the Qur'an, so treat them with respect," the mullah reminded him; he nodded in agreement.

Karmoo took the talismans home that evening, and his mother prepared them for the children. She took two clean pieces of cloth and soaked them in molten wax that she made by heating a candle in a small pot. As the wax cooled down, the cloth was stiff and water-resistant. She sewed two small bags, one green and the other white, and each contained a string to be tied around the boys' necks. The talismans were wrapped in the waterproof cloth and sewn inside the bags. The white taweez was given to Chandan and the green to Madan. The boys were not only protected from the evil eye-their health improved after that day, but it was easy to distinguish between them!

***

Notwithstanding the wonderful life of his family, Juma was depressed for no apparent reason. While he worked in the field, he was mostly quiet; when Juma was asked about something, he was startled as if awoken from sleep. As he fed the cattle, opened and closed irrigation channels, dug holes, and cleaned weeds, he was sunk deep in thought. No one knew what was bothering him. Even his parents had noted that something was bothering him, but they were hesitant to ask him. Someone asked Karmoo why his brother was so quiet, but he could not offer any explanation either.

Karmoo's mother sat on her charpoy, cracking betel nuts, and the twins played nearby. When her daughter-in-law passed by, she asked her to sit down for a minute. Juma's wife picked up the corner of her dupatta and wiped her nose as she perched on the corner of the charpoy.

"I have noticed that Juma is very quiet these days. He doesn't talk much while he is at home and doesn't even play with the boys."

"You are right, Amman; he doesn't talk much these days," replied her daughter-in-law.

"Is everything okay between you two?"

"I can't think of anything being wrong."

"That's what I thought. But you know," Karmoo's mother was nervous and looking for words. "Men are complicated, and sometimes they have problems."

"Oh, what problems?"

"You know ..."

She thought that her daughter-in-law was dumb. How long would it take her to understand? She started breathing heavily, and sweat appeared on her forehead.

"You know what I mean," she repeated. "When you two are alone ... is everything okay?"

She lowered her voice and talked in whispers. Juma's wife understood precisely what her mother-in-law was alluding to. Her cheeks turned red; she blushed, and her chin almost touched the collarbone as she lowered her eyes. *What kind of question is that?* She could not find suitable words for the reply. She wished the ground under her feet would split so she could jump into it to avoid further embarrassment.

"You don't have to feel shame in front of me, *bahoo*," said the old woman. "I am like your mother. If you don't talk to me, to whom can you tell your problems?"

"You don't have to worry about anything like that," she said and got up and walked to the kitchen.

Karmoo's mother was satisfied. At least that reason was ruled out. What else could be bothering Juma? She waited for the evening when her sons were back from work. It was long after dark, and the twins had already gone to bed. She spread the mat in front of the kitchen while her husband and the two sons washed their hands for dinner. Juma's wife was making fresh chapatis as the men sat down. Juma was quiet, as usual. He watched his father as he finished pouring potato curry on his plate. He picked up the pot and put it in front of Karmoo before taking his turn.

"You don't talk much these days, do you?"

Juma lifted his head and looked at his mother as she spoke. "Are you talking to me, Amman?"

"Yes, I am talking to you."

He did not say anything.

Karmoo was encouraged by the conversation his mother had initiated. "Someone asked me the same question today," he remarked, as he moved the pot in front of his brother. He wanted the conversation to continue. Juma did not answer; he picked up the ladle and poured some curry onto his plate. There was a long silence.

"There is nothing wrong," Juma finally said in a low tone, as if he wanted to close the subject. They continued eating quietly as his wife put a fresh chapati in front of them.

"There must be something wrong; otherwise, why you would start observing the fast of silence for no reason." said his father. There was another long pause.

Finally, Juma decided to settle the matter. "It is just that I want to leave the village."

"What do you mean, you want to leave the village?" Ibrahim raised his eyebrow as he looked at his son.

Juma hesitated. He did not want to hurt his family. "Times are changing, and we should change too."

"And how are times changing?"

He did not like his father's tone. He was still scared of his father, and even though he had stopped beating him after Juma got married, he still remembered the force of his father's slap. He wanted to settle the matter without making his father spank him in front of his wife.

"People are moving to the city," he said apologetically. "There are piles of wealth in Aligarh, and it will be a pity if we don't take our share."

"What do you need money for? Are your children starving here?"

Juma could not come out with the answer right away. He did have an answer for him but felt threatened because his father was getting angrier. He did not want to upset him during the meal.

"I asked you if your children are starving here or if your wife is not clad properly." His father demanded the answer.

"No, I can't complain." Juma tried to calm his father. "How could I offend God by denying His blessings? But how long shall we keep living in this mud house? I can work in Aligarh and make enough money to build a brick house, right here in the village."

His father did not answer right away. He kept thinking, putting the pros of his son's intentions in one pan of the scale and the cons in the other pan, and watching how the balance tilted. Juma's wife kept bringing fresh chapatis, and her mother-in-law sat quietly, waving the hand fan to keep flies away from the food.

"I don't understand." The old man finally gave his verdict. "We have served this village for generations. Our fathers and forefathers walked on this ground. Your grandparents are buried here. How can you even think of abandoning their graves?"

Ibrahim felt a lump in his throat. How could his son think of leaving the family? What would they possibly do with money, and what was wrong with a mud house? It was big enough for the family. Perhaps Karmoo would not get married, and his grandsons would not have any problem working in the field.

"I am not abandoning the village, Abba." Juma understood his father's reservations. "It is just that I will be working in the city. I will send you money, and you can start building the house. You do not even need to move. Just break these walls slowly as money comes in, and replace them with brick walls."

That was the end of the conversation. Juma was unsure what his father had finally decided, but his silence was a good indication of his approval, even if it was half-hearted. For the time being, he was satisfied. The three men got up to wash their hands and rinse their mouths. Karmoo's mother picked up the plates and rolled the mat. She was going to eat with her daughter-in-law inside the kitchen.

The family spent the night gazing at the starry sky. They all pretended that they were sleeping in their beds comfortably, but their eyes were wide open. As shooting stars played dart games in the sky, and birds sat in meditation on tree branches, they rolled in their beds to change sides, each one of them contemplating the consequences of Juma's decision.

Karmoo kept thinking about his brother working in the city. *Maybe he will be able to send enough money to build a brick house. We will even think of building the house close to the landowners, just outside the compound, where tailors live. I will work hard to build the house myself. There is plenty of help available in the village, and they will not demand any money in return. However, I will need money to buy bricks and cement.*

Juma's wife kept tossing and turning in her bed all night. The thought of her husband leaving the family was painful. *Will the family continue being kind to me while he is away? The boys will miss him. No, it is not the right decision. Maybe he will change his mind and decide to stay.* She disapproved of her father-in-law not being stern with him. *He should have put his foot in the path of his son's intentions. However, maybe it is right for the family. I could trust the judgement of my husband. After all, he is not stupid.*

Once, in the early days of their marriage, she had overheard her mother-in-law complaining to Juma about her, but he had handled the situation wisely. He had told his mother that he was not going to take sides. If there was any problem among them, they should resolve it themselves. *That was a wise move. All mothers-in-law are bossy, but they can be handled tactfully, provided their sons do not act foolishly. After that, she never said anything against me, and I did not have the guts to complain about her in front of him. No, Juma is right. He should go out to make some money to build a brick house. But what if he finds another woman in the city!* She kept changing her mind as she opened her eyes from time to time to guess how much of the night had gone by.

Ibrahim continued weighing the pros and cons. *The boy is right; Times* are *changing. Maybe he should go out and try his luck in the city. On the other hand, Karmoo is timid and foolish. People call him Kaana Karmoo behind his back and make jokes about him. On the other hand, Juma is brave and strong. Nobody can lift a finger against us. They respect Juma. On the other hand, why will they lift a finger against us in the first place? We do not come in anyone's way. We keep to ourselves and do not hurt anyone. On the other hand, you never know how some quick-tempered vagabonds will behave once Juma leaves the village. On the other hand, Karmoo could smarten up. Once he knows that his brother is not around, he will become more responsible.*

Karmoo's mother did not have much to think. It was a matter to be decided by the men. *What was it about changing times? I do not see any change. It is the same village, the same life, the same people, and same problems. What did Juma mean when he said that times are changing? Maybe times are changing. I am getting old, and so is Karmoo's abba, but who is not getting old? People always get old and die, and the young ones grow up. The grandchildren will grow up one day and will be married. Will they also move to the city, and everyone else in the family? Then what will we do here? I am never going to leave the village.* Her tears rolled down, wetting her pillow, but then she thought. *As if we are going to live forever. I am sure we will be long gone by the time the kids grow up and are ready to leave the village.* She took a deep breath of relief as she rolled over.

Juma himself was on cloud nine, dreaming about the anticipated change in his life. He had been to Aligarh once when he rode with the caravan of bullock carts hauling Khansab's wheat to the market. Aligarh was beaming with life. *I will bury myself in the crowd and will go places; I will visit the exhibition and watch the cinema; I will sit in the tea-house and smoke cigarettes, like the city folks. I will have fun for a few days before I start looking for a job. I am sure I will find something. Aligarh embraces the poorest of the poor, and nobody goes hungry. Even beggars can manage to lay their hands on chicken curry.* Then he suddenly felt gloomy. How could he eat chicken curry while his family lived on lentils and potato curry? *But then, it won't be for long. I will send them enough money to raise a few hens and a rooster and make egg curry. They can slaughter one every week and cook chicken curry. No, I am not going to touch chicken curry until they can afford it.*

As the stars got fainter, and the first rooster in the village crowed, The mullah woke up in the mosque with a start and washed at the ablution's place; he climbed the stairs to the top of the minaret and thrust his fingers in his ears to say Azaan for dawn prayers. Ibrahim got up with the first words of Azaan and started preparing to go to the mosque. Karmoo left his bed as he heard his mother call his sister-in-law to check if the twins had wet their bed at night. They all got up as if they had spent a restful night. Juma pretended that he was still sleeping. He wanted to spend a few extra moments in bed since he had a few more dreams to dream.

***

It was a large bowl of buttermilk, containing a whole loaf of cornbread, broken into little pieces. Karmoo's mother soaked the bread in buttermilk to ensure that it became tender. She added tiny bits of *gurh* to sweeten it. Her husband insisted that she should not stir it so that he could feel pieces of gurh in his mouth with every spoonful. She could not remember a day since she got married, and that was almost forty years earlier, that she had ever missed preparing breakfast for her husband. When Juma got married and his wife took over the kitchen, she still kept making breakfast for her husband. As Ibrahim sat on the charpoy, she brought the bowl and put it in front of him. Perched on the edge of the charpoy, she waited for his usual comments about the bread not being tender enough or the gurh dissolved without leaving any solid pieces, but he kept eating without saying a word. His silence showed that he was worried.

"So what have you decided?" she broke the silence.

"Decided about what?"

"About Juma."

"What about Juma?" He kept avoiding the conversation, but she kept insisting on talking about the problem.

"I ... I don't know," he said after a long pause. "I am going to consult with Khansab."

After he finished his breakfast, he got up and put his shoes on. As he passed the water-pot stand, he picked up the tumbler and dipped it into the pot. He took a mouthful of water and swished it from side to side between his cheeks. After he spat the water on the dirt floor, he drank the rest of it and replaced the tumbler as he walked out.

***

Khansab just came out of the house after his breakfast and sat down in his chair to take another look at the day-old newspaper. Fattu had just brought the hookah, freshly charged with his favourite blend of tobacco. Even though the December sun shone in his face, the pale sunlight warmed the air and felt good. As he took the first puff of the morning, he saw Ibrahim coming up the stairs.

"What brings you here so early in the morning, Chacha?" he asked loudly.

For some reason, Khansab thought that Ibrahim was hard of hearing. He always spoke up when he talked to him.

"I have to discuss an important matter with you," he said, as he prepared to sit on the floor. Khansab got up from his chair and touched Ibrahim's shoulder.

"No, Chacha, you sit here in the chair," he said and pointed to the chair in front of him. Ibrahim knew that Khansab always asked him to sit in a chair, but courtesy demanded that he wait until he asked.

"How are your grandchildren? I hear they keep you busy."

"Oh, yes! They have brought great joy into my life."

He was hesitant to bring up the subject at hand and talked instead

146

about the news that electricity was coming to the village. Khansab knew that he had not come to him so early in the day just to talk about electricity. There must be some serious matter that had brought him.

"So, what else is new?"

"Well, I wanted to talk to you about a serious matter."

Khansab rotated the hookah to point it in his direction. Ibrahim moved it back with a gesture of gratitude. He knew his limits, and just because Khansab respected him on account of his age, he had no intention of smoking in his company.

"My younger son wants to go to Aligarh," he finally said.

"So what is the problem if Juma wants to go to Aligarh?" asked Khansab. "Let him go."

"But he wants to leave Birehra and work in the city." His hesitation showed that he was worried about Khansab's displeasure over losing one of his workers.

"Every boy wants to leave Birehra," replied Khansab. "Have you talked to him?"

"Yes, but I cannot dissuade him. I thought that he would listen to you."

"I suggest that you let him go to see the world. Times are changing, and you cannot keep young people in the village."

"Times are surely changing." Ibrahim sighed, but he was relieved that the matter was settled amicably.

"Maybe he can go with the grain next week and help them unload it. He can stay back when the carts return."

He looked at Fattu, who stood nearby. "Get twenty rupees from Chhoti Begum, and give the money to Juma. He will need it while he looks for a job."

Fattu nodded in agreement. Ibrahim stood up to leave; he thanked Khansab for his generosity. He wanted to give the news to his son. On one hand, he was happy that Khansab did not mind, but on the other hand, he had wished that someone could persuade Juma to stay.

***

Karmoo missed his brother, who had never come back from Aligarh. Juma did send money to him as he had promised, sometimes five rupees, sometimes ten, every other month or so. Ram Das, the postman, had been bringing mail to Birehra since he joined the Indian Post's service at twenty. As far as people could remember, he had used the same bicycle and the original mailbag for the last thirty years. He knew three generations of everyone in each of the ten villages he served. Whenever Ram Das brought a money order from Juma, he usually stopped Karmoo while he was going to the well with the empty mashak hanging on his shoulder. "I have got some money for you, Karmoo."

"Oh, it must be from Juma!"

"No, it has come from London," said Ram Das sarcastically with a smile. "The king of England has personally signed it and has requested you to accept it as a gift!"

"That is what you say every time."

"What else can I say? You always ask me where it is from. Of course, it is from your brother. You are not a guru or a saint, so people will send you money unnecessarily!"

Ram Das reached into his leather bag and pulled out the money order form. He looked at the address carefully to make sure that he was delivering the right money order. Karmoo wiped his right thumb, dried it by rubbing it against his wet shirt, and looked at it to ensure it was clean. Although he was a dark-skinned man, his palms were almost milk-white and leathery. The skin had started splitting since his hands were always wet. There was a long cut on his thumb, through which a narrow line of blood was visible. He made a fist and stuck the thumb out. Ram Das pulled out a fountain pen from his pocket, removed the cover and examined the nib. It was almost dry. He unscrewed the back cover and felt the rubber tube that held the ink. He squeezed the tube gently, and a drop of black ink appeared on the tip of the nib. As he released the tube, the ink was sucked back but the nib was now wet. After he screwed the cover back, Karmoo extended his thumb, and Ram Das rubbed the nib's back all over it to spread the ink.

Even though Karmoo could not read or write, he knew exactly where he was supposed to put the thumbprint. He had done it so many times that he knew where each entry was. Ram Das rested the form on his bag, and Karmoo pressed his thumb on the right spot. It appeared as a perfectly opaque smudge on the brown paper, with only one line at the centre of the black impression that showed exactly where the skin on his thumb was split. Ram Das examined the thumbprint and nodded with approval. He took a small roll of money and pulled out two notes: a ten and a five. "Here are fifteen for you," he said to Karmoo, handing him the money.

"Oh, Juma must have saved quite a bit of money this month. He usually sends five or ten."

"You have a nice boy for a brother," replied Ram Das. "I hope you are using his money wisely."

"I am. Every paisa Juma sends me goes to building the brick house."

Ram Das tore the bottom portion of the money order form and handed it to Karmoo. "Here, he has also sent you a letter."

"Why don't you read it for me?"

Ram Das took the form back. "It says, 'Dear Bhai Sahib, Salaam. Everything is fine here. I hope everything is fine there. I am sending you fifteen rupees this time. I got many generous tips this month. A wise customer had advised me to get more tips if I am extra nice to customers. I am following his advice. Please give my regards to Amman and Abba and the boys and everyone else at home. Your Brother, Juma.'"

He had included his wife among *everyone else at home.* It was impolite to ask about his wife while writing to the older brother if someone felt that he cared more for his wife than his parents.

"I am glad that everything is fine with him," said Karmoo. "Could you please write a reply on my behalf?"

"I am running a little late today, but tell me what you want to say, and I will write it when I get back to the post office."

"Please tell him that we are glad to know that everything is fine with him and wish to tell him that everything is fine here as well. Tell him that I spend his money wisely. We have already replaced the old mud walls with brick and will raise the roof soon. Also, tell him that his hands will not touch the ceiling anymore when he returns and raises his arms to yawn. I have made sure that the walls are high enough."

"Don't worry; I will write a detailed letter to him and give him all the news in the village."

"In that case, let him know that Bilal's cow has given birth to a dead calf."

"Oh, that is too bad! Don't forget to express sorrow to Bilal on my behalf," replied Ram Das. "I will make sure to see him when I come here tomorrow. What else do you want me to write to him?"

"Tell him that the sugarcane season is here. I brought a whole pot of sugarcane juice from Khansab's crusher, and Amman cooked sugarcane pudding. The boys overate and got diarrhea. They are okay now."

Ram Das had a sigh of relief. "They must have liked it a lot," he remarked, as he clipped the pen back into his pocket.

Karmoo gave him a two-anna coin, three paisas for the reply postcard, and the rest was his baksheesh for reading the letter for him and writing the reply. "All you owe me is three paisas to buy the postcard." Ram Das searched through his pockets to return the change, but Karmoo insisted that he should accept the small token for his appreciation.

"You are so kind to me," he said. "You read to me Juma's letters and take the time to write back to him."

"This is the least I can do for you, but I appreciate your generosity." Ram Das gave up his attempt to look for change.

"Don't forget to write that the boys are okay now; otherwise, he will worry unnecessarily."

"Don't worry, I will take care of it," he replied as he left for the rest of the mail deliveries.

***

Karmoo visited his brother in Aligarh. He was dazzled by the city life and felt like a boy, walking on paved roads, riding on a lorry, going to the cinema, and spending time with Juma. He rode a *yakka* to the exhibition. It was a strange-looking horse carriage, hardly a three-feet-square plank of wood, mounted on two wheels, with an umbrella on top. The yakka driver sat on the poles that connected the carriage to the horse's back. There was hardly room for two people on it, but he kept calling for more passengers, and they kept climbing on it until there were four of them tightly squeezed, their feet hanging off the sides. Karmoo thought that the yakka was full, but he was wrong. The driver kept welcoming more passengers until they started sitting on the laps of those who had already occupied the plank. Karmoo watched him with interest as he stood patting the horse gently with one hand. He was a tall, skinny man wearing unkempt kurta pyjamas and a shabby cap. As he chewed paan, he had collected a mouthful of juice and did not want to lose a single drop. He raised his chin as he called for passengers, fearing any juice would drip out when he opened his mouth. Wet streaks of crimson colour had appeared on the corners of his lips as he chewed paan, and his voice came out gurgling through the juice. *Aik shawaari numaish ki ... Aik shawaari numaish ki.* He was asking for just one more passenger for the exhibition. It was a hot day, and the sunshine was bright as usual. The occupants were getting restless as they kept mounting one another. Streaks of sweat ran along with their faces. "Miyan, enough is enough," said one of the passengers angrily. "Where will you seat another passenger? On your head?"

"Jusht one more. I have to make enough money to buy graash for da horsh," he replied, looking at the sky. Even though he was trying his best not to lose any paan juice, he could not save the few droplets released in a spray as he opened his mouth.

"We have already lost a lot of our oil," grumbled another passenger, wiping sweat from his face with a dirty handkerchief.

The yakka driver accommodated everyone who could sit, perch, or hang somewhere. As long as there was room for someone to stick the front of his foot in a slot or a hole, he was allowed to hang on. By then, there were eight passengers, and the yakka was on its way to the exhibition. Each passenger paid one anna for the trip.

Juma and Karmoo entered the exhibition through the Muzammil Gate, named after a Nawab from the Sherwani tribe, who had built it. They were captivated by the hustle and bustle of people. They had to cut through the crowds to make way for themselves as they stroked forward through the flood of bodies. Every stall was equipped with loudspeakers blaring music. It was hard to pick out any song's words because they were mixed up with the neighbouring stalls' music. They spent the whole day going from stall to stall, eating spicy chaat, watching the magic shows, bursting balloons with the airgun, and buying gifts for Juma's boys. It reminded them of the old days when the two of them were young boys. They never had so much fun after their adolescence said goodbye to them.

When Karmoo returned to the village, he was bubbling with excitement; he decided to move to the city, but it was not easy. He needed money to rent a house and pay for expenses until he found a job. There were thousands of jobs for him in the city. He could haul a rickshaw, or work as a labourer, or he could even work in a restaurant serving tea to customers, just as Juma did. He had a good memory and could remember the bill for every customer; as the customers would line up to pay at the counter, he would sing their bills loud and clear, moving at the same time from table to table distributing tea:

One anna from the friend in the red cap;

Six paisas from the bearded guy;

The brother in the green shirt didn't eat or drink anything,

But he broke a glass.

Charge him four annas.

Karmoo chanted loudly, mimicking Juma's style, as he pulled the bucket from the well to fill his mashak. Suddenly, he realized that he was talking to himself. He looked around in embarrassment to make sure that nobody was listening. Fortunately, no one was around; otherwise, people would start doubting his sanity. He had seen Juma holding six cups and saucers, one on top of the other, on each palm, as he worked through the tables. It was ingenious; he was sure that his brother would be generous enough to teach him the art! The question was where he would find enough money to move to the city.

After he fed several buckets of water to his mashak, it was full. He tied the leather strap around the spout and loaded it on his back. *Will I ever be able to save enough money to move to Aligarh? Maybe Khansab will help me as he helped Juma, but why would he do that? I do not work exclusively for him. How else can I get enough money?*

There was a train of ideas passing through his mind, compartment by compartment, as he jogged his way back and forth, delivering water to his customers and returning with empty mashak to the well. He met several people on the way but did not bother to talk to them. They thought that he was too tired even to respond to their greeting. On his way back from a delivery, he did not even remember whose house he had been to and whether they had asked him for lunch. He walked back slowly to the well to pick up another load, his mashak hanging on his side, and his eyes pinned to the dirt on the ground. *What if I start charging for my service! It is not fair that they do not pay me for water. I think that is what I will do. I will tell them. No free water anymore! Even if I charge two paisas per mashak, I can collect enough money to move to Aligarh. There are four paisas in one anna and sixteen annas in one rupee. Now let me see how much money I will collect.*

Karmoo spent several days trying to determine how much money he would make. He delivered a minimum of two mashaks a day to each home; some took three. *Neem Haveli* was the largest customer; they took four mashaks, sometimes five. After a few complex calculations, he established that his daily delivery was close to thirty mashaks. He tried to convert mashaks into paisas, paisas into annas, and annas into rupees, but the arithmetic became more complex. When he finally arrived at the answer, he realized that it was not enough money. *I think I will charge one anna per mashak. I think they can afford it, and what will they do even if they cannot? I am the only water carrier here.*

At last, he decided to make his move. He was initially afraid that people would not like it, but his resolution got stronger as the days passed. He had thought about seeking advice from his father, but he knew that the old man would reject the plan. Khansab was the first one to get the news. "Times are changing, and we should change too!"

Khansab listened to him with patience and did not show any sign of displeasure. That was an encouraging sign. Khansab was the toughest nut to crack, and if he had accepted the arrangement so easily, he would have no problem with others.

People were not happy when Karmoo told them that he would charge one anna per mashak for delivering water. They said that he was greedy, but they could not do anything about it; Karmoo had a monopoly over water. They agreed reluctantly, and told him that he should keep track of how many mashaks he had delivered in a month. He decided to bill them at the end of the month. Karmoo was excited. He was the first entrepreneur in Birehra and a pioneer. The coming generations of emerging entrepreneurs would be proud of him!

***

As the new sun rose, it brought a new beginning for Karmoo with new plans, new resolutions, and a new life. He went back and forth all day, making deliveries, greeting everyone on the way. By the end of the day, he had counted twenty-seven mashaks. How many rupees did it come to? *Let me see; if I had delivered thirty-two mashaks, I would have made two rupees. Now since I am five short, it would make one rupee and eleven annas. That is a lot of money for one day. However, I have to keep track of individual accounts.*

Four mashaks for Neem Haveli, two for Central Haveli . . . It was becoming too complicated. He was sure that he would forget the whole arithmetic by the end of the month.

When he came home in the evening, he took one of the little notepads he had bought for his nephews at the exhibition in Aligarh. He even found a piece of a pencil. The boys had scribbled everywhere on the notepad, but there were still enough blank pages for Karmoo to write his accounting records. Although he did not know how to read and write, that was not a major problem. He allocated one page for each house and assigned a sign to it. The circle was for *Outer Haveli* and a cross for *Neem Haveli*. After he finished assigning an account number for each customer, he started entering the loads by putting a vertical line. That was simple. He would draw a line every time he delivered and count each customer's loads at the end of the month. He felt proud of himself.

Karmoo had stopped being part of evening gatherings when his friends sat down to smoke a hookah and chat about the day's events. They thought that Karmoo was perhaps displeased to find out about someone bad-mouthing him, but they all denied that anyone had said anything bad, as that would hurt Karmoo's feelings. They were aware that he had started charging for his services and that nobody had liked the idea, but they did not know that he spent his evenings at home, updating his daily journal.

Karmoo suspected that the Sherwanis had prepared a diabolical plan to make sure that his enterprise failed. What happened was that Khansab's relatives, who had gathered one evening for their daily chat, talked about Karmoo's issue. It was the second or the third day for the new water delivery arrangements. They felt that Karmoo was not fair. Why did he need money? His needs were met, and his family was cared for adequately by all households?

"We should stop catering to his family."

"No more free rations!"

"We should make sure that he pays for every grain of wheat, every drop of milk, every pinch of salt, every inch of cloth, and every block of gurh!"

"Tell the ladies that they should not offer him a single morsel of free lunch!"

"He should get tit for tat!"

Khansab agreed with his relatives. Karmoo was attempting to upset the equilibrium they had established over many generations.

***

It did not take long for Karmoo to find out what was happening behind the scenes. It came as a shock to him when nobody asked him for lunch. That was not a big deal; free lunch did not mean anything to him. The Sherwanis were displaying their bad manners! They were supposed to feed those who served them. *But am I really serving them?* he asked himself. After all, it was business-money in exchange for services. Maybe it was not too bad. He could drop in at home for lunch. That is what he would do from the next day on.

When he went home after the day's work, he was tired and hungry, but another shock awaited him. He greeted his father, who sat on the charpoy, gurgling his hookah. He mumbled something in reply and started churning the fire in the hookah with a twig. He approached his mother, but she turned her face and went away without saying a word. He asked his sister-in-law why his parents were in such a foul mood. She told him that his mother had gone to Khansab's home to get milk as usual, but she was told that she should buy milk from Shubrati's store.

"So did she get the milk?" he asked her.

"Yes, she did, but then Chhoti Begum told her that it was the last time she was getting free milk."

"I see." Karmoo stopped the conversation. He felt that the whole village was plotting against him. What was so bad about him wanting to improve the lifestyle of his family?

Just then, he heard his father calling him. He approached his father and stood near his bed. Karmoo started feeling uneasy; he knew that the news had reached his parents.

"What is it that I hear about you charging them for water?" asked his father, as he gestured him to sit down.

"Yes, they will pay one anna for each mashak."

Before his father could say anything more than a thoughtful "Hmm ..." Karmoo raised his voice to deliver his lecture. "You don't understand, Abba; times are changing, and we must change too. I will make enough money so that we can move to Aligarh."

Karmoo's father removed the hookah from his lips and raised his eyebrow. That is how he used to express his displeasure, but he decided to keep quiet and let his son finish his story.

"You know, Abba, Juma is doing so well there. I will go first and send you money. Eventually, we will rent a house, and you will move there too. We will have a good life. I will take you to the exhibition, and you will ride in a lorry. We will all have fun. The boys will go to school."

He was excited to see that his father quietly listened to him and thought about what he had said. Encouraged by how the conversation was going, he started talking again. "You don't know, Abba; city life is good and comfortable, and we will be together. Juma has been away from his children for so long; he will also like the idea." There was nothing more to say. Karmoo had come to the end of his argument, and his father's silence was pounding in his chest.

He finally got the verdict. "You must be crazy. What do you know about city life? People are murdered there every day, and they say that the roads are paved with hungry beggars. What will you possibly do in the city?"

"I will work there like Juma. He has such a busy life. He has nothing to worry about." Karmoo had decided to keep the volume of his voice high. That was the only way to win the battle.

"I knew that it was your brother who has poured poison into your ears. I already regret that I allowed him to go to the city, and now you have caught the same disease," replied his father, angrily.

Karmoo was disappointed. He avoided further confrontation with his father and returned to the kitchen, where his sister-in-law had already prepared his plate. His mother sat there too, eating quietly. The way his father had opposed him raised the strength of his resolution. He wanted to show everyone that he would succeed.

"I have never been so humiliated in my life," said his mother, as she broke a piece of bread. Karmoo did not respond. He knew that she would explode as soon as he opened his mouth. "I could have never imagined that anyone could refuse a bowl of milk for my grandchildren."

She waited impatiently for Karmoo to say something. He looked at his sister-in-law, but she looked the other way. The silence grew upon him until he could not take it any longer. "Don't worry, Amman; you can buy milk from Shubrati's store. I will have plenty of money to give you." She did not reply and kept eating silently. Karmoo finished his dinner and came out with a tumbler of water in his hand. After rinsing his mouth, he sat down to enter that day's transactions in his journal. He decided to see Khansab the next day and ask him for his opinion. Khansab was a reasonable man; he would surely understand his viewpoint.

***

The sun did not rise on the next day with any good news. When he arrived at the well, he found that Fareed, one of Zakaria Khan's servants, was drawing water from the well. He had already filled one large bucket and had started pouring into the second one.

"What are you doing here?" asked Karmoo with anger in his voice.

"Taking water, what else?" replied Fareed in the same tone.

"What for?"

"What do you use water for?"

Karmoo did not like it when his questions were answered with questions. "Don't you know that this is my well?"

"Did your father dig it for you?"

"Don't you dare try getting to my father; otherwise, I will break your bones."

"Oh, yes? It is a public well, and you cannot stop anyone from taking water from it."

Tempers flared, voices were raised, and the two men were ready to tangle when the mullah came running from inside the mosque. He had seen them through the arch over the well and knew that they were about to get into a fight. Even though Karmoo had never fought with anyone, Fareed was a quick-tempered young man.

"You two, don't you have any shame, raising your voices near the house of God? What is the matter with you two?" asked the mullah, standing at the gate and avoiding getting any closer, in case he was caught between them.

"Karmoo thinks that this well belongs to him," said Fareed, pointing his finger at Karmoo.

"I have been using it exclusively since I was a boy, and now I am told that it does not belong to me," Karmoo complained in return.

The mullah gave his verdict. "This well is in the mosque and belongs to everyone." Nobody has the right to stop anyone from drawing water from here."

Fareed lowered his arms to pick up the buckets and grumbled at Karmoo as he left.

"Why don't you two hug each other and shake hands before you leave," the mullah called to them, but Fareed did not turn back. Karmoo was still furious. He was now sure that the landowners were conspiring against him. *Landowners are landowners. They do not care for anyone;* he said to himself as he dropped the bucket into the well.

By the time he had made a few deliveries, his anger had subsided. He had decided to meet Khansab to test the waters with him. When he arrived at Khansab's home, he found him in the men's quarters, having lunch with two other guests.

"What brings you here, Karmoo?" asked Khansab as Karmoo stood at the door.

How rude and how un-Islamic, thought Karmoo. *He continues eating without inviting me.*

"Are you being paid promptly?" asked Khansab when Karmoo did not reply.

"I came about another matter."

"Yes?"

"I wanted to draw your attention to my shorts. They are worn out now and will have to be replaced soon." Karmoo just wanted to see his reaction. That was the ultimate litmus test to know his opinion.

Khansab wiped his fingers with half a chapati that was in front of him. "Oh, yes! I can see that. You should replace them soon," he said with a smile. "Why don't you go to the city and buy yourself a new pair of ready-made shorts? They have everything ready-made there. Ready-made clothes, ready-made shoes, ready-made relationships. Since you have decided to move to the city, you should get used to a ready-made life."

Karmoo did not have an answer. He left in despair, with his face down. He wanted to cry. He was angry that the people he had served since his boyhood behaved as if they did not recognize him anymore. Even his friends disapproved of his idea of change. *What is so bad about change? Who said that things should stay the way they are? The whole world is changing. The British are leaving, and the country will be free soon.*

Karmoo's disappointment grew by the day, as he noticed that his daily loads had gone down noticeably. People were conserving water. They were sending their servants to the well with their buckets. He could not stop anyone. Even the mullah was on their side. Everyone had boycotted him socially and financially. When he entered homes, he kept his gaze down, ensuring that he did not offend women. Things were already rough, and he did not want to stir them further. Women, on the other hand, missed his naughtiness. They complained to one another that he did not give them an opportunity to curse him. They had always enjoyed the old routine when he looked at them, like a thief stealing their charm, and they cursed him in return. They loved the way he smiled with his face down to hide his guilt. Where was that good old Karmoo?

The payday brought even greater despair for Karmoo. He told them their balances on the first day of the month, and they all paid promptly, without any hesitation. He counted the final intake. It came to seventeen rupees and twelve annas. That was not enough for him to buy groceries and save enough money to move to the city. His business venture had failed miserably, and he was ready to declare bankruptcy, but he was not prepared to admit failure since his honour was at stake. How could he tell his customers that he was prepared to go back to the old arrangement? Would they not think that he was stupid? Would his friends not ridicule him? Should he try for another month?

I thought that I was a pioneer in answering the call of changing times. How stupid of me! I should have at least sought someone's advice before I opened my mouth. He kept blaming himself. *That is why the elders say that you should weigh your words before you move your tongue.* No, he could not dare to ask his customers to forgive and forget, *unless one of them advised him to do so!* Then he would at least have an excuse to oblige them.

The opportunity came the next day when he went to make a delivery to Khansab's Haveli. It was a hot day, and Khansab was sitting in his room, reading his newspaper as usual. He saw Karmoo entering the house and kept an eye at the door.

"Come here, Karmoo!" Khansab called him when he came out of the house. He walked slowly and stood, staring at the ground, in front of Khansab.

"How is business?" He could feel a hint of sarcasm in Khansab's tone.

"What business, Khansab?"

"I mean your business of delivering water."

"I am not a businessman. I am just a poor labourer trying to make a living," Karmoo mumbled. He did not want to be disrespectful to Khansab. He wished that the earth could split, and he could fall in to save himself from Khansab's interrogation.

"I just want to know if you are saving enough money to move to the city."

Just then, Karmoo decided to raise his arms and give himself up. "No, I guess I had miscalculated my earnings."

"I suggest that you go back to the old arrangement and get yourself out of this mess," Khansab said and relieved him of his burden.

"Whatever you say, Khansab." Karmoo felt that the elephant sitting on top of him had suddenly decided to get up and walk away.

As Karmoo descended the stairs out of Khansab's place, he thought moving to the city was a stupid idea! How could he even think of leaving his friends with whom he had grown up? His roots were in Birehra. He remembered his father's words when he had told Juma years ago that it was not wise to abandon his grandparents' graves. He suddenly realized that his father was a wise man. As he returned to the well for another load, he saw from a distance that Fareed stood at the edge, pulling water from the well. He ran as fast as he could and knocked the bucket that Fareed had already filled.

"I have told you once before that I don't want to see you near my well!" He was trembling with anger, and words were caught in his throat. Fareed threw his arms around Karmoo's waist and dropped him on the ground.

"How dare you stop me?" He gnashed his teeth as he dug his fingers around Karmoo's neck. The mullah rushed to rescue them once again and pulled Fareed back. Karmoo coughed to relieve the pressure on his throat.

"I have warned you once before not to fight near the mosque!" the mullah yelled at them. "If you want to kill each other, go away from here and crack each other's skulls!"

"He started first!" Fareed pointed his finger at Karmoo.

"I have told him a thousand times not to come to my well, but he keeps polluting it," replied Karmoo.

"Okay, both of you sit down," The mullah pushed them down with his hands on their shoulders. "The Prophet has said that when anger takes you over, sit down if you are standing, and lie down if you are sitting."

They complied with his instructions; they could not be disrespectful to the mullah. "Karmoo, I have told you that this is a public well, and you do not have exclusive rights to it."

"But Fareed does not have to come here. I will be delivering water to Zakaria Khan's place."

"Now listen to me, Karmoo," the mullah said and put his hand gently on Karmoo's shoulder. "You charge for your service, and everyone has the right to save their money."

"But from now on, I am not going to charge for my service."

The mullah was taken aback at the new development; he wanted to find out what made Karmoo change his mind. Karmoo told him that Khansab had advised him to stop charging for water, and since he respected Khansab, he could not reject his advice!

"So finally, you have come to your senses. You made a wise decision." The mullah told Fareed to go home and say to Zakaria Khan that Karmoo would be bringing a full mashak shortly.

By the time people came to the mosque for evening prayer, the news had already travelled through the village. The mullah confirmed that Karmoo had decided to abandon his enterprise. They all appreciated his decision and promised him that his family would be well fed. Fattu told him that he was instructed by Khansab to go to the city and get a new pair of shorts for him. Women started cursing him once more for staring at them, and he started getting free lunches once again!

Who says times are changing? he thought while loading his mashak on his back.

Plus ça change, plus c'est la même chose. The more things change, the more they stay the same.

The Moneylender

Khansab's relatives had an instant need for money to meet legal expenses whenever cousins were locked in petty rivalries over the years, settling scores after scores in the courts. Party A had filed a lawsuit against party B, accusing the latter of killing their cat. Party B did not deny it but insisted that the cat had wandered onto their property, and they had every right to deal with it the way they chose. The trial had been going on for seven years, and while the carcass of the dead cat lay at the police station as exhibit one of one, money flowed like water to meet legal expenses. The two attorneys were not interested in getting the judgement and kept calling their clients to the court in Aligarh, as hearings were scheduled and postponed on an ongoing basis.

While the legal battles continued, the landowners had to feed their workers. They also had to spend big money when their farmers' daughters got married. The more lavish the wedding, the bigger the name and fame the landowner achieved. They competed in ensuring that the entire village talked about the marriage for years to come.

The revenue from their meagre lands could hardly support such activities, and they turned to Lala Ishvari Lal, the moneylender, to rescue them. He was always generous in financing them at an exuberant interest in exchange for a piece of land as collateral. As they borrowed more and more, the interest grew, and so did the principal until he was ready to take over the land. He divided it into small chunks and leased it to the same farmers who were already working there. It did not make any difference to them whether they worked for the landowner or Lala.

When the two warring parties got the word that their land was gone, it was time for reconciliation. As they hugged and said sorry to each other with wet eyes, the whole village knew that Party A had decided to withdraw the claim, despite advice from their attorney that the court decision was imminent. Everything was forgiven and forgotten, and life went on, except the two parties became the responsibility of their relatives who still owned land. Khansab supported many such relatives who had lost their land to Lala.

While life was good for Lala, he had a problem that he could not do anything about: He was obese. Even "obesity" was an understatement when it came to Lala Ishvari Lal. It appeared as if all his wealth was piling up on his body as fat. The richer he grew, the fatter he got, until he could not even stand on his feet. He sat on his patio all day, under the shade of a neem tree, clad only from under his waist in his white silk dhoti with a golden border. He kept a small wooden desk, about a foot and a half high, in front of him. Apart from serving as his lunch table, it contained records of his transactions. Customers came to him to borrow more money or pay the instalment of interest at the harvest time. He lifted the cover of his desk and pulled out their file as he dealt with them. Two servants fanned him continuously with hand fans as sweat flowed in streams on his naked body. Several folds of fat had formed on his belly, so deep that his entire hand disappeared as he drove it inside an itching fold to scratch it. A water carrier brought a mashak twice a day and poured water over him to keep him cool. It was his routine throughout the year, summer or winter.

Even with his obesity, Lala was quite mobile. He went indoors only to sleep at night or to pay an unscheduled visit to the toilet. He tilted his body slightly to the left, raised his right buttock, moved it forward, and repeated the movement with the other side of his body. He had mastered the art of walking on his buttocks so well that it appeared quite natural for him. As he moved inch by inch, the two servants took their positions on his sides and walked majestically with him.

Despite being rich and powerful, he was humble and cheerful. He was never rude to his debtors who failed to pay their instalments. Instead, he sent one of his servants to call them and offered them a thousand apologies. "Miyan, I could never dare to put you through this trouble." He always addressed Muslim landowners as Miyan to show them respect. "But you know things are tight these days, and I find it hard to cope with my expenses."

"I realize, Lalaji, that we missed the payment, but you know that the harvest has been very poor this year, and the workers come first."

"Oh, yes. I know that. Your servants have never complained."

"By the time I took care of their needs, there was not a single grain left."

"I am sorry to hear that. I know that you are a good man, and you will have a good crop next year."

"I hope so."

"So what have you decided about the payment?" he would ask, insisting politely for some commitment.

"I am sure we can arrange something."

"I wish I could wait for the next harvest, but you know I have to survive too."

He was always sympathetic to his customers and showed concern for their problems. "You know that I am a fair person," he said with a smile. "I will give you another thirty days to pay the instalment."

Lala was a man of his word. He waited for thirty days as promised before he opened his desk and pulled out the loan document. It was crystal-clear. The thumbprints of the borrower and the two witnesses were visible. He handed the paper to a servant and sent him to Aligarh. The clerks at the Land Registry Office knew Lala Ishvari Lal very well. They always welcomed his servant, who came to the office with a treasure van of gifts for them: large blocks of sweet gurh with almonds and coconut, and canisters of pure ghee made from buffalo's milk. They knew that no one could ever challenge Lala's documentation. He always made sure that he had dotted every "i" and crossed every "t." Within a few hours, the servant was on his way back with a piece of paper, declaring that the land title had been transferred to Lala. The debtor knew only the next morning when one of his faithful workers came to report to him, Lala's men were on the land to announce that the farmers would be working for him from that day on.

Lala never left his home except once a year, when he went to Benaras to take a dip in the holy River Ganges. It was always an event in the village when an elephant with colourful drapes hanging on both sides and wearing bells around its neck came to take him to the pilgrimage. It was a female elephant named Chandni. Everyone in Birehra recognized her since she had been coming to the village every year to take Lala to Benaras.

Children got out of their homes as they heard the bells and followed Chandni, clapping and running behind her. The *mahavat* sat on her neck and warned them not to come too close as he looked down at them. Lala was ready for the trip. He dragged himself to the edge of the patio by the time the entourage reached his place. Nobody knew if it was a mere coincidence or if he'd had that patio built in such a way that when Chandni was anchored against the wall, she was exactly at the same level as the patio. Walking on his buttocks, he slid gently onto the elephant's back, and his servants took their positions, one in front of him and the other behind him.

Many people gathered to say goodbye to Lala, and some of them brought urns containing the ashes of their departed relatives so that he could spread them over Ganges' holy waters. He never refused anyone and sometimes carried as many as a dozen of those urns. Children joined the celebration and ran in circles, chasing one another. When the mahavat was sure that everyone was seated comfortably, he knocked on Chandni's head gently, and she started moving. As people waved goodbye, Lala bowed to everyone with a smile and joined his palms in salutation. Children followed behind until they reached the boundary of Birehra and were turned back.

Every year, this ritual occurred when the same mahavat brought the same elephant to take Lala to bathe in the Ganges. They reached Benaras late in the evening and stayed at *Dharamshala*, an inn for pilgrims. It was the same Dharamshala where Lala stayed every year. The innkeepers remembered him very well because of his obesity. Even though he never left big tips for them, they respected him due to his humility and good nature. As he disembarked from the elephant and slid onto the patio, the servants at Dharamshala escorted him to his living quarters. They promised him that his stay would be as comfortable as ever. They woke him up at dawn to get started early and reach the waters in time for sunrise.

As Chandni made her way through tens of thousands of bare, dark-skinned pilgrims, Ishvari Lal joined his hands in prayer, closed his eyes, and recited the prescribed mantras. The mahavat led the elephant carefully into the dark water, as people moved aside to give way and made sure that the elephant did not trample anyone. Chandni descended into the depths of the polluted Ganges until the water reached just above her back and up to her occupants' waists. She kept her trunk up so that she could continue breathing. Lala joined his palms into a cup and lowered them to pick up water. He raised his hand as water dripped and prayed to the rising sun. Chandni dipped her trunk in the water, sucked in a trunkful, and raised it again, pointing backward. She breathed out a gush of water on the occupants as they rubbed the holy water on their bodies. As the sun came up, the air was filled with a serene hum of prayers and the intensity increased. There were men, women, and children wading through the riverbank and praying. Lala's servants took out the urns of ashes and emptied them one by one as they chanted their mantras.

When Lala returned, people of the upper caste gathered on his patio to greet him. He felt humbled and told them about his trip, as his servants passed them bottles of holy water and little pieces of sacred relics. "Kashi is such a holy place," he said. "It has thirty-three hundred million shrines and a half a million images of the deities."

"They say that Musalmans destroyed many of those shrines," someone remarked, referring to the Muslim armies of Qutbuddin Aibak in 1194.

"There are still plenty of them," replied Lala. "You need a lifetime to visit all of them. But unfortunately, I cannot see any of them since I cannot move much."

"If one wants to visit all the holy sites, it is wise to go there and never leave the place."

"That is true, and if one is fortunate enough to die in Kashi, he achieves *jivan mukti*. He becomes liberated and lives forever."

***

One year, when Lala returned from his pilgrimage, a foul odour started coming out of his body. As days passed, the stench became stronger, and even though the servants sniffed every part of his body, they could not locate its source. They consulted Vaidhraj Ramachandra, the Ayurvedic healer in the neighbouring village, and he prescribed an oily concoction for bath oil. Water carriers were brought in, and they swished loads of water as servants rubbed his body with mops soaked in the oil. Nothing helped, and Lala kept stinking. People talked about his problem. Everyone had his theory. "Someone at the mosque was saying that God has cursed Lala for his sins," said Karmoo Bhishti.

"What has poor Lala done?" asked Nathu. He did not like a Muslim criticizing a Brahmin. "He is a nice man and does not hurt anyone."

"But he lives on interest and grabs other people's property," replied Karmoo. "Interest is a sin. How can God forgive someone who charges interest?"

"I disagree. Lala goes to Kashi every year. All your sins are washed away when you bathe in the holy water, even if you have murdered a Brahmin. And what could be a greater sin than murdering a Brahmin?"

"My father had once gone to Kumbh Mela," said Chaita. "He used to say that Lord Vishnu himself had bathed in the Ganges."

"But that was in Hardiwar. Lala goes to Kashi," someone tried to correct Chaita.

"What is the difference?" Chaita did not like the remark. "The entire river is holy. It does not matter whether you bathe in Hardiwar or Kashi."

They talked until late at night but could not arrive at any conclusion. There must be some deeper reason for Lala's problem.

Several days passed, and Lala continued stinking. His customers did not express any reservation about the odour since their need for money was more important. When someone felt nauseous, he took a corner of his shoulder cloth and put it on his nose, as if he just wanted to wipe it. The daily ritual of bathing Lala with the Ayurvedic preparation continued. The water carriers started to fear that the well would get dry soon if they continued pouring tons of water on him. The vaidhraj, who had provided the oily medicine, came himself to examine Lala. He scanned every inch of his body for signs of disease but could not find anything. Finally, he suggested that they continue with the treatment and wait for results.

One day, as they were sponging Lala's body, one of the servants suggested that they should reach deep into the fatty flaps on his belly. Two servants lifted each flap from the sides as the third one sponged it with the mop and poured water. Suddenly, a dead fish fell out from a fold, and the mystery was solved. It had been rotting there for days. It was not clear whether the Holy River's pollution killed the fish, or it was choked to death when caught in Lala's belly. People kept talking about the poor fish for many days, and Lala's servants were relieved that their daily toil had ended.

Phagna the Menace

The day cooled slightly as the sun dipped to touch the distant neem trees' highest branches on an August afternoon. Karmoo, the water carrier, had just brought the second mashak of water and had started splashing it on Khansab's patio. He knew that he would have to go back to the well a third time before the sun-baked ground would show any sign of its thirst being quenched. Khansab opened the door to the patio after he woke up from his nap. He usually took his lunch inside the house, in the women's quarters, and stayed in Chhoti Begum's room for the afternoon nap, but today he had a visitor from out of town. Barrister Banerjee, his lawyer, had come from Aligarh to discuss a pending court case with him. Khansab had told Chhoti Begum that he would have lunch with the guest in the men's quarters. Barrister Banerjee was an old man who even knew Khansab's father and had fought a few cases for him.

Fattu stood in the far corner of the patio, watching Karmoo twisting his waist for every swish. When he saw Khansab open the door, he walked away to bring a glass of *sattoo* for him. It was a refreshing drink, which Fattu made by stirring a tablespoon of powdered barley and a spoonful of sugar in a tall glass of cold water. Today, he was going to make an extra drink for the guest from Aligarh.

"Salaam, Khansab!" Karmoo greeted Khansab, who stood in the door.

Khansab nodded to acknowledge the greeting and left the door open as he went back into the room to wake the barrister, who slept in the cot beside his.

Just then, he looked back through the open door and noticed two of his workers from the field coming up the stairs. They were holding Chunnu, another worker, who was staggering as he walked. When the three men turned to face Khansab, he saw that Chunnu's face was covered with blood. "What happened?" asked Khansab as he stepped out of the room.

"It was Phagna," replied the man on Chunnu's left. "He hit Chunnu on the head with his club."

"*You* tell me, Chunnu, what happened. I know that you are as wild as Phagna. You must have done something wrong."

"*Bhagwan ki kasam*, I can swear by God that I am innocent." Chunnu raised his head and looked at Khansab. Blood was still oozing out of his forehead. "I was just going my way when Phagna passed by. I didn't say a word, but he swung his club and hit me on the forehead. Anyone could tell that he was drunk."

The two men on his sides nodded to confirm his statement. Meanwhile, Fattu stood behind the men, holding a tray with two glasses of *sattoo*. He waited for them to be dismissed. Khansab asked them to take Chunnu to Doctor Ali Hussain to put some tincture iodine on the wound. As they left, Fattu entered the room. The barrister sat in a chair as he took his glass of sattoo. "Go and bring Phagna with you," Khansab instructed Fattu.

"Who is this, Phagna?" asked the barrister.

"He is a menace," Khansab replied calmly while sitting down in a chair and taking a sip of his drink. "He has been terrorizing this village since he was a young boy. I have been protecting him all his life, but he is beyond rehabilitation. I would have kicked him out of Birehra long ago, but I keep thinking of his dead father, who was innocent as a lamb, and respected by everyone, even though he was a poor woodchopper."

"Is he the son of Bhagwan Das, whose mother nursed you when you were a baby?" asked the barrister.

"You are right," replied Khansab.

"Yes, your father had told me that an untouchable woman nursed you."

Khansab did not seem to hear what the barrister had said. He was in deep thought, and then his lips quivered.

"Phagna's mother tied a rakhi around my wrist, and I have always protected her as a brother would," he replied. "I always think of her when I am harsh to her son."

"Why don't you put him to work?"

"I have tried everything, Barrister Sahib, but nothing has worked."

***

Everyone in Birehra was afraid of Phagna. When he walked through the street, people avoided him; children ran into their homes when they saw him coming. Azad looked at him through the eyes of a child, and Phagna appeared ten feet tall, or even taller. He was fat too, with a big belly. He had long, bushy moustaches, properly starched and oiled, which always pointed at ten past ten. Phagna was always angry. Even if someone asked him politely how he was feeling, he would start yelling at him. "It's none of your business how I am feeling! You should care for yourself!"

His eyes were always bloodshot. People speculated that he must have committed a murder. "If you kill someone, your victim's blood shows through your eyes," they said. "That's how the police catch murderers."

Phagna grew up, constantly being reminded by everyone, every day, that his father was a humble man who had never caused any trouble in the village. *So what!* he thought. *Did anyone care for me? Whenever I ended up with a bleeding nose or cracked skull while fighting bullies, everyone told me that it must have been my fault; even my mother yelled at me!*

But now, he had grown up and was old enough to get even. He got drunk now and then and started beating everyone who crossed his path. People hated him and preferred to stay out of his way. Whenever he picked on someone, that person would complain to Khansab, who would send someone to call Phagna. Khansab was the only one in the village who Phagna had any respect for and would listen to his rebuke, standing quietly and looking at the ground until Khansab told him to get out of his sight.

They said that Phagna was born feet first. According to the local superstition, if you had a bad back, you would get someone born feet first to kick you in the back; your backache would be gone instantly! People with bad backs went to Phagna regularly and requested him to give them a kick in the back. That was the only time he showed any courtesy to them. He obliged everyone, regardless of their race or religion-Brahmins, Muslims, untouchables-and he never asked anyone for money. Even though some people tried to pay him for his services, he always declined the offer, saying that it was a God-given gift, and he would surely lose his power if he started charging them.

Deep down, Phagna was a lonely man. He had no friends around him, just scared people who only came to him when they had sore backs. He felt that his heart was like the endless dunes, with blowing sand and blazing sun, in which deadly scorpions clung to his bruised self-esteem. He often saw himself laughing and at peace with himself, but that was only in his dreams. When he woke up, his aspirations were swept away like a dried bush rolling in the desert wind. He longed for a friend with whom he could share his heartache but did not dare to break the shell he had built around himself.

***

When Fattu told Phagna that Khansab was boiling with rage, he knew why he had been summoned. Khansab looked outside as he saw Phagna on the stairs. He came to Khansab's door and stood there, looking down at his feet. He knew that he was going to get an earful.

"You have done it again, Phagna." Khansab was unexpectedly calm and spoke in a low voice. He just wanted to show his guest that he was in control of the situation. "I am asking you now to leave Birehra and never show your face here again."

Phagna raised his head and looked at Khansab in disbelief but lowered his eyes again.

"If you are ever seen in this village again, I will get your moustache shaved, your face painted black, and get you to ride through the village on a donkey, facing its tail." That would be the ultimate humiliation for Phagna, and he would never be able to show his face to anyone. Therefore, he turned back and left without saying a word.

At first, Khansab thought that Phagna would avoid facing him for a few days, but he would not dare leave the village. When he found out that Phagna had left Birehra, he was stricken with guilt. He sent several men to neighbouring villages to look for Phagna, but they returned without finding any trace of him. For several days, Khansab kept thinking about Phagna's father, whom he had always loved because he was his milk brother. *Forgive me, my brother. I could not take care of your son.*

As time passed, Phagna was forgotten, and people went on living in peace. They talked about him sometimes, though, and speculated as to where he might be. "Perhaps he is in Calcutta or Rangoon." It was easy for bums like him to survive in those big cities. "You never know; the city life might have taught him valuable lessons."

"It's possible that he has found a woman and is happily married."

"He must be making tons of money. I bet someday he will show up in the village with gifts for everyone."

"Don't be silly. Phagna bringing gifts for everyone? You must be dreaming a fool's dream." The conversation about Phagna always ended that way.

***

Eventually, they forgot Phagna altogether, until one day, he suddenly returned to the village a year later. This time he was a changed man. He wore a turban and had his long beard parted in the middle, with the two sides folded up neatly over his cheeks and tucked under his turban. He carried a long spear and a dagger and wore a bracelet on one wrist. Dressed in spotless white trousers and a parrot-green *kurta* with golden embroidery for the shirt, he looked like an honourable guest from the city, maybe a government official. He went straight to Khansab and told him that he was Phagna. Overcome by emotion, Khansab was taken aback. *Where have you been, my son?* He wanted to ask him. His hands moved forward to embrace Phagna, but then he pulled them back. After all, Phagna was untouchable!

Phagna said that he had become a Sikh and could even speak Punjabi. He promised Khansab that he would live peacefully if he were allowed to stay there. When he sat down on the floor, Khansab invited him to sit in the chair as usual. Since Phagna had changed his religion, he did not belong to the untouchable class anymore. "Do you know that your mother died last month?" Khansab did not want to be the first to break the news to him, but someone had to. Phagna did not show any reaction. He kept looking at Khansab with

180

a blank look on his face.

"Pneumonia took her life," said Khansab. "We come from Him, and to Him, we shall return!"

Phagna was still quiet. Khansab approached him and touched his shoulder. He was startled and got up from the chair. Khansab embraced him. "Don't think that you are left alone in this world." Khansab could not stop his tears. "You will always be like a son to me."

When people found out that Phagna was back in the village, they expressed reservations about him. "He will start causing problems again," someone remarked.

"I have still got this big scar on my head," said Karmoo. He lifted his cap and bowed down to show the hairless circle on his head. "After all this time, I still get headaches."

"Khansab should kick him out again. We're better off without Phagna."

"I bet he'll be even more violent now that he has become a Sikh."

People wondered if he retained his therapeutic value for their bad backs since he had abandoned his old religion. They discussed the matter for hours on cool nights as they sat in a circle around the fire after their evening meal. Some people did not believe that he could still heal sore backs. Others thought that it was immaterial what religion he was. After all, he was born feet first. They sat there roasting corn and exchanging stories of Nawabs, Maharajas, and Englishmen, and of course talking about Phagna, until late at night when the burning wood had turned into ash, and the cool breeze had started penetrating their shawls. As far as Phagna was concerned, they decided to wait until someone got a sore back. They would find out for sure then if he still possessed his healing power.

***

It was said that Khansab's great-great-grandfather was a big Nawab. He was called Nawab Sahib since he owned a lot of land. He had several thoroughbreds in the stables and many water buffaloes, which provided milk and butter for the entire village. A large part of the estate was wiped out in feeding the households of his servants. The rest of the land was lost to attorneys, as his descendants fought legal battles with one another. Every cousin, nephew, and niece claimed a piece of the pie. By the time Khansab came into his inheritance, the estate was reduced to thirty acres of land and two mango trees. Those trees, nicknamed *Black Bombay*, were famous near and far. Their fruit was sweeter than honey, and each weighed as much as a seer. All you needed was one mango and a loaf of chickpea bread, soaked in pure ghee, to make a heavy lunch for the heftiest appetite. One could finish off his meal with a tumblerful of buttermilk, wipe his moustaches with his sleeve, and lie down under a shady tree for a blissful nap.

When the season came, the fruit was picked with the utmost care, without dropping it on the ground, and packed in crates to be sent to friends and relatives in nearby villages and towns. There was one crate for every household. The Deputy Collector used to get two crates since he was a big officer. Once the fruit was picked and shipped out, the rest of the crop was distributed among the people. They enjoyed the mango of Black Bombay as they kneaded it all around, squeezing it between their fingers and thumbs until the juice inside was loosened. Finally, they pinched a little skin on the top to make a little hole; the mango was now ready. They took a bite of chickpea bread, put their lips on the mango and squeezed it. A gush of thick juice came out rushing and sweetened every bit of their morsel. "This year, Black Bombay is sweeter than ever," they remarked, as they sucked the juice while chewing their bread. The juice covered their hands and flowed down their arms, dripping from their elbows, as they squeezed the fruit.

Khansab offered a job to Phagna; he asked him to watch for children in the village, who used rocks and bamboos to drop unripe fruit from Black Bombay. Phagna brought a rope bed and set it under the arch between the mango trees. He sat there all day, smoking his *hookah* and yelling at any kid who came within rock-throwing distance. People were surprised to see how Phagna had changed. At first, they were reluctant to approach him but were encouraged by the courtesy he extended to everyone. They wondered why he still smoked a hookah.

"What kind of a Sikh are you?" they asked him. "You are not supposed to smoke."

"Yes, smoking is not allowed in the Sikh religion," someone else remarked.

"My guru has given me special permission," replied Phagna. "I told him that I have smoked all my life and can't quit now."

"But don't you feel bad about it?"

"I repent every time I charge my hookah and ask God for forgiveness after every puff!" He raised his hands and touched his ear lobes to express his repentance.

When he realized that the arch under the mango trees would be his permanent abode, he requested that some fellow villagers build a shed to move his cot under it when the sun was too hot. They made a small shed from dried wood, straw, and mud. Then they dug deep into the ground to erect four wooden poles and tried to shake them off to test how sturdy they were. The poles stood there solid as steel. Finally, they mounted the shed on top of the poles and guaranteed that no earthquake or hurricane could dislodge it from its position.

Whenever it rained, Phagna moved his cot under the shed. He also built a small *chulha*, shaped like a horseshoe, from mud and placed an old aluminum kettle on it. He made a kettleful of tea in the morning and kept it hot all day. As visitors dropped in, they helped themselves to a cup of tea. Whenever he noticed that the fire under the kettle was about to die, he put on some more wood and dried cow dung to keep it going. In another corner, there was a large earthen pitcher full of water. Whenever it was empty, he asked someone to carry it to the nearby stream and fill it up. That was his entire household. His life revolved around the cot, the shed, and the hookah.

Phagna did not have any relatives. He was the only child of his parents, and neither of them had any siblings of their own. People asked him from time to time when he would get married and start a family. He said that an astrologer had told him that there was no woman in his life. He had become wiser and had started talking like a philosopher after having gone through tough times in the city. "I do not have any relatives, and I will not leave any descendants," he used to say. "I am like a lone cactus in the desert. No one knows where I came from, and one day I will be gone, leaving no trace of myself on the ground!"

***

Phagna was hired to guard the two mango trees on the outskirts of Birehra, on one side of the only dirt road that led into the village. Travellers used the trees as a milestone to know that they were entering Birehra. It meant that anyone entering or leaving the village had to pass through Phagna's checkpoint. People returning from trips brought candies for him, and he kept them in stock for children. Whenever they passed by, he called them over and gave everyone a few candies. Sometimes they hovered around his shed, hoping that he would call them. They often tried to sneak out to the neighbouring village to buy kites, but Phagna shouted at them and chased them back into the village unless an adult accompanied them. However, he could not stop them every time. They would often make it past his post while he dozed off for an afternoon nap on hot summer days. His meals came from Khansab's home. Chhoti Begum ensured that the maid packed three large loaves of cornbread, pickled chilli and lemon, and a jug of buttermilk for his lunch. Nobody could keep his eyes open after such a heavy meal.

Phagna maintained a mental inventory of everyone in the village. If a stranger came in, he found out whose guest he was and how he was related to the host. Nobody could enter or leave the village without his knowledge.

Gone were the days when mothers used to scare little children by mentioning the name of Phagna when they misbehaved. Everyone noticed that he had become extremely humble and docile after returning from Punjab. Suddenly, he had a job and a purpose in life. As people passed by, they stopped to talk to him. He knew about everyone and asked about the well-being of their families. "How is your grandfather? Is he still coughing?" "I haven't seen little Munni for a while. Has she started losing her teeth?"

People discussed their problems freely with Phagna. Mattoo talked about his water buffalo, which had suddenly stopped producing milk. Mohan told him that he was living hell since the day he got married; his mother and his wife quarrelled all day and drove him crazy. Old Jaggoo Daada told him that he had lived as a widower for five years and felt that he could not live any longer without female companionship. Phagna gave free advice to all, and they trusted him with their problems.

The farmers working in nearby fields dropped in all day for a chat and smoke with Phagna. He shared his hookah with everyone, regardless of caste or religion. His guests held the pipe at one end of their fist and put their mouth at the other end to ensure that their lips did not touch the pipe as they took turns to take puffs.

Ram Lal, a local potter, who claimed that his family had been making pottery since the days of Darpana the Great, made the potter's wheel sing while his hands danced around the clay, squeezing it, moulding it, smoothing it, and trimming it. When he built Phagna's hookah, he constructed the flask from special clay that came from a mine in Southern India and baked it with the utmost care in his kiln. He claimed that if the flask were dropped from the top of the palace of the Maharaja of Udhepur, it would land on the ground below without any crack.

When he showed the hookah to people, he said that even though the tobacco bowl was paper-thin, it could withstand any load of burning coal. "If it ever shows any crack, you can shave my moustache with the urine of a jenny."

Bilal, the carpenter, had built the pipe for the hookah. He chiselled a long piece of wood into a cylinder and drilled a hole through it. His sixteen-year-old, newly married daughter-in-law wrapped a fine golden thread around the pipe. It was said that the touch of a young bride, who had just discovered ecstasy, contributed to the trance that smokers experienced after a long and deep gasp. Bilal showed the pipe to people with great pride. The job was done with such expertise that no two turns of the golden thread overlapped, and neither was any space left between turns. He took off his glasses and handed them to the people sitting in his shop at that time. They were the thick glasses that the doctor gave Bilal after his cataract surgery. They used it as a magnifying glass and went over the entire pipe inch by inch. Indeed, they could not find a single flaw in the wrapping of the golden thread and acknowledged that Bilal was lucky to find such a talented girl for his son. The pipe connected the flask to the tobacco bowl. Bilal built a second pipe that was flexible like a rubber hose and was covered with golden thread.

When the hookah was ready, Ram Lal and Bilal presented it to Phagna. Everyone sitting on the cot with him looked at it and appreciated it. They acknowledged that they had never met a potter as talented as Ram Lal, or a carpenter as good as Bilal. From then on, Phagna and his guests enjoyed the gurgling sound of the new hookah all day.

When the tobacco turned into a charred cake, and the fire cooled down, it was time to recharge the hookah. Phagna took the task very seriously. The difference between good smoke and bad smoke came from the patience and love with which the hookah was prepared. He took the tobacco bowl off to empty it and scraped off any burnt tobacco sticking to it. He placed the bowl upside down and left it until it cooled down to room temperature. In the meantime, he detached the pipes from the flask and emptied it on the ground nearby. The water was all brown and smelly. At times, someone who had an open sore on his foot would use that water to wash the wound. It was supposed to be antiseptic and prevented infection. Phagna rinsed the flask with fresh water from the stream a few times and then filled it before mounting the pipes back on it.

He carried stocks of many types of tobacco: strong, light, sweet, and bitter. Each variety came with several fragrances. Even those who did not smoke made sure that they brought back some fancy tobacco for him whenever they returned from a trip. They stopped at Phagna's shed and gave him the tobacco before entering the village. When he prepared his hookah, he asked his visitors what kind of tobacco they wanted to try. He opened several canisters, and people smelled the black lump inside each one. Once they approved a brand, he took a piece of it out, spread it in the bowl and put a few pieces of red-hot coal and dried cow dung from his chulha on top of the tobacco. Phagna's hands were so rough and leathery that he could pick up a burning coal with his bare fingers. The hookah was now ready; people took turns to smoke it and appreciated the aroma. They sat there for hours, smoking and gossiping.

***

No one in a thousand villages could challenge Sharfu's expertise in shoemaking. His father was a low-caste Chamar and had lived in the area of untouchables, but then he converted to Islam and built a shack in another neighbourhood, where working-class Muslims lived. He took comfort in the fact that he enjoyed an elevated social status. He could go to the mosque and pray with wealthy landowners. He could even hug them and get preferential treatment on Eid and Baqreed. Chamars specialized in tanning and leather making. They relied mostly on wealthy Muslim landowners who gave them free hides whenever a goat or a cow was slaughtered; otherwise, they would have to rely on dead animals, the possibility of which was minimal. As they say, no cattle can die a natural death in a land where Muslims live. In return, Sharfu made shoes for his benefactors and did not want to charge them any money, even though he accepted token payments as a gift when he could not persuade his customers to forget about money. Every family had its own Chamar where all the hides went.

The Chamars of Birehra had enough business since they could collect enough hides and sold their leather products in other villages. The day of *Baqreed*, when goats and buffaloes were slaughtered for sacrifice, was of special importance for them since they collected an entire year's supply of hides and spent months preparing the leather. The practice had continued for years until the mullah at the mosque declared that the hide from a sacrificial animal could not be given to a Hindu. It could be donated only to a needy Muslim, and he could sell it to whomever he wanted. There was no restriction on routine slaughtering, and the hide could be given to anyone. It raised serious concerns among the Chamar community since the day of Baqreed was the major source of their raw material. Khansab asked the mullah about his fatwa. "Can I buy the hide from my sacrificial animal and give it to a Chamar as a gift?" he asked.

"I don't see any problem with that," replied the mullah, "as long as you give the money in charity."

"Can I give that money to a Hindu?"

"You should give preference to fellow Musalmans, but it is okay to give it to a Hindu if you don't find a needy Musalman." The problem was solved, and everyone was happy. Chamars received the hides as gifts and money as charity.

Sharfu was proud of his Chamar heritage. He claimed that he could tell the source and age of leather with his eyes closed, just by smelling it, and that no Chamar in the world could match the quality of shoes that he made.

Not everyone in the village wore shoes. Farmers, for instance, never wore shoes. Their feet became so leathery that they could extinguish a smouldering cigarette by crushing it with their big toe. They still got a pair made for themselves but used them only when they were visiting relatives in other villages. That was part of being cultured and making a good impression upon their relatives. They kept their shoes tucked under their armpit as they walked barefoot and wore them only when they reached the doorstep of their host. This way, they managed to keep their shoes clean and longer-lasting. One pair of shoes was enough for a lifetime.

Nevertheless, Sharfu had enough business from Brahmins, upper-class Muslims, and young men who had learned to read and write. They all wore shoes. Whenever Khansab needed a new pair of shoes, he called Sharfu and gave him the hide of a freshly slaughtered young goat. Sharfu dried it and tanned it himself. It took a whole month for him to design shoes that fit Khansab's feet like a pair of gloves. When someone got new shoes, they usually bit the wearer, and he had to put pieces of cotton at bleeding spots for a few days. Sharfu boasted that his shoes never bit the wearer. "If you ever get a sore, I will lick my spit," he claimed. Young men usually requested him to make *churr-murr* shoes that made a churr-murr sound as they walked. One could hear the churr-murr of Sharfu's shoes for a mile. Girls were incredibly crazy about those shoes. When a young man walked by wearing churr-murr shoes, the village girls knew that he was wearing a new pair of shoes made by Sharfu. As a pair of shoes grew old, the sound usually died down; but Sharfu claimed that his shoes kept churr-murring until they were worn out and thrown away!

Even though nobody could doubt that Sharfu had mastered the art of shoe-making, his true reputation was established as a storyteller. He was famous for his wit and articulation. People gathered around him at night when he sat down to tell them stories of witches and wizards. They became especially attentive when he described how Afrasiab, the great wizard in the Koh Qaf Mountains, fought an army of headless monsters single-handedly. Every time Afrasiab extended his arms and pointed his open palms forward, a bolt of thunder emerged from each of his fingers and set ten headless monsters on fire!

There were no streetlights in Birehra. If you stood on the dirt road in front of Khansab's home on a pitch-dark night and looked away to where the two mango trees stood, you could see a glow from Phagna's hookah every time someone took a puff. You could also hear oohs and aahs at times, and it was a sure sign that Sharfu was telling them one of his stories.

Old Sharfu was the wittiest man in the village until something happened that brought great shame to him, and he was too embarrassed to face people. It was discovered that his unmarried daughter was pregnant. At first, Sharfu and his wife tried to hide it by keeping their daughter indoors, but the news leaked out soon when women started noticing her pregnancy. Sharfu was furious when his wife gave him the news. He poured a canister of kerosene on his daughter and tried to set her on fire. But his wife got in the way to save her life. Now that the news was out, it had become the talk of the village. Sharfu could not do anything about it. He came to complain to Khansab that it was the son of Fareed, a servant of Zakaria Khan, who was responsible for his daughter's pregnancy. Some boys in the village had testified that they had seen Sharfu's daughter and Fareed's son enter the sugarcane plantation at the village's back several times. Some people went through the field and found a four-by-six-foot patch that had been cleared to serve as the refuge where the young lovers spent time together "blackening their faces." Of course, it was a natural hideout; you can hide a whole army in a sugarcane plantation without any fear that it will be discovered. Azad could never understand why they were said to be "blackening their faces"; he was too young to have been told that extramarital relationship is a major sin, and sinning is just like blackening one's face. He visualized them sitting face to face in the patch, rubbing pieces of coal on each other. *Grownups are strange people,* Azad thought.

Khansab called Fareed to inquire about his son. He said that he was himself so embarrassed that he could not face anyone in the village. "You know, Khansab, that I come from a noble family."

"Yes, I am a witness to your nobility and the nobility of your parents," replied Khansab. "But, I cannot say that your nobility has passed on to your son."

"You are right, Khansab. He is a true copy of his mother, and you know what a bitch she is."

"So, what do you suggest now?"

"I am at a loss myself. My son ran away as soon as we found out about it, and I don't know where to find him."

Khansab called a few people and asked them to go into neighbouring villages to look for Fareed's son. "In the meantime," he said to Fareed, "you will take care of Sharfu's daughter. You will pay Sharfu her living expenses until your son is found. As soon as he returns to the village, get the girl married to him and let him take care of her and the baby." Fareed went away, but he and Sharfu still did not talk to each other. Fareed spent his days in isolation. He maintained silence in front of everyone except Phagna, who listened to his account quietly, like any good counsellor, and nodded his head in agreement, as he heard Fareed's complaint. "It is not fair what Khansab has asked me to do," said Fareed. "I am a poor man and cannot carry any more burden."

"I agree." Phagna always agreed with everyone. "However, you should understand that it was your son who made this mess, and you have to be accountable for it."

"I do not deny my responsibility," replied Fareed, "and that is why I did not say anything to Khansab. You know that my son is a bum, and his mother has spoiled him. You know that a thousand bitches died when she was born."

"I know that your wife is very hot-tempered. Why don't you give her a good beating once in a while to keep her in line?"

"You must be joking. My wife will kill me if I even think of raising my finger to her. Do you remember the wound that I carried on my forehead during the last rainy season?" Fareed touched the scar on his forehead.

"Oh yes, it had become infected, and your eye was closed shut."

"You are right. I almost lost my eye."

"As far as I remember, you had hit your head on a rock when you fell."

"That is what I told everyone, but how can I hide anything from you, Brother Phagna?" Fareed moved a bit closer to Phagna to share the secret. "My wife had thrown a brass tumbler at me, and it hit me like a boulder. For a while, I didn't even know whether I was coming or going."

"I didn't know that she beats you."

"You better believe it. I told you that my wife is a real bitch, and my son is following in her footsteps."

"I sympathize with you, Fareed. I hope that your son will come back soon, and you will get him to marry Sharfu's daughter."

"I hope so," Fareed replied with a sigh and got up to leave.

***

As time passed, the gathering at Phagna's shed kept growing. Someone brought another cot and left it there for additional guests. Phagna arranged for a second hookah so that people did not have to wait long for their turn. They stopped there for a smoke while on their way and sat for hours. When there was no more room on the two cots, someone would get up and leave to make room for newcomers. As night approached, the sounds of Birehra became muffled. The farmers were back from their fields, the cattle tied to their posts, the chicken put in their coops, and birds rested quietly in the trees. The street in front of Khansab's home and the alleys of Birehra were shrouded in darkness. The only sound that broke the pitch-dark silence was the song of a chirping cricket. Even on those dark, quiet nights, someone at the other end of the alley could still see the faint glow from the lantern hanging under Phagna's shed. One could not see anyone in the dark, but every gust of cool night breeze coming from that direction brought a faint sound of laughter with it.

"I hear that the *Engraze* are leaving Hindustan," someone commented, referring to the departure of the British from India.

"That's what they say," replied Phagna. "They say that the country will be divided into Hindustan and Pakistan."

"What I don't understand is how they will divide the country," said Chunnu. "You can divide the money. You take your share and put it in your pocket, and I take my share and walk away with it, but you cannot put a part of Birehra in your pocket."

"Don't be silly," replied Sukhdev. "It is just that the area where you and I live will be called Hindustan, and Kareem Chacha's house will be in Pakistan."

"I guess you are right," said Kareem. "Birehra is not going anywhere. We will just call it by different names."

"What do you think, Fattu?" asked Phagna. "You are a wise boy and read the newspaper."

"I don't know, Phagna Bhaiyya. Things don't look good. Do you know that strange people have been coming into Nagla from the city for meetings with the boys there?"

"What strange people? What meetings?" asked Sukhdev.

"They are making flags and banners and chanting slogans."

Silence followed. No one commented. *The Engraze will be gone. Everything will be okay.*

Not many of Phagan's visitors were aware of the storm that was gathering over the country. They could not have imagined at that time that their lively conversation would soon be laced with talk of blood and death and that their sittings would eventually end.

BOOK TWO
PARADISE LOST

Rising Storm

As smoke rose from the garden in Reich Chancellery just outside the Fuhrerbunker in Berlin, an acrid smell with a hint of bubbling fat entered the nostrils of German soldiers guarding the area. They could not identify the odour, and the thought that the bodies of their Fuhrer and his wife had been set alight never crossed their minds. A week later, when Germany signed the Instrument of Surrender, hundreds of thousands of Brits celebrated the victory in London's streets. The Mall was packed from Trafalgar Square to Buckingham Palace, where King George VI appeared on the balcony to greet the cheering crowd. Prime minister Sir Winston Churchill accompanied him. The spectators watched them with their palms over their foreheads to shield their eyes from the bright sun. No one in the crowd realized that the sun, which had never set on the British Empire, had suddenly started descending into the western horizon behind the palace.

The jubilation continued until reality dawned on Britain. It had suddenly lost the greatness that it had boasted of for centuries. The economy was in tatters, the Exchequer was as empty as the womb of a barren woman, and the infrastructure was left in rubble after German bombings. The raw material from the colonies, which fed the factories in Britain, could not be used fast enough to meet civil service payroll. Once a jewel in the British Crown, India had suddenly become a liability. The size of the Indian Army had soared from prewar 200,000 men to 2.5 million by the end of the war.

Their payroll could not wait for the wheels to start turning again in the factories of England. Every clang and ring of an NCR cash register felt like a fist striking the heart of His Majesty's Government. The only way out was to cut and run, but it had to be done with class-like everything else that Englishmen do-provided the Indians allowed them to exit with honour. So the British decided to grant freedom to India.

"Over my dead body," said Churchill-perhaps not precisely in those words, but who cared about him anyway? He had won the war but lost the election. Clement Attlee, the incoming prime minister, thought that the sky was falling on India, and he had to get out of there before the fallout affected the United Kingdom.

"Not so fast," declared the Indian political leaders. The All India National Congress-the largest political party, led by Nehru-which claimed to be a secular party, was challenged by Jinnah, who had left the Congress earlier, saying that Hindus had dominated the party, and the rights of minorities were not safeguarded. He had joined the All India Muslim League, which represented the Muslim minority, comprising fourteen percent of India's population. Jinnah claimed that he was looking after all minorities' interests, including Sikhs, Christians, Buddhists, and the untouchables.

Lord Wavell, the British viceroy, who was assigned to supervise Raj's liquidation, was overwhelmed by Indian leaders' squabbling. The League and the Congress rejected every proposal coming from each other. They had perhaps decided amongst themselves not to give the opportunity of an easy exit to the British. The final straw that broke the back of the British Raj was the Cabinet Mission Plan, proposed by three cabinet members in England. According to that plan, India was to be divided into three administrative, self-governing blocks, joined by a loose federation. At first, the plan was acceptable to both the Congress and the League, but they both rescinded it later.

The people of India did not know, at that time, that Lord Wavell was soon to be fired and sent back to England in disgrace.

***

The monsoon should have already started, but it was still hot and dry. Khansab sat alone in his chair, reading the newspaper that Fattu had just delivered to him. He picked up his handkerchief; it was already soaked in sweat. He rubbed it along his neck to wipe away the sweat. There was no relief from the heat. He unbuttoned his shirt and started fanning his folded newspaper over his chest. He felt cool as the sweat evaporated slowly. He looked into the street below to see if any of his regular visitors were on their way, but no one was in sight. He spread the wet handkerchief over his knee and unfolded the newspaper again.

The servants had put the usual number of chairs on the patio, but Khansab knew that many of them would remain empty. The Brahmins of Nagla, who had been part of the lives of Sherwanis for several generations, and his friends, with whom he had shared dirty jokes all his life, had suddenly started treating him formally. He could see it in their eyes. Their once smiling, laughing eyes were now filled with sadness and agony. There was polarization even among his relatives. They could not cut off their blood links, but arguments and debates replaced their friendly chats. Khansab remembered the time when they used to depart late at night, with sleep in their eyes. Now they had started leaving early in the evening with anger on their eyebrows and a bad taste in their mouths.

It seemed as if an evil spirit had cast its shadow upon Birehra. People had started speaking in whispers, in case they offended anyone. Khansab was so immersed in his newspaper that he did not hear the footsteps of Noor Khan climbing the stairs. He raised his head when Noor Khan pulled up his usual chair. Every visitor, coming for the regular evening gathering on Khansab's patio, had become accustomed to sitting in the same chair each time. If someone else sat in another chair by mistake, he made sure to get up when the rightful occupier arrived; otherwise, he was politely reminded that he was sitting in the wrong chair.

Noor Khan exchanged greetings with Khansab and picked up a section of the newspaper. They sat quietly, reading their papers.

"Have the children left for Aligarh?" Khansab finally broke the silence.

"Yes, they left this morning," replied Noor Khan as he put the newspaper aside. "The university will open in two weeks, but they left early to get ready for their classes."

"I see," Khansab said and turned back to the newspaper. There was a long silence. They could enjoy each other's company, even without saying a word for hours.

"So what does today's paper say?" asked Noor Khan.

"The Cabinet Mission Plan has failed."

"So, what is new? Everyone knew that the Plan was doomed from the start. Even a child knows that the Congress has been playing games from the beginning."

"Why do you blame the Congress?" Khansab was the only supporter of the Indian National Congress among the Sherwanis of Birehra. All his relatives were on the side of the Muslim League. "The Muslim League is just as responsible for the failure of the Plan."

"Bhai Sahib, you know deep down that it is not true. The Congress leaders cannot make up their minds. Sometimes they accept the Plan, sometimes they reject it, and sometimes they offer their interpretations for it. Even the viceroy is tired of their games."

"And what would you say about the Muslim League?" Khansab was becoming defensive. "Jinnah Sahib says that he will have to take direct action to oust the British."

"So, what is the alternative?" Noor Khan snapped back. "The viceroy has given up, and the Congress won't budge; what can poor Jinnah do?"

Noor Khan did not realize that he was raising his voice. He had always treated Khansab with respect, but he could not stay calm when discussing politics.

"Why can't Jinnah Sahib work with the Congress?" said Khansab.

"Is that not what he has been doing all along? He even headed the Congress before Nehru and Patel entered the scene. They are the ones who have pushed him against the wall, and they are the ones who want to kick out Jinnah Sahib and make him take his Pakistan with him."

"You cannot even imagine how much blood will be shed," Khansab remarked.

"Only the Congress leaders can avoid bloodshed if they stop being so obstinate."

Khansab did not respond. After all, Noor Khan was his cousin, and he could not let politics come between them, even if they disagreed. Noor Khan finally broke the long silence. "You know, Bhai Sahib," he said politely, "that Mr. Jinnah has been the champion of Hindu-Muslim unity for years, while the Congress has been playing dirty from the beginning."

"And now Jinnah Sahib has reiterated his demand for Pakistan. There goes the Hindu-Muslim unity."

"What choice does Jinnah Sahib have? Lord Wavell has tried his best to persuade the Congress, and you know that he has been sincere, but the Congress has sabotaged every effort made by him."

"Pakistan is not the solution." Khansab was not prepared to concede. "Have you ever had any problem with Hindus? We have lived together for hundreds of years. We respect their ways, and they respect ours."

"You can say that because you are living in your paradise. You know what is happening in the cities and towns around you."

"But I don't live in a city. India lives in villages, not in cities, and it is those villages that will determine India's future."

"Bhai Sahib, you are talking like Gandhiji, but don't forget that nobody cares what Gandhiji says. Even the Congress does not care for him. To them, he is just an old, senile man who lives in his world. They can turn him into a god and put his statue in temples, they can worship him, but that is all that gods are good for."

"I disagree. Gandhiji is a great man. He has proved himself in South Africa."

"There is a difference between India and South Africa."

"I am aware that the destiny of India does not lie in Johannesburg. It lies in our villages."

"Please permit me to disagree." Noor Khan was not willing to give up. "Decisions are made in cities, not in villages. The destiny of India does not lie in Birehra and Nagla; it lies in Delhi and Calcutta. If our cities burn, the whole country will burn. If Hitler had managed to capture London, the entire British Empire would have fallen."

"Gandhiji believes that the destiny of India lies in villages," said Khansab.

"I agree with you, at least on that point. However, we should not forget that Gandhi's movement has nothing to do with independence. He is preparing for a social revolution to bring down the walls erected by old dogmas. His movement would have been relevant even if the British were not ruling India. He is using independence only as a backdrop to attract the masses to him."

"But he is the leader of the Congress and supports the party."

"The question is, does the Congress support him? They are using him only as a tool to promote their agenda; otherwise, it has no interest in his movement. They are both sick and tired of each other."

"When he came from South Africa, he chose to join the Congress," Khansab reminded Noor Khan.

"Bhai Sahib, you know that it is not true. When he disembarked the ship at Bombay port, it was Jinnah Sahib who went to welcome him. He advised Gandhiji to stay away from politics and watch for a few months before deciding, but he headed straight to the villages to preach his message. It was the Congress that duped him into joining the party; Gandhiji is too naïve, too innocent, to play dirty politics."

"Don't forget that-" Khansab suddenly stopped as he saw Pundit Uday Lal coming their way. He was a towering personality with a clean-shaven head, and he wore a milk-white dhoti as usual. People thought that he always wore freshly laundered clothes; he walked every evening from Nagla to spend time with Khansab. Everyone addressed him as *Punditji* out of respect.

Uday Lal was the most educated Brahmin in Nagla. He was fluent in Sanskrit, Urdu, and Persian and was an avid reader. Even though he was a Hindu, nobody could refute him when discussing Islamic jurisprudence and quoted from different schools of thought about an issue. However, his main interest was history, and he remembered accurately the year in which any Indian king was crowned, dethroned, or decapitated. He spoke like a true historian without passing judgement. Uday Lal should have been a supporter of the

Congress, but he watched events like a historian in the process of collecting his thoughts as history unfolded. As a follower of Doctor Ambedkar-an untouchable intellectual who had shunned untouchability and the caste system - Uday, Lal became agnostic and abhorred Gandhi, whom he had labelled as a hypocrite for supporting castes.

"Have you two been fighting again?" Uday Lal remarked as he pulled up his chair. "I have heard your voices for a mile."

"Come, Punditji, we thought you were not going to show up tonight," said Noor Khan as he pushed his chair to the side to make room for Uday Lal's chair.

"Okay, continue your argument, but don't ask me for arbitration." He reserved his right of impartiality.

"It looks like Partition is inevitable," Khansab said, as he picked up the folded newspaper and fanned it in front of his face. "The Muslim League has withdrawn its support for the Cabinet Mission Plan."

"Who cares about Partition?" said Uday Lal with a smile on his lips. "I support Partition, and I say that we should have three countries. We do not care if they take their Hindustan and Pakistan, but they should give us our Birehra. We don't bother anyone, and let no one come to bother us."

Uday Lal laughed as he passed his judgement, looking at Noor Khan and then at Khansab. He expected them to appreciate his sense of humour, but they both remained serious.

"Your joke aside," replied Noor Khan, "Punditji, you have put your finger on the pulse of the matter. India has never been one country. Neither the Mughals nor the British could erase state boundaries."

"I beg to disagree with you," Uday Lal said and raised his eyebrow. "You will have to admit that India was a single country during the golden rule of Chandragupta Maurya,"

"Be serious, Punditji." It was Noor Khan's turn to laugh. "Chandragupta Maurya died over 2000 years ago. Rajas and Maharajas have always ruled India. The Mughals ruled India for over 300 years, but there was not a single day when they were not fighting somewhere. The Mughals took over India through force, and the British established their empire through treachery. It's a shame that we let the British come and rule us for nearly 200 years, but we should be proud to say that there was not a single day when they too were not fighting in one corner of India or the other."

"Khansab, what are you trying to say?" Uday Lal looked at Khansab for support.

"I sincerely believe that the Partition of India is not the answer. Once you start carving up India, there will be no end to disintegration. There is no guarantee that she will not be subdivided again, and what is the guarantee that Pakistan will stay together? Keep India united, and she will grow in strength."

"I agree with you one hundred and ten percent," Noor Khan said and moved forward in his chair. "Who wants to carve up India? Jinnah Sahib does not want to do that. All he wants is a surety that the Hindu majority will not overrun the minorities, and remember that Muslims are not the only minority. You have Sikhs, you have Christians, you have Buddhists, and you have untouchables. Provide them security, and they will work together to build a strong India. But no sir, Nehru wants absolute power-"

Uday Lal was getting restless to jump in, but Noor Khan was too excited to let him interrupt.

Khansab interrupted his cousin instead, to give a chance to Uday Lal. "What do you say, Punditji?"

"Who cares what I say? I should tell the British to leave India as they found her. They should find some Mughal prince and put him on the throne. They should leave all Nawabs and Maharajas alone. India will determine her course. Would you agree, Khansab?"

"No, Punditji, I disagree with you. You want history to repeat itself, but unfortunately, history never repeats itself, contrary to what they say. Invaders bring with them irreversible changes. Time can only move forward. You cannot turn the clock back. The old empires can never return. Every invader has enriched our land, and so have the British. We should make their contribution a part of our heritage and move only forward."

Noor Khan gave his verdict. "Maybe something good will come out of it." "If two brothers cannot live in the same house, it always helps if one brother moves out. When they have their own space, they find it easier to be brothers again."

"I hope you are right." Khansab adopted a reconciliatory tone. "But I am afraid that Pakistan will be a thorn in the heart of India for all times to come. How can you cut a piece of your flesh without bleeding?"

Uday Lal and Noor Khan responded with silence. They all knew that troubled times were ahead. Still, they could not have predicted at that time that those whose hearts bled when their friends and neighbours experienced even slight pain would suddenly leap at each other's throat like rabid dogs, and the soil of Mother India would be tainted with the blood of its offspring.

Undoing History

Fattu was right, thought Phagna, when he noticed that strangers had started passing through Birehra on their way to Nagla, almost daily. They were mostly young men and talked like city folk. Usually, they came in groups of three or four, but he counted many more on some days. His curiosity rose as he saw them coming day after day and leaving late at night. Even though he knew everyone living in Nagla, he had never met those people before. He kept asking himself who they were and where they were going. It was his job to keep an eye on the village, and he considered it his business to know everyone who passed through Birehra. He stopped a few of them and asked them who they were but did not get any satisfactory answer.

"Oh, we are just passing through," was the usual answer.

"I know you are just passing through, but where are you headed?"

"Do you have any problem with us?" asked one who appeared to be a bit aggressive.

"No, I do not have any problem, but I am curious," said Phagna. "I am just a friendly person, and I know everyone who lives here; I even know their relatives who come to visit them."

"Good for you," replied the young man. "It is a good idea to mind your own business."

That evening, he decided to discuss the matter with his friends, who gathered at his place for an evening chat.

"Chaita, do you know if something strange is happening in Nagla these days?" Chaita Dhobi went into homes in Nagla to pick up their laundry every day and knew everyone there.

"What do you mean by something strange?"

"I see a lot of boys passing through Birehra, and they are all on their way to Nagla," Phagna replied. "Do you know where they go?"

"Oh, they are friends of Pundit Uday Lal's son. You know he is back from the city after finishing his education. His friends from the city come to visit him."

"I see, but I don't understand why they are so secretive about it."

"What makes you think that they are secretive?"

"I asked some of them, but they were rude to me; they did not tell me where they were going."

"You know how young people are these days, especially educated ones. They think that we are just stupid."

Phagna's curiosity was not satisfied. The next day, he went to Khansab and told him about the strange comings and goings.

"Why are you so concerned, Phagna?" asked Khansab.

"Something tells me that they do not have noble motives," replied Phagna. "People who keep secrets should not be trusted. They always have some hidden agenda."

"What could be their hidden agenda?" Khansab smiled at Phagna's unnecessary concern. It seemed that they were just a bunch of boys coming to visit their friend.

"Still, why don't you ask Uday Lal what his son is up to?"

"Uday Lal is away on a pilgrimage for a month," replied Khansab.

"I will ask him when he comes back."

Phagna left Khansab's home, as unsatisfied as he had come. His sixth sense was telling him that something sinister was brewing.

***

Uday Lal's son, Amrit, met with two of his friends, who had come from the city. They should have been jovial and talking about mundane things at their age, but they were discussing serious matters in whispers - Ajit, who had gone to the university with Amrit, and Darpan, whom Amrit had met on the train while coming back from Calcutta. They had continuously talked during their two-day train ride; they had concluded that they had a lot in common and thought alike about most issues.

"Let us make sure that there is no violence," said Amrit.

"May I disagree?" asked Ajit, who sat next to Amrit. "You cannot achieve your objective without cracking a few bones."

"Why bend your fingers when you can pick up the butter with straight fingers?"

"And then, we do not want to attract the police," interjected Darpan,

"That is right," Amrit agreed. "We cannot afford to get into trouble with the law until we gain enough power to dictate the law ourselves."

Darpan nodded in agreement.

"Remember that our objective is just to create harassment and not to kill anyone," Amrit continued. "It is okay to beat up anyone who comes in our way, Hindu or Musalman. However, we have to make sure that no blood is shed and no bone is broken. I am writing a strategy paper that will list the guidelines and the action plan to move forward. I will share it with you before circulating it to the group and starting the training of our workers."

"How important is it to stay underground?" asked Ajit.

"Now is not the time," replied Amrit. "A lot is happening in the country. The independence is at our doorstep, and right now, there is an uneasy calm before the storm. Let us not stir the pot at this point."

"Okay, Amrit. I have to leave now so that I can get back in time," said Darpan.

"Why don't you stay here tonight?" asked Amrit. "You can leave in the morning after breakfast."

"Tomorrow is a working day, you know. We do not have the luxury of being on our own."

"Let us meet one week from now. In the meantime, please call a meeting of the group in a couple of days to discuss what we have decided today," said Amrit as they got up to leave. Amrit came out with them to see them off.

***

Amrit had inherited his intellect from his father, who had schooled him at home and had taught him to be a freethinker. The father and the son used to discuss every issue without reservation. They believed in the human race's universality, without barriers of religion, creed, or colour. According to them, the world was a single entity, and geographical borders were artificial. Amrit was full of enthusiasm and had a definite opinion on every issue.

Uday Lal's wife had died of cancer three years after their marriage when Amrit was only six months old; Uday Lal had raised his son like a mother and had decided not to remarry. After Amrit finished his high school curriculum, he wrote the entrance examination and got admission to the University of Calcutta, one of the country's oldest universities. He returned to Nagla every summer during the vacation, and his father noticed that his thoughts and ideas were going through a transformation. He had become a nationalist and also talked frequently about religion. The father and the son disagreed more frequently than they agreed in their conversation. Uday Lal attributed it to the intellectual growth of his son. It also indicated a generation gap, which was positive. He thought that if a father and son agree on everything, it suggests that the family has stagnated.

Even though Uday Lal owned acres upon acres of land, he did not have any interest in agriculture. His manager, Muneemji, handled all land and money matters, while Uday Lal was occupied with his intellectual pursuits. On the other hand, Amrit was passionate about farming. Now that he had graduated from the university, he decided to settle back in the village and take charge from Muneemji, whom Amrit considered a cunning old man who had slyly taken over even Uday Lal's family matters. Muneemji understood clearly that his master's son was a threat to his employment and started treading carefully.

Uday Lal was back from his "pilgrimage." His trip to India's old temples did not have any spiritual significance, and *he* could not call it a pilgrimage, but others did. He was merely interested in those temples' history - their architecture and the mythology that surrounded them. He was fascinated by Hindu mythology and knew the genealogy of every god and goddess.

No one could enter Birehra without being noticed by Phagna. When he saw Uday Lal's horse approaching, he came forward to greet him. Uday Lal nudged slightly on the reins, and the horse stopped gently, stepping back with a soft poll. He released the reins immediately and patted the horse on the side of his neck to reward him. It seemed as if the horse could read the mind of his rider.

"How have you been, Phagna?" asked Uday Lal.

"Everything is as usual here, Punditji. How was your pilgrimage?"

"My pilgrimage was good." Uday Lal smiled.

"You had a lot of guests visiting your home while you were away."

"Is that right? Do you know who those guests were?"

"I have no idea. They told me that they were your son's friends." Phagna was satisfied that he had sown the seeds of suspicion in Uday Lal's mind.

When Uday Lal entered his house, he asked the servant to call Muneemji. After a quick shower, he came out onto the lawn. The servants had set up a table and chairs in the centre of the lawn as usual. Uday Lal was used to having tea early in the evening when the sun came down, and a gentle, cool breeze started blowing. Muneemji was waiting for him on the lawn and stood up from his chair to greet Uday Lal as he approached.

"How was your pilgrimage, Punditji?" asked Muneemji.

"It was wonderful. I spent a whole month in the Ajanta Caves this time and studied their architecture. You know that these caves are 2000 years old and depict the Buddhist culture beautifully." Uday Lal realized that Muneemji was not the least interested in the Ajanta Caves. "So, how are things here?"

"Nothing significant," replied Muneemji. "Ravi Nath's mother died, and one of our cows delivered a calf."

Uday Lal smiled, realizing that Muneemji implied that the newborn calf was Ravi Nath's mother's reincarnation.

"Where is Amrit? I have not seen him around."

"Amritji has gone to the city. He said that he would be back in the evening."

"I hear that he had some visitors from the city."

Muneemji did not respond. He had the opportunity to disparage

Amrit and wanted to choose his words carefully. "They were here for some meetings," said Muneemji with his eyes fixed on the ground.

"What meetings?" asked Uday Lal.

"I don't know. They were talking about pamphlets and flyers and about keeping their activities secret."

Uday Lal raised his eyebrow, and Muneemji looked at him. He was satisfied that his arrow had hit the bull's eye.

***

Uday Lal received several Hindi and Urdu newspapers from the city every day and read them when he woke up from his afternoon nap. The news was not good. Lord Mountbatten replaced Lord Wavell as the viceroy; he was a nephew of the king. The editorial in one of the newspapers stated that the new viceroy had resolved to get the last Englishman out of India in six months, and it was up to Indians to decide their fate.

The country was in turmoil; Partition was imminent. There were processions, slogans, speeches, and clashes everywhere. The Nawabs and the Maharajas of over 500 princely states were angry with the government. They had pledged their allegiance to the British government through written agreements, in which their autonomy was guaranteed. They wondered if their autonomy would be preserved in independent India, but the British had refused to offer them any guarantee.

Uday Lal looked up as Amrit entered the room. He picked up a newspaper as he sat down.

"I hear that you had been having some meetings here while I was gone," Uday Lal said, and looked at his son with a piercing stare.

"What meetings?" Amrit was startled. "It looks like Muneemji has been pouring poison in your ears again.”

“Tell me about your meetings.”

“There were no meetings. It is just that some friends from my university days have been visiting me. We talk about the general climate that is prevalent in the country these days.”

Uday Lal put the newspaper aside and turned his chair to face Amrit.

“Son, I raised you as a friend, and we never had any secrets between us. What is it that has changed you? You seem to be hiding something from me.”

“Why do you think that I am hiding anything from you? No, there are no secrets between us,” replied Amrit.

Uday Lal did not respond; he picked up a newspaper again and adjusted his glasses. Amrit also straightened his paper. There was a long period of uneasy silence.

“I suspect that you have joined RSS.” Uday Lal referred to Rashtriya Swayamsevak Sangh, an extremist Hindu organization that was responsible for Hindu-Muslim violence.

“What?” Amrit was taken aback. “I am disappointed that you are accusing your son of embracing violence. That only means that you are admitting your failure in raising me.”

“So you don’t believe in violence. Then what is your agenda?”

“You know that the British are leaving, and a new India is emerging. Ours is a think-tank of young people to play a role in the new country.”

“That certainly is noble,” said Uday Lal. “So, what role do you think is important for you and your group?”

“We have to take care of our people, who have been ruled by

foreigners for centuries. They have been deprived of their culture, their religion, and their identity. We have to help them regain their heritage.”

“I am trying to understand your viewpoint. Who has deprived us of our identity?”

“When the Musalmans invaded us, they converted us to Islam by their sword. When the Portuguese and the British came, they converted us to Christianity.”

“It is a myth that the Musalmans converted us to Islam by their sword,” Uday Lal interrupted Amrit. “If they had done that, then there would not be a single Hindu in India today.”

“Well, sometimes there was force, and sometimes there was bribery. They favoured those who converted to their religion. The British have done the same thing.”

“And how do you plan to bring them back to Hinduism after twelve hundred years?”

“The biggest barrier that we are faced with is the Musalman elite.” Amrit was encouraged by the openness with which his father was carrying on the discussion. “They act as a glue to keep poor people on their side. We should encourage them to leave us peacefully.”

“Where do you think they will go after being here for centuries?”

“There is talk of Partition. I support it. They should go to Pakistan.”

“In short, you want all the Sherwanis to leave Birehra and go to Pakistan.”

“That is it. They do not belong here.”

“What do you propose for their workers?”

“They are our people. They will revert to Hinduism after their masters leave. They will work on our lands, and we will take care of them."

"Aha! I get it," Uday Lal pointed his finger at his son. "You want to get rid of the competition."

"There is no competition between them and us. The market is big enough for everyone. It is a matter of ideology."

"You are planning to undo history, and you claim that you will do it peacefully, but I cannot think of any example where history can be undone without repression."

"It can be done, but not in one day. It will require patience in the new Hindustan," replied Amrit. "You are a student of history yourself, and you know well that decades, even centuries, are insignificant in history."

Uday Lal had started enjoying the conversation. "When these Musalmans revert to Hinduism, which caste will you put them in? Will they be Brahmins, Kshatriyas, Vaishyas, or Shudras?"

"We don't believe in castes. They will all be equal."

"That is noble. You seem to belong to Arya Samaj, but don't forget that Aryans introduced the caste system. They were invaders too, and remember that you too have Aryan blood flowing through your veins. So you also do not belong here."

"You are talking about pre-history."

"It does not matter. Invaders are invaders. It does not matter whether they came here yesterday or centuries ago. You said yourself that centuries are insignificant in history." Uday Lal picked up the newspaper to indicate that he wanted the conversation to end. Amrit got up to leave the room.

"Just remember," said Uday Lal, "that you and I are on opposite sides. Sherwanis are our friends. We have worked together and helped each other for generations. We do not have any problem with them, and they do not have any problem with us. I will not get in your way, and you will not get in mine. I will do whatever is in my power to protect my friends."

Amrit stopped momentarily until his father finished talking and then walked away without saying a word.

Clouds Begin to Gather

Hasan Khan was wide awake long before the first rooster in the village had crowed. He had spent a restless night, and even though his eyes were closed, his mind was awake. He had been tossing and turning all night long. Something was bothering him, but he could not pinpoint it. He sat on the edge of his bed with his feet on the ground and took the time to decide if he should go back to bed or start his day. Feeling tired and heavy-headed, he got up and went to the toilet to wash up. By the time he was ready to go out of the house, he had hoped that it would be dawn, and he would hear the call to prayer, but it was still dark. As he entered the mosque, he saw someone in the courtyard but could not recognize him in the dark. He took off his shoes on the stairs and walked up. When he got closer, he saw that the mullah was dragging a sack across the floor. "What are you doing, Mullanji?" asked Hasan Khan.

The mullah was startled and dropped the sack. He whispered, "Someone has slaughtered a pig in the mosque."

"Shh!" Hasan Khan put his index finger on his lips. "Let us make sure that it stays between us."

There was a streak of blood on the floor, indicating that the mullah had dragged the sack from inside the prayer hall.

"Let us take it to the back of the mosque and bury it outside," suggested Hasan Khan. "We have to wash the floor before others get here."

By the time they managed to dig a hole in the backyard and buried the dead pig, it was already dawn and time for the call to prayer. The mullah ran back and forth with buckets of water from the well, while Hasan Khan washed the floor with a broom. He reminded the mullah not to mention it to anyone.

When Noor Khan entered the mosque, he saw Hasan Khan and the mullah in the courtyard's centre, talking in whispers. He took his shoes off on the stairs and greeted them as he walked up to them.

"Are you two conspiring against someone?" he laughed.

There was no response from them. They stared at each other quietly.

"What is the matter," said Noor Khan. "Is something wrong?"

"Someone slaughtered a pig here last night," Hasan Khan said, finally deciding to share the news.

"Shh!" Noor Khan put his index finger on his lips. "Not a word should get out."

Slaughtering a pig in a mosque had become the most common method of inciting a Hindu-Muslim riot. A few homes would be set on fire, and a few rioters would be killed from both sides before everything was back to normal, but the culprits always remained anonymous and stayed quiet until a cow was slaughtered and fresh riots broke out.

The Qur'an forbade Muslims from eating the flesh of a pig, but the Indian Muslims went a step further and declared pig *persona non grata,* to the extent that it became sacrilegious to touch it or even utter its name. It was simply referred to as the "dirty animal." On the other hand, Hindus revered a cow as a sacred animal for being a milk source and a symbol of life. They kept an eye on their Muslim neighbours, who raised a cow to produce milk, in case it ended up being slaughtered for meat.

Cows and pigs were responsible, in a way, for bringing the British Raj to India in 1857, when the British issued new gunpowder cartridges to the Indian army. The soldiers had to bite the cartridges before loading them into their rifles. The rumour spread that the cartridges were greased with cow and pig fat, which inflamed both Hindus and Muslims. It started unrest in the army, which resulted in widespread rebellion. In the mutiny aftermath, the Mughal king was deposed, and the government was transferred to the British Crown. That was the beginning of the British Raj in India.

***

By the end of the day, most Sherwani men knew what had happened in the mosque the night before, and everyone was tense. Noor Khan and Hasan Khan met Khansab at his home that evening. The three of them sat quietly and kept passing the tip of the hookah to each other.

Khansab finally broke the silence. "I think we should share the news with the Hindus of Nagla." "Forgive me, Bhai Sahib," interjected Noor Khan. "I don't think it is a good idea."

"I also think that we should tell them," Hasan Khan finally expressed his opinion. "They are our friends, and we expect them to help us in case of trouble."

"I agree," replied Khansab. "It is safe to take them into our confidence, but we have to make sure that the news does not get to the common people, Hindus or Musalmans."

There was an uneasy calm among the Sherwani families. They were nervous for a few days but relieved that no incident had occurred because of the pig slaughtering in the mosque.

***

Lord Mountbatten, a friend of Nehru, gnashed his teeth in anger every time he thought of Jinnah. The hatred for Jinnah became a common bond between him and Nehru. They both wished that he would go away. Jinnah's problem was that he was a brilliant but shrewd constitutional lawyer, and the only language he spoke was that of law. Neither Nehru nor Mountbatten could stand his guts or match his wits, and felt intimidated while dealing with him; in return, he enjoyed their resentment like a cat playing with a half-dead mouse in agony. Finally, the viceroy announced in a press conference that the British Raj in India would end in two months, and the country would be partitioned into Hindustan and Pakistan.

The Muslim League protested over the haste of the decision. It alleged that the viceroy had conspired to create a truncated Pakistan that could not survive on its own because no country in the world had been created in two months. Mountbatten had a take-it-or-leave-it attitude and told the Indian leaders that his mandate was to get every Englishman out of India by a certain date. The announcement resulted in chaos and riots throughout the subcontinent and started a mass migration and the massacre of up to a million people on both sides of the border. It was uncertain whether Lord Mountbatten of Burma would go down in history as the Liberator of India or India's Butcher. It all depended on who wrote the history.

Among Pakistan's supporters, those who had heard the clumsy thief's story characterized Pakistan as Mountbatten's underwear. According to the story, a thief broke into a house late at night while the occupants were in deep delta sleep. He found out that it was a poor household, and there was nothing worth stealing, except some pots and pans in the kitchen. So he started collecting them, but he was so clumsy that he kept dropping a pot here and a pan there. All that noise woke the family, and they started yelling. "Thief! Thief!" The thief ran out of the kitchen, climbed the courtyard wall and jumped out of the house. The owner of the house ran after him, yelling, "Thief! Thief!"

When the neighbours heard the noise, they woke up and joined the chase. Before long, the entire neighbourhood was running after him, but nobody could catch him. They did not know that he was a marathon runner. No one could compete with him, except the immediate neighbour, who was himself a marathon runner. He kept getting closer and closer until he almost caught the thief - almost because he grabbed the back of his shirt, and it tore off. They had left the crowd far behind, but the neighbour continued chasing the shirtless thief until he came close again. This time the thief lost his trousers but kept running in his underwear. All that the neighbour needed was the final push, in which he got the underwear, and the thief ran away, stark naked, and disappeared in the dark night. Our hero stood under the street light pole, holding the underwear. When the crowd approached him, he raised his hand and yelled with excitement, "Look, at least I got his underwear!"

And that is how Jinnah presented Pakistan to his people.

***

Two young men entered Nagla and approached a group of boys playing. One of them had a pole in his hand with the orange, white, and green flag of India wrapped around it. The other had a bag hanging off his shoulder. He put his hand in the bag and pulled out a fistful of candies. As he handed them to a boy, the others stopped their game and dashed toward him. They encircled the two men and stretched out their palms.

"Don't rush," said the man with candies. "I have got plenty for everyone."

The other man unfurled the flag and handed it to the youngest of the boys. "Here, you take the flag and lead the procession."

"The leader will say *Hindustan,* and everyone will say *Zindabad.* The leader will say *Congress ki,* and everyone will say *Jai ho.* Now let us all practise." The children liked the new game, and the procession started moving, chanting their slogans:

Hindustan, Zindadad,

Congress ki, Jai ho,

Mahatma Gandhi ki, Jai ho,

Nehru ki, Jai ho.

"Louder," prompted the young man with the candies, and handed them another fistful.

The adults watched the procession with interest; more boys joined as they moved until there were twenty or so of them. When they entered Birehra, their slogans changed abruptly, as per the young men's instructions. They stopped at the doors of Sherwani homes and chanted, *Bhaag Jao Pakistan, Bhaag Jao Pakistan.* It was a message asking the Muslims to run to Pakistan. The two men who had organized the procession were nowhere in sight, and the boys kept singing and clapping until they realized that there were no more candies.

When the news of the procession reached Baldev in Nagla, he was furious. He thought about Khansab and his relatives and felt that he had to come forward to support them. After all, Khansab had saved his honour when Pratap Singh had come to attack him.

"What do you know about this incident?" Baldev asked the servant, who had told him about the procession.

"They say that some men gave them candies and taught them the slogans."

"Do you know who those men were?"

"No. There were two men, and nobody knows them," replied the servant. "They must have come from the city."

"Are they still in Nagla?"

"No, they disappeared when the children entered Birehra."

"Let me know if you hear anything."

"Yes, Thakurji." The servant took the cue and left.

Baldev decided to drop in at Khansab's home that evening. When he got there, he found that the mood was sombre. Hasan Khan was there, and so were Zakaria Khan and Noor Khan. Pundit Uday Lal from Nagla was there too. Khansab stood from his chair to greet Baldev and pointed to the chair next to his. As he sat down, he shook his feet to dust the dirt off his shoes.

"I say we ignore this incident," said Khansab. "It was merely a children's play and does not mean anything."

"You call it a children's play. The question is who taught them their slogans," asked Noor Khan.

"There is no doubt that there are some miscreants who want to cause trouble," said Baldev. "My servant tells me that there were two strangers in Nagla who gave candies to the children and organized the procession."

"We have to keep calm," commented Khansab. "The whole country is on fire, and we do not want that fire to reach us. I am sure things will eventually be back to normal."

Uday Lal was quiet. He knew who the culprits were and decided to confront his son again. He could not sacrifice the centuries of peaceful coexistence of the people in his neighbourhood for his interest.

"Some of you have not heard about what happened in the mosque last week," said Hasan Khan.

Uday Lal and Baldev looked at him. Everyone was quiet.

"Someone slaughtered a pig in the mosque."

"What!" exclaimed Baldev.

"Someone is trying to start a riot here," replied Hasan Khan. "Our families are terrified. You know what is going on in the country."

"It is a serious matter," said Baldev, "but we are with you. They will reach your throats only after our throats have been slit."

"Are you sure you will not be helpless yourselves when it is time to help us?" asked Zakaria Khan, who had listened to their conversation silently.

Baldev did not respond. He kept staring into the distance, absorbed in deep thought. Silence fell on them as if there was nothing else to discuss, no solutions to propose, and no decisions to make.

***

When Uday Lal woke up the next morning, the sun was already shining in his eyes. As the weather got warmer at the end of the short winter, he got his cot moved from the bedroom onto the veranda, where the cool, night breeze helped him sleep better. Following his morning routine, his servant brought a tumbler of water and the stack of day-old newspapers and placed them on the side table. Uday Lal took a mouthful of water to gargle and spat it into the spit bucket on the floor next to the side table. In the meantime, the servant brought a bolster with a green silk cover and put it on the pillow. Uday Lal sat with his back supported by the bolster and opened a newspaper. He sent a servant every day to the city to buy several newspapers, and by the time he got them, it was already late in the evening. Therefore, he read them all the next morning. The news was not good. There were riots everywhere, especially in Punjab, where village after village was torched, men were slaughtered, women were raped, and children's lifeless bodies were hung on spears. Uday Lal felt as if an alien force had taken over the country. The entire nation was suffering from mass hysteria.

As he picked up another newspaper, he looked at the crow sitting on the wall around the courtyard, cawing continuously. *As if a guest will come today,* he smiled when he thought about the old superstition, which said that if a crow caws on your wall, it is telling you that a guest is coming. Just then, Amrit walked in and greeted him.

"Are you a guest?" asked Uday Lal.

Amrit did not understand what his father meant and kept looking at him for further explanation. Uday Lal pointed to the crow. Amrit smiled at his father's remark and sat down as he picked up a newspaper. The servant brought a cup of tea as usual and put it on the table.

Uday Lal recollected the conversation at Khansab's house the night before and looked at his son. "Are you aware of what has been happening around us?" he asked Amrit.

"You mean the riots?"

"No, I mean the events in Birehra."

"What events?"

"Someone slaughtered a pig in the mosque." Uday Lal knew that his son was behind the trouble but wanted him to confess. "Yesterday, a bunch of children roamed around, asking the Sherwanis to go to Pakistan."

Amrit did not answer. He kept his eyes on the newspaper, assuming that his father did not expect a reply.

"There were two men from the city who were coaxing the children to form a procession," said Uday Lal.

"What is wrong with suggesting to Sherwanis to go to Pakistan? Now that they have their country and can live there the way they want to."

"So you want all Indian Musalmans to go and pack themselves in that tiny piece of land that you have given to them like they throw a bone to a dog. Is that the idea?"

"When did I say that I want all Musalmans to go?" replied Amrit. "We want only their elite to leave."

"We have had this conversation before," said Uday Lal.

"Yes, we did."

They turned pages of their newspapers simultaneously. Uday Lal's tea was getting cold. A fly had dived into the cup and was struggling to get out, but its wings were too wet to let it break free. Uday Lal finally broke the long, uneasy silence. "I had raised my son to be open-minded and free from taboos and prejudices." He seemed to be talking to himself. "I could have never imagined that he would grow up to be a terrorist."

"A terrorist?" Amrit retaliated. "I do not believe in violence. Ours is a peaceful movement."

"You don't have to kill people to be a terrorist," replied Uday Lal. "You are terrorizing peaceful people, who have nothing to do with politics. They have been our friends for generations and do not get in our way."

"And that is the way we want it. They should live peacefully in their home, and we will live in our home. They won't be in our way, and we won't be in theirs."

"I am shocked to see what has become of you," said Uday Lal.

Amrit folded his newspaper and put it aside. "I am entitled to my opinion just as you are entitled to yours."

"I do not dispute your right, but I cannot allow my home to be a source of plots and conspiracies."

"I guess that means that we do not belong under the same roof," said Amrit, as he got up from his chair and walked away.

Uday Lal did not respond. He remembered that the servant had put a cup of tea on his table. He looked at it and noticed the fly. It had given up its struggle, and its lifeless body floated in his tea. He turned back to the newspaper. Amrit walked past him with a suitcase in his hand and walked away without looking at his father. Uday Lal was startled. He had not realized that their argument would go that far. *Come back, son.* He struggled with words, but his voice was muffled in his throat.

***

Uday Lal had spent his life as a lonely man since his wife died three years after their marriage. He was only nineteen years old when he got married, and Nina was two years younger than he was, but the child within her was still very much a child. She treated life like a toy and looked for any excuse to burst into uncontrollable giggles. Her laughter was enchanting and made Uday Lal feel like thousands of tiny silver bells were ringing in his ears. It did not take much to make her laugh. Sometimes, he would come quietly behind her and say, "Boo!" That was enough for her to burst into laughter. And now, Nina was gone. It had happened twenty-five years earlier, but he felt as if she had died just yesterday. He had lived with himself all those years and made sure that his pain stayed with him. Whenever there was a sign that his wound was healing, he prodded it with a fingernail to keep it fresh.

He got up from the bed and decided to take a walk in his garden. He passed through a long arched canopy, built from bamboo and covered with bougainvillea. The vines were loaded with bright red, pink, orange, purple, white, and yellow flowers, shimmering under the sun. He thought of Amrit as a baby and saw himself sitting in a chair with his son on his lap, his arm supporting Amrit's neck and holding a bottle of milk in the other hand. Whenever Amrit fell asleep while being fed, Uday Lal nudged his arm gently, and Amrit started sucking on the nipple again.

As Uday Lal walked through the garden, he remembered how they used to play hide and seek when Amrit was three years old. He would stand facing the wall while Amrit would run to hide in the closet. Uday Lal would pretend that he did not know and would call out to him:

"Ready or not, here I come.

Where are you?

I know. You are under the bed.

Oh, you are not under the bed.

You must be behind the shelf.

Not there.

Ah, you must be in the closet.

Just then, Amrit would come out giggling and wrap himself around his father's leg. Uday Lal recollected event after event, and every event added to his gloom. He reached the outer gate of the garden. Amrit had not bothered closing it on his way out. He looked outside; the street was deserted. Far away, on the edge of the village, he could see the back of a young man with a suitcase walking away. Uday Lal stood there as long as his eyes could follow his son, and then turned back, leaving the gate open.

Unanswered Prayers

No one could remember when Phagna had first started coughing. They advised him that he should cut down on his hookah and start drinking more buttermilk. As time passed, his cough worsened. He felt weak and sluggish and lay on his cot all day. When he tried to get up to welcome his guests, they would extend an arm and put a hand on his chest to stop him from sitting up. They helped themselves, making sure that the hookah was freshly charged and the kettle contained enough tea. Phagna was sick. Someone was always there, massaging his head and wetting his hair with oil. He would feel fine in the morning, but his fever went up as the day progressed. His guests suggested several remedies for his cough and told him about their own experiences. "My uncle's cough was much worse than yours and went on for a whole year. Then someone suggested to him dried ginger root, and he chewed it only once or twice. He has never coughed since then." It was considered rude if you visited a sick person and did not suggest a cure for him.

Everyone brought some medicine for Phagna: small pills, large pills, sweet syrups, bitter concoctions, herbal preparations, and home remedies. He opened his mouth for everyone while keeping his eyes closed, and they shoved their medicine down his throat. Someone suggested that Khansab be told about Phagna's health, but he forbade him strictly. "Don't you dare let him know," he said, lifting his weak hand and pointing his finger at them. "He will take me to a city doctor, but I don't want to go anywhere." As he coughed day and night, he became so weak that someone had to help him whenever he tried to sit up in his bed. They hoped that Phagna would be well soon, but he did not show any sign that he would get better.

When his visitors noticed blood in his spit, they knew right away that it was tuberculosis. The news spread, and Khansab found out that Phagna had been throwing up blood. He called Wafati, the bullock cart driver, to bring his cart to Phagna's shed immediately after dawn prayers the next morning. He asked two other people to be there, to escort Phagna to Aligarh. As they departed at dawn, Khansab followed them on his horse. It was late in the afternoon when they arrived at the clinic. The doctor examined Phagna and declared that it was tuberculosis. Khansab asked him if he could take him to a TB sanatorium. "It is too late," said the doctor. "The x-ray shows that TB has consumed his lungs. He is not expected to live for long." The doctor prescribed a few medicines to relieve the pain and gave detailed instructions for making sure that other people in the village were not infected.

They brought him back to his shed and helped him settle down in his bed. Fattu was assigned the job of staying with Phagna. He was instructed to make sure that, when Phagna spat on the ground, he put some dirt on it right away.

When Khansab came home, he was exhausted. He gave special instructions to Chhoti Begum about Phagna's diet. "The doctor says that he should get a healthy diet. Give him a lot of milk and juices of fresh fruit," he told her. "Phagna has been like a son to me. He has always respected me, and I have always loved him, even though I have never admitted it. I can't see him die so helplessly." Khansab wept bitterly like a baby.

"You can't do anything in this matter," his mother-in-law consoled him. "Every living soul has to taste death," she quoted from the

Qur'an.

"I realize that, but somehow I cannot accept it."

"Even the Prophet had to die. And don't forget Noah, who lived for nine hundred years. Even he had to go eventually."

Khansab was overcome with guilt. He thought of Phagna's father, Bhagwan Das the woodchopper, who was his milk brother. He was a Hindu. *So what?* he thought. *I shared his mother's milk with him, and he was my brother, but I did not take care of him. I did not even take care of his son. How can I let Phagna die like that?*

Chhoti Begum prepared Phagna's food very diligently. She crushed some apples and oranges and squeezed them through a piece of cloth to extract fresh juice. No more pickles and no more cornbread! He could get only rice, fish, and chicken soup.

Fattu took good care of Phagna, who slept most of the time. He poured milk and fruit juice and slid a spoonful through the slit between Phagna's lips. People still stopped by and stayed for a while for a smoke. They even spent time exchanging gossip and talking about city life, but Phagna did not participate. He lay in his bed with his eyes closed. When they lowered their voices, fearing that they were disturbing him, he opened his eyes and made a gesture with his hand, asking them to speak up. Even though he was too weak to participate in their conversation, he still wanted to be part of it. Sometimes, when he felt better, Fattu helped him sit up and tried to feed him some rice and fish. He asked Fattu not to give him any food since it was too painful for him to swallow.

Someone mentioned to Khansab that Phagna wanted to see Azad. When he visited Phagna, Azad was shocked to see a tiny, frail body lying in the cot. His arms were thin as sticks, and there was a deep pit where his stomach used to be. Was this the same big, fat Phagna with bloodshot eyes, who had once appeared twenty feet tall? As Azad stood at his bedside, Phagna opened his eyes slowly and looked at him. "I know that you used to get scared of me." Azad could hardly hear him, so he moved closer. "I wanted to talk to you, but you always ran into your house when you saw me coming." Azad did not have anything to say to him. He just stood there, looking at Phagna's weak body.

"Are you still scared of me?"

Azad shook his head from side to side without saying a word.

"May He keep you under His protection," he said and raised his hand in prayer. "Remember to be like your father when you grow up."

Tears started flowing on Azad's cheeks. Even though he had always treated Phagna as someone to be avoided, he was devastated to see how someone as strong and scary as Phagna could break down just like that.

When people gathered at his shed that evening for their late-night chat and smoke, they saw that Phagna was breathing with a gurgling sound. They asked Fattu about it, and he said that he had noticed that sound too. Perhaps he had not been able to swallow the last spoon of chicken soup that Fattu had tried to pour down his throat. They did not know that his lungs were filled with fluid, and he was taking his last breaths. It is said that everyone who has ever lived and who will ever be born is brought into this world with a prescribed number of breaths. No matter how sick you get, you have to complete the number of your breaths. Even though Phagna was hardly alive, he counted the breaths he was blessed with when he was born. His eyes were closed, and he kept gurgling all night.

***

As Azad woke up at dawn, he looked around. His parents were still sleeping. He could hear his grandmother's heavy breathing too. That was odd. *They usually wake up before I do. It must be a bit early.* He tried to go back to sleep, but his eyes were wide open. He could hear the roosters' cock-a-doodle-do. Some farmer was on his way to the field. Azad could listen to the dull sound of a bell tied around the bullock's neck. He must be carrying his plough on his shoulder and holding his bullock's harness on the other hand. They were not in any hurry. The farmer must still be half-asleep, and his lazy bullock must be wondering what kind of a day was ahead. *Poor bullock! It must get tired of pulling a plough in the field all day. It's hard work.* He thought about his visit to Phagna's shed the night before. Poor Phagna could not care anymore who came into the village and who left. Azad remembered the times when they would go past him, and he would give them candies. He never meant any harm, even when he yelled at them as they tried to sneak out of the village.

Azad's eyes became wet with tears; he swallowed hard as he lay in bed, thinking about Phagna. *Oh, God! Please make him feel better. You know that he used to be mean at one time, but now he is nice to everyone.* Just then, he heard the call to prayer from the mosque. He started praying for Phagna. One must always pray for others when one hears the call to prayer. That is a special time when God answers your prayers. He knew that Phagna would get better. That is why he had woken up so early and prayed for him. They say that God pays special attention to children's prayers since they have such a pure heart. Indeed, he could remember a few sins that he had committed, but they were all small sins.

Once, he had managed to slip out of the village, with other kids, to buy a kite from the neighbouring village that was three fields away. When his mother asked him where he had gotten the kite, he had told her that he had given money to Shubrati's grandson to buy a kite for him. He admitted to himself that he had lied to his mother, but that was also a small sin, and he was sure that it would not be a big deal for God to forgive him.

O God, please do not hold it against me, and make Phagna feel better, Azad whispered as he fell asleep, not realizing that Phagna was about to breathe his last.

***

Back under Phagna's shed, Fattu, who was sleeping on the cot next to him, was unsure how he woke up. It was either the call to prayer from the mosque or the fact that he had stopped hearing Phagna's breathing. Whatever it was, Fattu opened his eyes all of a sudden. He looked at Phagna's cot and noticed that the gurgling sound had stopped. Phagna was not breathing anymore. He ran toward the dirt road. A farmer walked to his field with a plough on his shoulder and his bullock's bridle in his hand.

"Phagna is dead!" Fattu choked as he cried. The farmer dropped his plough and came running. As morning approached and farmers passed by, they found that Phagna had died. It was still dark as they gathered under the mango trees. Birds were chirping, and the morning dew was dripping from the leaves, the sun rising behind a thick patch of clouds. By that time, the entire village knew that Phagna was dead. They remembered when he used to be a rogue and terrorize the whole village, and then they talked about his transformation to a loving and caring person who cherished life. Everyone commented on his life after death, according to his faith. Muslims believed that he would go straight to heaven. He was undoubtedly a good man and deserved a better life in the hereafter. Hindus believed that he would be reincarnated as a higher form of life, possibly a saint or a peacock. They looked up at thick clouds in the sky. Even though the rainy season had started, not a drop of water had fallen from the sky. Farmers had been waiting for rain, but the sun had been ablaze for days. As Phagna's body lay under the mango trees, the cloud cover up above was a good omen. It proved that Phagna was indeed a good man.

It was not until mid-day that people started wondering what they should do with Phagna's body. There were no fewer than a hundred people there, and they could not agree whether they should burn the body or bury it. Hindus wanted cremation while Muslims were insisting on burial. However, Phagna was not a Hindu, and neither was he a Muslim. He was a Sikh, and no one was sure what Sikhs did with their dead. There were no Sikhs around to help them. As time passed, arguments started gathering heat, and voices began rising.

"Sikh religion emerged from Hinduism, so they must be burning their dead," someone remarked.

"But Guru Nanak, who founded the Sikh religion, had gone for a pilgrimage to Mecca," came the reply.

"Guru Nanak was a Hindu."

"But he was a Musalman at heart."

Fattu insisted that Phagna had told him, just two days back, that he wanted to be buried, but nobody heard him. Everyone was shouting, and Fattu sounded like a parrot in a drum house. While people argued about the disposal of Phagna's body, the pundit at the temple declared that, since Phagna was not a Hindu, he would not get involved in any ritual of cremation. According to whatever little he knew about religion, the mullah in the mosque said that Phagna was not a Muslim. He hesitated to lead the funeral prayer or to show his involvement in any way if they decided to bury the body. People cared neither for the pundit nor for the mullah at that time. The immediate task was to win the debate.

"Phagna was a Hindu before he became a Sikh."

"His parents and forefathers were all Hindus."

"So we should cremate his body."

The argument did seem to carry weight, and the Muslims gave up. They were disappointed at their defeat but accepted the proposal for cremation. It was mid-morning when some elders in the village were dispatched to the temple to convince the pundit to perform the ritual. The clouds got thicker, and the cool breeze carried them gently across the sky. People kept reiterating that it was a sure sign of Phagna's good life after death. Someone pointed to the pundit, coming with his troupe. It seemed that the elders were able to convince him to perform the cremation. As they arrived, their yellow-orange robes fluttered in the gentle breeze. The pundit started giving orders and making haste since it was already late. He sent a group to *marghat*, the cremation ground, to prepare a pyre. Another group laid the corpse on the ground and sat down to chant the scripture. The word came from the marghat that the pyre was ready. They put the body on a stretcher, and four men lifted it on their shoulders. The rest of the procession followed them as they sped along. They chanted and rang bells as they ran-*Raam Naam satt hai*. It appeared to be a celebration. Death is something that should be celebrated. Death does not mean the end of life. It merely points to another phase in the cycle of reincarnation. Besides, Phagna was a good man. He might have even come out of the web of reincarnation and had achieved *nirvana:* the divine state. The ever-blazing sun was hidden behind huge clouds, and the air was loaded with moisture. It indeed was a good day for Phagna's funeral.

***

A *tateeri* flew past. It called with a shrill sound as it passed. It was said that a tateeri had a hole in its throat and could not swallow water. Whenever it tried to drink water, it fell out through the hole. A tateeri was always thirsty. "The only way it can quench its thirst is by pointing its beak upward and opening it when it rains," Nanijan had told Azad. The rainwater could get through its throat easily. If it did not rain for a long time, a tateeri got extremely thirsty and prayed for rain. "Ta-tee-ri, ta-tee-ri, ta-tee-ri," it yelled out its prayer as it flew in search of water. No one had ever seen a tateeri. It flew so fast that one moment you would hear its cry on your left, and by the time you raised your eyes to locate it, you would hear it far, far away on your right. If you heard a tateeri, it was a sure sign that rain was on its way. It was said that Indra, the Hindu god of rain and thunder, despite all his power and might, was helpless when a tateeri pleaded for rain. Muslims said that the hearts of angels were torn when they heard a tateeri's eerie cry. God could not ignore the thirst of a poor, helpless bird and would order angels to send down the rain.

The children in the village had come out to play in the street. As the wind picked up speed, they enjoyed the cool breeze and looked up to watch the gathering clouds. The wind formed little eddies that lifted the dirt, whirling in circles. They chased every eddy to hurl in pieces of paper and see them rise. They competed to see whose paper went higher up before the eddy lost its force, and the dirt fell back to the ground. They knew that they would soon be able to bathe in the rain and cool down the heat rashes on their bodies. The tateeri was continuously flying and crying bitterly: *"Ta-tee-ri, ta-tee-ri, ta-tee-ri."* It only meant that rain was imminent.

As Phagna's funeral procession entered the cremation ground, it headed straight to the pyre. They put the body on the pile of timber and splashed oil all around; the pundit and his group chanted verses from the Vedas. When everything was ready, the pundit asked who was going to light the fire. It usually was for the deceased's eldest son to set the fire, but Phagna had no son. Some people suggested that Fattu had served Phagna like a son during his last days, so it should be his privilege to light the pyre. As Fattu was given a burning stick saturated with oil, someone pointed out that he was a Muslim. How could a Muslim perform the cremation of a Hindu?

There were arguments and counter-arguments until Fattu's grandfather, who was considered a wise old man, said that if Phagna could talk at that time, he would certainly give his approval. That was how much Phagna loved Fattu. Everyone agreed.

As Fattu approached the pyre, the chanting became louder. He touched the pyre base with the burning stick, and the oil-soaked wood caught fire right away. Then suddenly, it seemed as if someone had squeezed the clouds up above like a sponge. Water came pouring down in buckets, and the entire ground was ankle-deep in water within minutes. The fire was out before it could reach the corpse. Someone brought a sheet of waxed cloth and spread it over the pyre to keep it dry, but it was drenched with water by that time. People ran here and there for cover and waited under trees. It seemed that the rain was not going to stop soon. It kept falling with the same intensity until the ponds started filling, and the streams began running. The ground that was baking in the sun for months opened its pores to absorb every drop of water that it could. Farmers had smiles on their faces as they looked up, and children ran in the street chasing each other and chanting rain songs-*chhaai badarya meh barsaa.*

People started talking as they waited under the trees looking at the cold pyre in front of them.

"Is this rain ever going to stop?"

"Even if it stops, do you think that you will be able to light the fire soon?"

"Maybe God did not want Phagna to be cremated."

"You mean to say that he was a Musalman."

"I don't know, but what would you say about this rain?"

"Maybe you are right. Maybe God did want Phagna to be buried."

The argument caught on. More and more people started believing that such heavy rain was a sure sign that God intended Phagna to be buried.

"I already told you that Phagna wanted to be buried!" shouted Fattu.

"When did you say that?" someone asked.

"I did, but nobody would hear me."

"Fattu is telling the truth," said Chaita Dhobi. "I heard him myself saying that Phagna wanted to be buried."

The pundit got angry. If they wanted to bury the body in the first place, why did they waste his time? Some people still felt that the body should be cremated, but they kept quiet as the rain kept falling with the same intensity. It was finally agreed that the funeral is taken to the graveyard. The pundit and his troupe left in anger. The elders who were given the task of bringing the pundit, were now requested to go to the mosque and convince the mullah to lead funeral prayers. Two gravediggers were asked to rush ahead of the funeral and start digging the ground.

As they were talking, the rain stopped as suddenly as it had started. Some people suggested that they try making the fire again, but others said that the decision had already been made. They had received a clear omen that Phagna's body should be buried and not cremated. Everyone agreed. The clouds were moving away fast. They were travelling to quench the thirst of another land and another tateeri. The air had been washed, and the soil that had been baked by the sun smelled fresh. The trees looked greener as the leaves fluttered in the cool breeze.

Even though it was late afternoon, it seemed as if it were after sunset. The body was lifted from the pyre and put back on the stretcher. The funeral procession started moving slowly. The mood was sombre as people came forward to give a shoulder to the stretcher. Everyone in the funeral procession was supposed to put a corner of the stretcher on his shoulder, even if it was only for a moment. It was a reminder that we all have to die one day. The mullah would remind them, "Death is a gateway to life in the hereafter. We must do good deeds in this life to find a place in heaven and should refrain from bad deeds to save us from hellfire."

When the procession reached the graveyard, it was found that the ground was filled with water up to people's knees. The gravediggers stood there helplessly with their spades on their shoulders. Even though the mullah was already there, he was reluctant to perform the ritual. He said that he did not believe in signs and omens and still felt that Phagna was not a Muslim, but agreed that he was a good man and deserved a respectable burial. The question was how to prepare the grave. His body had lain for the whole day, and it was important that it should be buried before the nightfall. "It is not necessary to bury the body here," said the mullah.

"Mullanji is right," someone remarked. "We should find high ground to dig the grave."

"What can be a better place than Phagna's shed for his grave?"

"Yes. The mango trees are on high ground, and it must be dry over there."

The gravediggers were rushed to the new site, and two elders were dispatched to get permission from Khansab. After all, the trees belonged to him. How could he object to it, since he had treated Phagna like his own son? By the time the funeral procession got there, the clouds had moved away, and the sun was setting. An orange glow had filled the horizon. A flock of birds passed slowly in a V-formation as they flapped their wings majestically in the air. As the stretcher was laid beside the shed, people lined up in a straight line for funeral prayers. Hindus waited on the side until the prayer was over and then came forward as the body was lowered into the grave. Everyone took a fistful of dirt and slid it gently into the grave. "It is important that we should all touch the dirt and participate in a burial," said the mullah. "It reminds us that we too have to die one day."

By the time the grave was filled, it was dark. A bunch of incense sticks were lit and put on the grave. The mood was gloomy, and people hugged Fattu as they departed, holding back their tears and wiping their noses. Fattu decided to stay back and be in the company of Phagna, whom he had served as he would have served his own father.

***

Who could have imagined at that time that Phagna would eventually gain the status of a saint, and his grave would become a shrine? Fattu would dedicate the rest of his life to taking care of the shrine and would receive thousands of pilgrims-Muslims, Hindus, and Sikhs from near and far, who would come there to pray and worship. Women would pray for husbands to love them or for their mothers-in-law to be kind to them; men would pray for wealth and their barren wives to give birth to sons. Everyone would get his wishes fulfilled, and those who would not consider it their own misfortune. The fruit from the two mango trees would become sacred, and pilgrims would buy loads of them to take home. Fattu would be known as the disciple of Phagna and showered with the pilgrims' gifts and money. He would become rich with all the wealth that would come his way. After all, he served Phagna selflessly and deserved the reward.

The Last Straw

The moonless night was pitch black. A dark cover of clouds made it even darker. It was already past midnight, and the people of Birehra were in a deep sleep. Chunnu was still at Phagna's shed, keeping company with Fattu. He found it difficult to keep his eyes open. He got up to leave and let Fattu get some sleep.

The farmers who slept in their fields had also retired, except a few whose hookahs were still gurgling. They sat in their cots with sleepy eyes for a few more puffs. Sukhdev, who guarded Khansab's fields, was one of them. The tobacco cake under the smouldering coal in his hookah had turned into ash, and all he was smoking was hot air. He put the hookah aside, and as he lay down on the cot, he heard someone yell from a nearby field.

"Charhai ho rahi hai!" The attack is imminent.

Sukhdev was perplexed. What kind of attack was imminent? He got up and repeated the announcement, as he was supposed to. The entire area was filled with the eerie sound of *"Charhai ho rahi hai. Charhai ho rahi hai."*

"What do they mean? There is no sign of a storm." Chunnu opened his eyes. The strange announcement had alerted him.

"I am sure some prankster is pulling off a trick," replied Fattu.

"That is dumb," said Chunnu.

"You are right. No one will believe when there is a true emergency. We should take such things seriously." They decided to ignore it.

***

Noor Khan, who had chronic insomnia, was the first one to hear the announcement. He ran out of his house in a panic and went from house to house, knocking on doors and warning his relatives that the rioters were coming. Men came out, half-asleep, and when they found out what the problem was, they were wide-awake. Fear gripped their senses as they ran amok in the alley, knocking on doors. Every gust of wind from the fields brought the message- *Charhai ho rahi hai*-and their panic grew.

"Who could have thought that we would have a situation like this in Birehra?" asked Zakaria Khan.

"We don't have time to think," replied Noor Khan. "Let us prepare to defend ourselves."

"What do you suggest? I don't have a gun,"

"Let us not waste time. Let us gather whatever we have: sticks, knives, guns, whatever."

"It is important to stay calm," suggested Hasan Khan. "Go back and get your families. Let us all gather in the mahal. It is secure."

Hasan Khan referred to his residence, built like a fortress with walls over thirty feet high. Everyone agreed with his suggestion. Khansab sped to his home and woke Chhoti Begum and Nanijan up.

"Is everything all right?" asked Chhoti Begum.

"We are under attack. The rioters are coming."

"Oh, God! The rioters are coming?" She got up with a start and ran to pick up Azad. Khansab asked her to get her jewellery box since that was her most valuable possession. He picked up Azad and put him on his shoulder. They came out in the empty street. The night was so silent that not even a cricket chirped. As they ran through the darkness, Azad woke up and could not understand the situation. He was overcome by intense fear when he found that someone was running, carrying him on his shoulder. He started crying bitterly. Khansab pulled him away from his shoulder and put his hand on Azad's mouth to muffle his crying. Who knew where the attackers were hiding in that darkness? He did not want to alert them. Azad squirmed against Khansab and became hysterical. Khansab could not manage to keep him silent, but they had reached the mahal by that time. He stopped at the door to let Nanijan and Chhoti Begum enter first. Azad had stopped crying, and Khansab put him down so that he could walk by himself.

When they entered the courtyard, it was bathed in light. Petromax lanterns were hanging all around. Several families had already arrived. Servants were busy setting up beds for the men in the courtyard. Hasan Khan told Nanijan and Chhoti Begum that all the women and children were in the main hall. Azad followed his mother into the women's quarters.

Khansab settled down in one of the rattan chairs that were set up in a circle. A servant had already started serving tea. As the night crept slowly toward the dawn, Khansab thought that tea would take away whatever sleep was left in his eyes, and he wanted to salvage it. Then he saw that nobody was prepared to go to bed anyway, so he accepted a cup. The mood was sombre, and everyone was in deep thought.

"Who are these rioters?" asked Zakaria Khan, addressing no one in particular.

"You know that the whole country is falling apart," replied Noor Khan. "Our forefathers settled here, and we have worked hard for generations to cultivate this land and feed the people, but let us face it. We do not belong together."

"I am sure it is just a temporary phase," replied Khansab. "Things will be back to normal."

"I don't think things will ever be normal. The wheel of history churns only in one direction. You cannot reverse it," said Noor Khan.

"We should discuss the situation with our Brahmin neighbours and see how they feel," said Zakaria Khan.

Hasan Khan interrupted the conversation and suggested that they try to get some sleep before the mullah's call to prayer. "In the meantime, I think that you should consider moving your families here at night until things settle down."

"You are right," said Khansab. "We cannot resolve this matter tonight. So we will talk about it in the morning."

Khansab got up from the chair and lay down on one of the beds. Others got up one by one, while a servant started dimming the lanterns.

***

The people of Birehra were unaware of what had happened with the Sherwanis. Those who had heard the announcement from the fields had ignored it. They thought that it was a prank and did not deserve any reaction. However, the message did reach the people for whom it was intended and had achieved the desired result.

It was almost dawn, but not quite. The roosters were still silent, and the mullah was perhaps still asleep in the mosque. The night was shrouded in silence, and the familiar odours of the village were swept away by a cool breeze. Chunnu walked barefoot in the street, covered with a thick layer of dust. He had never worn shoes in his life, even though he still had a pair that old Sharfu had made for him. He had worn them only once or twice but could not understand why anyone would wear shoes. As he passed Khansab's house on his right, he noticed that the door was closed. That was odd. He knew that there was a room behind the door, with another door at its back, locked from inside at night. However, the outside door was always open. He walked closer to the house and saw a large padlock on the door. He stood there for a while, and as he crossed the alley, a man approached him from behind the sidewall.

"Who are you?" asked the man.

Chunnu stopped and came closer to the man. He could see the face of the stranger in the light of dawn but did not recognize him. The man was certainly not from Birehra or Nagla.

"My name is Chunnu," he replied.

"What do you do?"

"I work on Khansab's land."

Suddenly the man took a step forward and punched him hard on the side of his nose. It was a well-balanced punch, delivered with full force. Chunnu's head was snapped back, and he could see stars dancing in front of his eyes. At first, he was frightened by the unexpected attack, but then the fear gave way to intense hatred for the attacker, followed by a feeling of humiliation. As he prepared himself for retaliation, two other men appeared from behind the wall. One of them stood on his right, and the other positioned himself behind the man who had attacked Chunnu. It did not matter. Even if there were a dozen of them, he had to take revenge to restore his honour.

Chunnu knew right away that his opponent was strong but not an expert in fist fighting. Being left-handed, he moved slightly to the right to avoid his punches being blocked by the opponent. It also made his opponent's face a clear target for his left hook. He turned slightly to the left, tilting his right hip forward and targeted the right jaw of his attacker. His fists were in place, and his blood was getting saturated with the adrenaline rush. He could not wait any longer but had to maneuver his opponent to give him free access to the blow.

Just then, the man moved to Chunnu's left, exposing the other man standing at the back, who came forward, holding a long flick knife. His thumb was on the ejector button. As he moved closer, he pressed the button, and a six-inch blade appeared. Chunnu's fight or flight strategy changed immediately. The man on his right was relatively short and appeared weaker than him. That was his escape route, but he did not want those men to know that he was planning to run away. As his opponent slowly moved forward, waving the knife, Chunnu knew that his chest was the target. He moved his fists higher to cover his chest and exposed his abdomen. The hand carrying the knife moved immediately downward, aiming for his abdomen. That was precisely what Chunnu's strategy was. He was preparing to kick the knife out of his opponent's hand, to knock the man down on the right with a punch in the stomach, and to run away from the scene as fast as he could. He readied himself by moving his left foot back and tilting his body slightly to the left so that he could kick the attacker's right hand, which was holding the knife. He was aiming for a spot halfway between the wrist and the elbow. A swish from the left would knock the knife out of his opponent's hand. It was going to be a dangerous move, but Chunnu could handle it. After delivering the kick, he would be facing right, which would enable him to punch the man on his right without extra effort.

Suddenly, the man in front of Chunnu moved back and pressed the button on his knife's handle. The blade moved back into the handle.

"We mean no harm to you," he said in a soft tone. "Just consider us your friends."

Chunnu dropped his fists but could not suppress his anger; his adrenaline was looking for a way out. He yelled at the top of his lungs, "You bastards! What kind of friends are you? You almost broke my nose!"

"Shh! Let us not raise our voices," said the man on his left, who had punched him in the face. They were all strangers and spoke like city folk. Chunnu could not understand what their motive was.

"We just wanted to deliver a message to you."

"Could you not deliver the message without hitting me?"

"The punch was just to get your attention. It will not let you ignore our message."

"What are you trying to say?"

"Our message is that you will not work for Khansab anymore."

Chunnu was confused. What did they have against Khansab? He massaged his nose gently to relieve the pain.

"Why do you say that?" he asked. "How will I feed my family if I don't work?"

"Don't worry. You will find work."

"I don't know what you have against Khansab," said Chunnu. "I don't have any complaint against him."

"We do. Just remember that you should tell everyone in Birehra what we told you. Nobody is going to work for Musalman masters. If they do, we will beat them and their families."

"I don't like you people. You are trying to cause trouble in our village."

"You can believe whatever you want to, but we have given you our message. If you don't follow it, you will see the consequences." All three men turned back and walked away. Chunnu stood there watching them until they disappeared behind Khansab's house.

***

Irshad had entered Khansab's service when he was a fourteen-year-old brat, picking fights with boys in the neighbourhood. His father, who worked in Khansab's fields, was fed up with complaints from people whose children were bullied by his son, so he held the boy by his ear and brought him to Khansab to put him to work and teach him discipline. Khansab handed him over to the old groom, who took care of his horses. That was thirty years earlier when Irshad had started as a stable boy. He had taken over as the groom long ago, after the death of his old mentor.

Working with horses had taught him responsibility, empathy, and tenderness. Irshad was reticent by nature and did not speak unless someone spoke to him. It was not that he did not have much to share with others. On the contrary, he had plenty to talk about, but he spoke only to his horses. He told them stories, scolded them when they misbehaved and expressed appreciation for their excellent conduct. It appeared that the horses understood every word. They always agreed with whatever he said and responded to his comments with an occasional nod, nicker, or snort.

There were five stalls in the stable, but only three were occupied — first, *Raja*, a sabino horse with pink skin, dark eyes, and an all-white coat. Khansab had bought him from an English lord, who traced the horse's mother's ancestry to the royal stables. He was Khansab's personal horse, and he did not allow anyone else to mount him. The only exception was Irshad, whom he treated with respect and gentleness. Khansab's friends, who claimed to be expert horse trainers, were thrown off his back within moments, when he reared unexpectedly, standing on his hind legs. The rider would be hurled back like a projectile from a catapult! If the rider managed to stay on Raja's back, the horse would simply balk, refusing to move even an inch. Then there was *Chandni*-the moonlight-a Marwari mare with a dark brown coat and white pinto patches. The third occupant of the stables was *Mushki*, a seal-brown horse, trained as a polo pony and once known, on Khansab's team, for his agility. With his roached mane and braided tail, he stood sixteen hands high at the withers and looked taller than any other horse on either team. He followed the ball's line so closely that, when Khansab swung his mallet, the ball never missed the goal. He had earned many ribbons for Khansab, but those days were long gone. Mushki was already thirty-seven years old and was on his last legs.

Irshad paid particular attention to old Mushki and treated him as his elder. "How is the old man feeling today?" he asked as he patted Mushki's neck gently after he entered the stable every morning. Mushki always responded with a soft nicker, which in horse talk, meant "Welcome back!" Among other issues, Mushki was also struggling with arthritis. There were days when his knees were swollen like balloons, and he spent the nights moaning gently in pain. Whenever Irshad heard Mushki's moan, it tore his heart. It reminded him of his grandfather, whose fingers and toes had stiffened and curled due to arthritis, and who also moaned all night in pain.

Sleeping next to his grandfather, Irshad often woke up and picked up the lantern. As he turned the knob to raise the wick, a faint light would fill the room. He'd walked to the kitchen, carrying the lantern with him, put a pile of firewood in the *chulha*, and pour on kerosene oil from a bottle. When Irshad threw a burning matchstick, the firewood would catch the flame instantly, and he would put a pan of water on the chulha. When it started boiling, he would pick up the pan and bring it to his grandfather-still half asleep, tossing and turning, moaning and groaning with pain in his bed. Irshad would dip old rags in hot water and wrap them around his grandfather's knees. Sitting on the edge of the old man's bed, he often fell asleep and woke up with a start to find that the wrappings around his grandfather's knees were now cold, but his pain had stopped, and he had started snoring. Irshad would get up, with his eyes barely open, and go back to bed.

After the old man died, Mushki took his place in Irshad's heart, and he served him with the same dedication. When he entered the stable in the morning, he went straight to Mushki's stall and examined his knees and fetlocks. If he found any swelling, he applied hot compresses until the horse felt comfortable.

Most of Irshad's day was spent in cleaning the stable and giving each horse a brisk massage. He started by spreading his fingers and keeping his hands on the side of Mushki's neck until the horse felt relaxed. Then he moved his palms slowly, following the contours of the body. As Mushki's head drooped, Irshad knew that it was falling into a relaxed trance.

"Feeling sleepy, old man?" asked Irshad. Mushki raised his head gently.

"It is okay. Just relax." Irshad started massaging the body with his fists and elbows, kneading every muscle gently. The intensity of the massage increased until he started sweating. It was a tiring job, and he had to take a break after massaging each horse.

Chandni sighed as Irshad approached her, which meant she was preparing to enjoy the relaxing massage she was about to get.

"Is my queen ready to be served by her slave?" asked Irshad.

She responded with a friendly snort as he patted her on the back.

"I know that you enjoy your massage more than those two," he pointed his thumb to Mushki and Raja. "At one time, there was another horse whom I loved serving. He loved me as much as I loved him."

Irshad worked on Chandni's muscles, leaning into her body, pressing each muscle with his forearm and releasing it with a jerk.

"Let me tell you about Pehelwan," said Irshad. "Pehelwan was Khansab's polo horse before Mushki. What a majestic horse! When Khansab descended on the polo ground, dressed in breeches and wearing a polo hat, the female spectators oohed and aahed. Pehelwan earned many ribbons for Khansab!"

Suddenly Mushki raised his head and neighed in a high pitch, showing protest and anxiety. Irshad burst into laughter. "Did you see that?" He stepped back and gestured towards Mushki. "Did you see that? The old man got jealous when I talked about Pehelwan!"

Irshad could not stop laughing. Chandni and Raja raised their heads and nickered as if they were laughing with him! He walked toward Mushki and choked with laughter, "Don't worry, my old man. He was not as good as you were. You also earned many ribbons!" He patted Mushki on the neck to calm him.

He finished his daily chores by early evening, and then it was time to take Mushki for a leisurely ride around the fields to keep his joints working, and muscles stimulated. He tied the horse with a head collar rope and started brushing his body with a comb to remove any dirt or caked mud, finishing the job with a soft brush. After he combed the mane and the tail to remove any tangles, he put a pad on Mushki's back and the saddle on top of it. Finally, he attached the girth to the straps and fastened it securely. Mushki was now ready to go. Irshad brought him to the front of the house and called for Azad, who was already waiting for him.

"Will you help me, Irshad Chacha?" asked Azad. He was a bit afraid of climbing on a horse, especially after falling once while he tried on his own.

"No, you will climb up yourself," he replied. "Eventually, you will have to get on it yourself."

"Yes, when I grow up. But now I cannot even reach it," said Azad in a pleading tone.

"Let us try, anyway."

Irshad used to pick up Azad and put him on the horse's back, but he had started insisting that Azad should learn to climb up himself. He interlocked his fingers to make a cradle and asked Azad to put his left foot in the cradle and raised it until he could reach the stirrup. "Now, put your right foot in the stirrup and swing your left leg on top of the saddle, up, up!" That was a difficult move for Azad, but he would eventually master it.

"Now pat your horse gently on the neck to greet him," said Irshad.

Azad leaned forward and patted the horse. Mushki gave the nod and snorted gently.

"Mushki is welcoming you and is ready to take you for a ride."

Irshad walked in front of the horse, holding the lead rope. Mushki followed at a slow pace, with his head drooping as if in deep thought.

"Are you feeling okay, old man?" Irshad looked back at the horse.

"Why do you call Mushki an old man?" asked Azad.

"Because he reminds me of my grandfather. I used to call him an old man."

"That is bad. You should not insult your elders. That is what Nanijan tells me."

"Oh, he did not mind. We were friends, and he always smiled when I called him an old man."

When they reached the village's boundary, Irshad increased his pace, hoping that he would get Mushki into a trot for a little extra exercise. He was disappointed to see that the horse did not respond to the lead rope's extra nudge. When he realized that he was unfair to old Mushki, he felt guilty and stopped until the horse caught up with him. He patted Mushki on the cheek and started to walk again.

"Is Mushki older than your grandfather, Irshad Chacha?" Azad interrupted his thoughts.

"In human years, yes," said Irshad. "Mushki is two years older than my grandfather."

Azad did not respond. He kept thinking about his horse. *It means that Mushki will die soon,* he thought and felt a lump in his throat.

Irshad kept on walking with the lead rope in his hand, looking down at the ground. They had left the fields at the back and were returning to the village. Neither of them bothered to see that the sun had turned into a bright orange ball, descending slowly into the horizon, and the sky looked like a watercolour painting, with thin streaks of gold and orange clouds. They did not even notice a flock of egrets passing in front of the setting sun, in a perfect V-formation, on their way to roosting.

***

The announcement of an imminent attack had become a nightly affair, but nobody paid attention to it anymore. The farmers sleeping in the fields were asked to find out who initiated those calls, but they could not catch the culprits. The fear among the Sherwanis persisted, and their families spent night after night in the mahal. When they left their homes unoccupied at night, the prowlers had a free hand to climb the walls of interior courtyards. They roamed freely, stealing whatever they wanted. Every morning when the families returned, they counted missing pots and pans. Their workers were constantly threatened and beaten up until most of them started staying away from their employers. They had planted corn a few days back, and the plants were already a foot high. Khansab hoped that the situation would be back to normal soon so that his field workers could return by harvest time. He could not blame them for being afraid of working on his land.

Khansab and his family had just returned from the mahal after spending another restless sleep, punctuated by nightmares and disturbing dreams. The rain had stopped overnight, but the morning was still damp and warm, which was a sign of more rain on the way. As he stepped out of the washroom after his morning routine, he heard someone shouting his name frantically, "Khansab! Khansab!" He was offended since he was not used to being called from outside. Visitors were supposed to knock on the door, and the maid was supposed to go and find out who the visitor was. This time, sensing anxiety in the caller's voice, he came out himself. Irshad stood motionless in front of him, his eyes bulging with fear, gazing in the air.

"What is it, Irshad?" asked Khansab.

"Ah ... er ... the horses ... er ... the horses." Irshad kept flinging his arms and making gestures. Nothing he said made any sense.

"What are you trying to say?"

"Em ... the horses ... yours!"

"What about the horses?" Khansab was losing his patience.

"Dead!"

"What do you mean? The horses are dead?"

"Yes."

Khansab pushed Irshad aside and ran through the outer door. He even forgot that he was wearing slippers. Irshad ran behind him as he reached the stable at the back of his house. He stood at the door, facing the open stalls, and could see the three horses lying on their sides. Mushki and Chandni were motionless, but Raja's body still twitched. He trembled as tremors came in waves. His nostrils were flared, and he was gasping for air. The bedding was soaked with feces and urine, over which the horse had no control. Khansab sat down and touched Raja's body. The back was cold as ice, and there was no motion in the hind legs, but the front side was burning with fever; his front legs trembled with each tremor. Khansab sat there, patting his back. As a tremor passed, Raja raised his neck and looked at Khansab with glassy eyes, as if pleading for help or trying to say goodbye to his master. Slowly and slowly, the intensity of the tremors subsided. Raja raised his neck, opened his mouth, gasped for air one last time and died. Khansab sat there with his hand still rubbing the horse's neck gently. Irshad stood behind him, with tears flowing down his cheeks. It felt like the earth had stopped moving, and time stood still as the two men in the stable mourned the death of their friends.

Khansab sighed and stood up as if he was awakening from a deep sleep. He walked to the feed bins and picked up a bunch of leaves spread over the regular feed. He turned to Irshad and raised his hand to show the leaves to him. "They have poisoned my horses!" he shouted as he shook his arm.

Irshad had never seen Khansab so angry. "They have poisoned my horses!" He raised his fist and screamed as he walked out of the stable.

***

Uday Lal had not visited Khansab since the day Amrit had walked out of the house. He spent the day reading newspapers and taking care of his garden; that day, he sat in front of the freshly prepared plot that he had cleaned and watered for several days, preparing it to plant pansies. He dug small holes with his trowel and transferred seedlings from the seedling tray into the plot. The young plants had already started flowering. Uday Lal was so engulfed in thought that he did not even notice the vivid colours of the pansies: deep purple, glowing orange, flaming red, and turmeric yellow. His hands worked mechanically, but his mind was elsewhere. He had heard about the harassment that the Sherwanis were going through but could not gather enough courage to tell anyone that his son was responsible for it. Sometimes he felt that everyone around him knew what was going on but were too polite to talk about it in his presence. He was deep in thought, unaware of his surroundings. When he realized that his manager had walked up to him quietly and stood behind him, he turned his head and looked at the old man. "What are you up to, Muneemji?" Uday Lal asked him.

Muneemji's lips quivered, but no words were heard. Uday Lal put his trowel aside and stood up. "Are you trying to tell me something?"

"Khansab's horses are dead."

"I see," replied Uday Lal. "How did they die?"

"They were poisoned last night."

Uday Lal did not respond. He knew what Muneemji was thinking. He picked up a pitcher of water and sprinkled it over the freshly planted pansies. "He had told me that his movement was non-violent."

"Maybe he thinks that killing animals is not violence," replied Muneemji sarcastically and walked away.

Uday Lal decided to pay a visit to his friends in Birehra. He would spend a few hours in Hasan Khan's library and would drop in at Khansab's on the way back.

When he entered the gate that led him to the mahal, he noticed a line-up of bullock carts in front of the annexe. He did not bother counting them, but there were twenty or so. Some people went into the annexe, while others came out with cardboard boxes on their heads and loaded them into the carts. He went inside the library and found that people were emptying shelves and packing books into boxes. Most of the shelves were empty by the time he got there. The old librarian was busy giving instructions to the workers. He overlooked Uday Lal, who went up to him and stood next to him.

"Adab Arz, Mudeer Sahib," Uday Lal said, and finally got the old man's attention.

"Oh, Adab Arz, Uday Lal," replied the librarian. "Where have you been?"

"What is going on here?"

"Oh, you didn't know. Hasan Khan has donated the library to the university."

"I see. Where is Hasan Khan?"

"He is in Aligarh right now, making sure that the new premises are ready."

Uday Lal appreciated that the library would get more readers in Aligarh, but he was sad to lose access to such a treasure.

"Why has Hasan Khan decided to part with his library?" asked Uday Lal.

"Oh, you didn't know," replied the librarian. "He is leaving for Pakistan."

Uday Lal felt as if someone had hit him in the chest. He was shocked as he tried to swallow.

"You must be disappointed, Mudeer Sahib, that you will lose your job."

"Not at all," replied the librarian. "Hasan Khan has arranged a job for me at the university. I will still take care of these books."

Uday Lal left him alone and kept watching as the shelves were emptied and books were packed. He was overcome with grief. Those books had been his companions, providing him refuge from political hypocrisy and social unrest. He had spent months in that library, absorbed in Rumi's *Masnavi,* with fifty thousand lines of poetry. As he walked out of the mahal with his head down, he whispered to himself:

Listen to the flute what it is saying,
It is complaining about separation.

"Ever since I was cut from the reed field,
Men and women weep when they hear my cries.

"I want a heart which is torn from separation,
So that I may explain the pain of yearning."

Whoever is plucked from his roots,
Is always longing to return one day.

He wondered if Hasan Khan and his relatives, who were leaving for Pakistan, one by one, would return one day. "I doubt it," he muttered to himself. "They will all turn into Rumi's flutes." He was startled by his voice. He looked up and around to make sure that no one had heard him.

***

Khansab had just finished his usual breakfast of crumbled millet bread soaked in hot milk and honey. He picked up the newspaper from the previous day and unfolded it; then he folded it back up and put it aside. *It must be the same old news: riots, refugee camps, massacres, villages set on fire.*

The maid was clearing the dishes when Noor Khan walked in and greeted Khansab as he sat down in a chair.

"Have you had breakfast?" asked Khansab.

"Yes, but I thought I would have tea with you," replied Noor Khan.

"Munni, why don't you bring tea, and make sure it is hot and strong," Khansab asked the maid. She nodded as she left with the dishes.

Noor Khan, the first cousin of Khansab, was only ten years old when his father had died. Khansab took care of him until he grew up, got married, and lived independently; he was fifteen years younger than Khansab and respected him as his elder brother. He sought Khansab's advice before making any decision, but he was nervous that day because he had made a major decision without consulting Khansab. It took him some time to gather the courage to share the news with him

"Bhai Sahib, I have sent the children to Pakistan." He looked at Khansab for his reaction, but he did not respond. Noor Khan's anxiety rose steadily. He could read displeasure on his cousin's face.

Khansab finally broke the silence. "Hmm! When did they leave?"

"Last Thursday."

"And you are telling me now?"

Noor Khan looked down, gazing at his shoes, thinking of a proper excuse. "I was under a lot of pressure," he eventually replied. "So much had happened that day. A Punjabi friend of theirs from the university was returning to his home in Lahore. He asked them to accompany him."

"So, what will happen to their education?"

"They will continue at the university in Lahore."

"I see." Khansab did not seem pleased. "Did you seek advice from someone?"

"No. It had to be decided in a hurry."

"It is always a good idea to share your decisions with someone. At times we get a different perspective, but in the end, you decide yourself."

"Yes, Bhai Sahib."

"A wise man has said that you should *always* talk to someone before making a decision."

"Yes, Bhai Sahib."

"And if you don't find anyone to talk to, just talk to a tree."

Noor Khan did not respond. He kept flipping through the pages of a newspaper. He could understand his cousin's feelings but had to think of his family first.

"I have decided to leave," Noor Khan almost whispered. "Things are getting rough here, and everyone is preparing to leave."

Khansab kept reading the newspaper. His silence was the indication of the storm brewing inside him. Noor Khan had no option but to offer him the opportunity to swallow the bitter pill. "Zakaria Khan and his family will also accompany us."

Khansab put the newspaper aside and looked at Noor Khan. "So, what will you do in Pakistan?" Khansab asked.

"God is the protector," Noor Khan responded with some hesitation, as he looked down.

"Indeed. God protects even your camel, provided you tie it to a post."

"The boys will finish university in two years, and I am sure they will find good jobs. Pakistan is a new country with tremendous opportunity."

"Are you sure that you are not hasty in uprooting yourself?" asked Khansab. "I think it is just a phase that will pass. Pakistan cannot survive on its own."

Noor Khan fell silent as if he felt that there was a grain of truth in his cousin's statement, but then his resolution returned. "Whatever will happen, will happen. History has given its verdict, and we have no choice but to follow our destiny."

"I don't believe in destiny. One makes one's own destiny."

"Will it not be wise to move to a safe environment under the circumstances?" asked Noor Khan in a whispery tone. "Why don't you come with us, Bhai Sahib?"

"Who, me?" Khansab laughed. "What will I do in Pakistan? I am already fifty-one years old, I do not have a western education, and the only skill I have is to rule the peasants. So what will I do there?"

"God is our master. We will do something together. Maybe we will open a shop or something."

"What do you know about shopkeeping?" Khansab guffawed loudly. "Can you think of anyone among our forefathers who is known to have run a business?"

Noor Khan did not have an answer. Khansab picked up the newspaper again and started turning its pages. His eyes scanned the words in the paper, but his thoughts were elsewhere. Was his cousin right? Were his days in his homeland over? Was his destiny really written in the lines of his palms? Question after question popped up like bubbles, awaiting answers that he did not have. He had been a staunch supporter of Gandhi and the Congress, but now his faith in the leaders seemed to dwindle at times. The idols that he had raised and worshipped were crumbling one by one. He felt as if he were changing his religion. His old faith seemed hollow, and he was challenging his ideals and his patriotism. Throughout his life, he had put his forehead on the ground of Mother India five times a day, and she was now on the verge of disowning her own son.

His gloom was suddenly taken over by anger. He was angry with Nehru. To him, Nehru was directly responsible for slicing the country like a master butcher, who skilfully trims off excess fat from a piece of meat. He was angry with Gandhi, who had initially declared that India would be partitioned over his dead body, but changed his position when Mountbatten said Pakistan was just a tent that he was putting up in a hurry. *Some Mahatma!* he thought. *But then what could poor Gandhi do? He is nobody as far as the leaders of the Congress are concerned.* He suddenly felt a wave of guilt for casting doubt upon Gandhi. How could he criticize a saint?

The chain of his thoughts was broken when the maid entered the room, carrying a small tray. She put two cups of tea on the side table. Noor Khan picked up his cup and started looking for words to break the silence.

"Hasan Khan has donated his library to the university."

"I see," replied Khansab while he kept looking at the newspaper. "What made him decide that?"

"He has decided to go to Pakistan."

"Is there anyone who is not going to Pakistan?"

"As far as I know, you are the only one left, Bhai Sahib."

"I see."

Noor Khan felt that his cousin did not want to talk anymore on that subject. He waited for further response, but Khansab continued reading the newspaper.

How can I leave him behind? Thought Noor Khan. *He is like a father to me. He has raised me, educated me, and got me married. I will live with guilt all my life if I leave him behind.*

"I have decided that I will not go to Pakistan." Noor Khan took his cap off and scratched his head.

"Why have you changed your mind suddenly?" Khansab folded the newspaper and put it aside.

"Because I cannot leave you alone here."

"Why? Am I a child, or you think that I cannot take care of myself?"

"Bhai Sahib, you once told me that on every grain of wheat is written the name of the person who will eat it."

"Yes, I believe that."

"I feel that there are no more grains left here with our names."

"I agree that times are tough, but I hope that it is a phase, which will pass."

"What if it is not?"

"We should never give up hope."

"I agree, but can hope alone change anything?"

"I do not have an answer for that," Khansab finally yielded.

Noor Khan was encouraged by Khansab's response. "Bhai Sahib, let us go together. If you think that we will suffer there, let us suffer together. We will overcome the suffering if we are together because we will be stronger together."

He was surprised that he had said all those things to his elder cousin. He thought that Khansab would take offence at being advised by someone younger, but he did not show displeasure.

"Tell you what," Khansab said. "Why don't you go ahead, and I will follow you."

"Why don't we go together?"

"Because I have to wrap up things here."

"What is there to wrap up?

"You can see that the crop is ready to be harvested."

"People have left with their crops standing. Nothing is being harvested this year."

"I owe it to my workers. They have to be paid; otherwise, how will they survive for the rest of the year?"

"You don't have any workers. They have all abandoned you. Your crop is drying up, and soon you will have nothing left to harvest. You don't owe anything to anyone."

Khansab listened to Noor Khan without interrupting him and did not respond right away. "Still, you go ahead. You have my blessing. I promise you that I will join you later."

***

After Khansab's horses were killed, Irshad had nowhere to go. Therefore, he was assigned the responsibility of the upkeep of the men's quarters. He made sure that Karmoo wetted the patio well and that the servants dusted the chairs before putting them outside on the deck just before sunset. There was a time when that patio used to be packed with visitors every evening, but those days were gone. He knew that most of those chairs would be put back at the end of the evening without being touched by any occupant.

When he noticed Uday Lal coming up the stairs, he noted that it was unusual for someone to drop in that early on a hot afternoon. There must have been some urgent matter. Irshad joined his hands and bowed slightly to greet Uday Lal, who returned the greeting with a nod of his head. Despite being an enlightened Brahmin, he still followed the social norm. It was not customary to join hands for a person of lower status.

"Is Khansab at home?" he asked Irshad.

"Yes, Punditji, I will let him know that you are here."

Irshad walked to the room in the men's quarters and opened the door. "Why don't you come inside, Punditji. It is too hot outside."

"Thank you, Irshad," replied Uday Lal as he entered the room. "You are a nice boy."

Uday Lal sat down in a chair and lifted a corner of his dhoti to wipe

268

the sweat off his face. The room was dark and cool. Irshad closed the door as he left to keep the heat out. Some light diffused in through the curtains on small ventilators near the ceiling. He picked up a hand fan that was lying on the side table and started fanning his face. It felt cool as the sweat evaporated.

The door opened, and Irshad walked in, carrying a small circular tray holding a silver bowl full of a pinkish white drink with crushed ice and rose petals floating on the surface.

"Khansab is on the way," said Irshad as he put the tray on the table. Uday Lal responded with a nod.

Just then, Khansab walked in and interrupted Irshad as he was leaving the room. "Do you want to treat Punditji just with a bowl of sharbat?" Irshad turned back for further instructions.

"Why don't you ask Munni to prepare lunch?" asked Khansab.

"No, no, don't worry about lunch," said Uday Lal. "You know that I stopped taking lunch long ago."

"Where have you been all these days?" Khansab was excited to see his old friend. He sat down in a chair in front of him and picked up another hand fan from the table.

"To tell you the truth, I have shut myself within my four walls. I don't feel like going anywhere or meeting anyone."

"Don't tell me that you are depressed. It is unlike you."

"Who won't be depressed under current circumstances?"

"I am not. You know the best cure for depression is hope. Just keep your hope alive, and depression won't come near you."

Uday Lal did not respond. Deep down, he knew that Khansab was just trying to pick up his spirits; otherwise, he was equally concerned at what was going on around him. There was a long silence. They were both considering what to talk about next.

Eventually, Uday Lal broke the silence. "Did you know that Hasan Khan has also decided to leave?"

"Yes, I found out only this morning."

"I am coming from mahal. He was not there, but his library is being packed up."

"That is what I hear," replied Khansab. "Noor Khan told me this morning."

Uday Lal picked up the bowl and took a few sips of the ice-cold drink. "Have you harvested your corn?" he asked Khansab as he put the bowl on the table and picked up the fan again.

"It is still standing."

"I thought you planted early."

"Yes, you know that I grow the sweetest corn in the area, and the secret is to plant it early and harvest it early."

"So why haven't you taken it down?"

"I don't have any workers. They have all been chased away."

"I knew that people are being harassed, but I did not know that it had gone that far."

"It has, and by now, my corn is worth nothing. Just yesterday, I checked some ears, and they are dry as tinder. There is hardly any sweetness left in the kernels. All I could taste was starch."

"Tell you what," said Uday Lal. "Let us take it down next week. I will make fifty men available to you."

"You will make me the happiest man in Birehra. I don't know how I can repay you."

"Don't even mention it. What are friends for?" replied Uday Lal as he got up to leave.

Khansab was overcome with emotion as he said goodbye to his friend. He would eventually be able to harvest his crop and feed his workers.

Let them all go to Pakistan, he thought about his relatives. *I cannot leave this village even if I am the last Muslim left here. It is my land, and it will remain mine, even after I am dead.*

***

It was a windy day when Khansab decided to go out for a walk through the neighbourhood. The air was warm, and whirlwinds formed dust devils that lifted dirt and garbage, leaving clean circular patches on the ground. He stopped at the entrance to the outer courtyard of Noor Khan's house. Khansab was born in that house, and so was his father. His grandfather had built it when he returned to the village after deserting from the army during the Great Revolt of 1857, which was crushed ruthlessly by the British. They hunted down poets, scholars, and Sufis and hanged them. Bahadur Shah Zafar, the last Mughal king, was dethroned, and his sons beheaded. Major Hodson, whose task was to quell the rebellion, brought the princes' decapitated heads on trays and presented them to the king. "Your Majesty, here is a gift for you."

"Descendants of Timur always come in front of their fathers in this way," replied the king calmly, as he looked at Major Hodson.

After fleeing from the army, Khansab's grandfather wandered from town to town, maintaining a low profile, until he was sure that the British had forgotten about him. He returned to his village, was married, and settled down.

The house had been renovated several times over the years, as it passed from one generation to the next. Khansab recollected that, as a child, he had played hopscotch in the courtyard with his friends. They used to draw a course with a piece of coal on the cement floor and take turns hopping through it. There was a veranda, spread on three sides, with several rooms for male guests behind it. Sometimes, while playing hide and seek, they would hide in the rooms and behind pillars until someone was caught. On one side of the courtyard was the house in which Khansab grew up. He had been married twice, but neither of his wives had lived for long. His parents had also passed on. Two years after the death of his second wife, he had decided to get married again. That was when Noor Khan left his job as an accountant with the Maharajah of Jaipur and returned to Birehra, and since he did not have a place of his own, Khansab gave him that house and built a new one for himself.

A gust of wind suddenly broke his train of thoughts. He noticed that the door to the interior of the house was open. That was odd. Did Noor Khan leave the door unlocked? He walked into the house. It was an eerie sight. Everything was where it was supposed to be. Even the beddings were wrapped neatly and kept on the heads of cots in the veranda. He thought about Noor Khan's children, two boys and a girl. He was very fond of them and used to visit them frequently when they were young. Noor Khan's wife covered her face in front of him as a sign of respect. It was just a ritual. She just lowered the edge of her dupatta over her forehead when he entered the house. He always announced himself before stepping in. "Anybody home?" The children ran out to the door and wrapped themselves around his legs. They knew that he never came empty-handed. As soon as he sat down, they gathered around him and put their hands in his pockets to look for candies. Noor Khan's wife asked him for tea, but he always declined. He was there to spend time with the children, but they had grown up and gone to the university-and now to Pakistan.

As he stood in that house, he felt like calling out. "Anybody home?" In return, he heard nothing but silence. There was nobody home. All his relatives had left, with their houses open, and he was left all alone. While going out of the house, he closed the door behind him.

As he walked out, looking down, he stopped for a moment and turned back. He slid the latch and opened the door again before he walked away.

Across the street, there was a small door in the boundary wall, which ran around the estate of Hasan Khan. Khansab entered the door and was in the open ground. The mahal stood on the far side. Once, it was a village within a village, full of life. There were always people walking in that ground, going about their business, but now, there was not a single soul there, as if the inhabitants had suddenly evaporated. As he walked along leisurely, a tumbleweed rolled past him. The wind had picked up speed and dust. He watched it as it moved fast and came to rest against the far corner of the boundary walls. A pack of stray dogs, wandering through the estate, had gotten into a fight. They barked and tackled one another until Khansab threw a stone at them to break up the fight. He felt sorrowful to see the place turn into a ghost town. When he reached the mosque, he noticed that the door was closed. He opened it and entered the courtyard. Several squirrels sat on the floor, chewing dates fallen from trees around the courtyard. The floor was littered with dry leaves and bird droppings. Khansab thought about the mullah, who would have chased those squirrels away. The mullah used to wash the floor every day before the evening prayer, but he was no longer there. He had left Birehra a few days earlier and had probably settled in some other village, in some other mosque, telling tales of his adventures to his new fans.

As Khansab got out of the mosque, he left the door open and walked away, deep in thought, contemplating his family's future. He stopped for a moment and looked back at the mosque. The door was still open.

***

There was no moon in the sky, and the stars were extinguished to prepare for dawn. The pitch-black night wore a shroud of silence, disturbed by occasional snorts from the cattle yards. No one was there to see three men entering the village from behind the fields. They had unfolded their turbans and wrapped them around their faces, leaving their eyes uncovered only by a slit. They tiptoed with large canisters on their shoulders. The wind had picked up speed. As they approached a cornfield, they walked around it and stopped on the side from which the wind was blowing into the field. They put down the canisters and stretched their arms to release the tension of carrying the weight. They spoke in almost inaudible whispers. One of them picked up a canister and entered the field. He started pouring out the contents, spreading the liquid over the largest possible area. The smell of kerosene filled the air. He walked back carefully to reduce the rustling of plants and picked up another canister. One of the men took a stick and wrapped a piece of rag around it. He dipped it in kerosene as the third canister was carried into the field.

Hardev, who slept in the neighbouring field, was in a deep sleep. He could not understand why he woke up suddenly. He sat in his cot, with his feet hanging on the side, wondering if there was something odd when he detected the smell of kerosene. Then he heard a loud sound as if something had fallen to the ground. It sounded as if a metal pot had been dropped. He got up with a start and climbed the *machan*, a raised platform on which he used to stand to scare off birds with a slingshot. He looked around, but it was too dark to spot anything. Suddenly he saw a faint light in the neighbouring field. Someone had ignited a torch; he could see silhouettes of three men quivering in the glow. Hardev shouted from his post to draw their attention. They threw the torch into the field and started to run. The area caught fire instantly, which was spread fast by the wind. Hardev jumped from the platform and ran to the village.

***

Chhoti Begum was the first one to wake up. Someone was knocking on the door repeatedly. Khansab's bed was next to her bed. Azad slept on the other side, and next to him was Nanijan's bed. Chhoti Begum called her husband, but he was in a deep sleep. She got up and shook his shoulder, but he turned to the other side.

"Who is knocking on the door?" he asked Chhoti Begum while still trying to get back to sleep.

"I don't know," she replied. "But whoever it is, sounds desperate."

Khansab got up and walked to the door. It was Irshad.

"Your field is burning." He seemed to be in a panic.

"What do you mean, burning?"

"Someone has set it on fire."

Khansab ran out into the street in his slippers and sleeping suit. No one had ever seen him dressed that way. Irshad ran behind him. The street was full of people running back and forth with large pitchers of water on their heads. Some people returned with empty pitchers and hurried to the well to refill them. When he arrived at his field, the blaze had covered most of it, and people were pouring water on the adjacent field, which was in the path of the wind. They had ignored his field since it was like a horse with a broken leg that could be saved only by being shot. Some people sat on the edge of his field, cutting down the plants to create a space between two fields. Fortunately, the fire stopped before getting to the neighbouring lot.

Khansab looked at the scene. The entire field was smouldering in bright twilight, and the smell of smoke hung in the air. People clustered around him and stood silently. No one had the courage even to say a few words of sympathy. He saw some of his workers in the crowd. It seemed that they were all remorseful at having abandoned him in his hour of need. Suddenly there was movement at the back. Hardev pierced through the crowd and came forward.

"I saw them, Khansab," he said.

"What are you talking about, Hardev?"

"There were three men. They set your field on fire, but they had their faces covered."

"They must be the same men who have been threatening us," said someone from the back. "They have been telling us not to work in your fields."

Khansab did not respond. He looked at the charred field and walked away, looking down and in deep thought.

Even though he had been known to be a big spender, leading a luxurious life, no one knew that he was not a rich man. How rich could one get with two mango trees and thirty acres of land? He was the leader of his community, and his land fed over fifty families. Whenever the daughters of his workers were married, he even took responsibility for their clothes and jewellery. Everyone got a share. He never let anyone know that he did not even maintain a bank account in the city. Whatever his land produced, he spent.

The world around him had suddenly changed. He walked back, thinking about his predicament. How was he going to survive for a year? How would his workers' families survive? He disagreed with Noor Khan when he had told him that he did not owe anything to his workers because they had abandoned him. That was not fair. After all, it was not their fault.

***

When Baldev approached Khansab's house, he expected that a servant would come forward to greet him, but there was no one around. He thought that it was odd. He knocked on the door several times, but there was no response from inside. As he was about to leave, the door opened, and Khansab came out himself.

Baldev was shocked to see that his friend looked pale and weary. "Are your servants all dead, so you had to come out yourself to answer the door?" Baldev tried to be cheerful, even though he knew what Khansab was going through.

"You can say that. I let Irshad go," Khansab replied and led Baldev to his room outside the house.

"So, what is happening?"

"Nothing much, I guess."

"I can read it all in your face," said Baldev. "I am disappointed. I always thought that you were invincible."

"God is the only one who is invincible."

"Since when have you become religious?" Baldev chuckled.

"Since I found out that you can fight everything and everyone except fate."

"I don't call it fate. I call it blindness."

"What do you mean?"

"What I mean is that you close your eyes when it comes to knowing your enemies."

"I don't understand," said Khansab. "Why are you talking in riddles?"

"Are you saying that you don't know who set your field on fire?"

"I know who did. These terrorists have driven all my relatives out of the country, and now they are trying to dislodge me."

"And you don't know who is behind it all?" asked Baldev.

"I have no clue."

"Have you heard the name of your friend, Uday Lal?"

"I don't believe you." Khansab looked offended. "Uday Lal is a man of peace."

"It is his son, who has joined RSS."

"Does Uday Lal know that?"

"Every child in Nagla knows it."

Khansab did not answer. How could he believe that a friend, one who had offered him help to harvest his crop, had let his son burn it down? He was shocked and angry. He remembered the evening when they all sat, chatting and taking turns on the hookah. Uday Lal had told them the story of Julius Caesar and how his friend, Brutus, had led his assassins to him.

Khansab muttered an old proverb. "A dagger under the armpit and Rama on the lips." "A snake is a snake, even if it lives in a flowerbed," Baldev responded.

***

It is said that the most precious possession of a man is his ego. He creates, builds, achieves, and destroys just to satisfy his ego. When his ego challenges him to conquer, he turns into Hulagu Khan, trampling land after land under his horse's hoofs, plundering treasuries, burning libraries, and killing citizenries. The same ego creates Mozart and Einstein. Some say that Mona Lisa's mysterious smile depicts her recollection of ecstasy the night before. Still, it was perhaps the final touch to the portrait to show the satisfied ego of Leonardo Da Vinci.

When a man's ego is bruised, he loses his manliness. The same man who once was a creator is now worthless. It is as if he had never achieved anything in life. The ego is the Achilles' heel of a man.

Khansab had been a man of action all his life. He was known as a leader, a friend, and a high achiever. Even though he carried countless scars in his heart, being widowed twice and having to bury thirteen children, he had never lost his ambition and strength. For the first time in his life, he was now a broken man, with a shattered ego. He felt shame and worthlessness as if someone had slapped him in public. He became exasperated quickly, and Chhoti Begum bore the brunt of his irritability. He went into a deep depression and built a cocoon around himself; every morning, he went out into his room and spent the day reading a book after breakfast. Sometimes, Khansab engaged in conversations with himself during long walks. His moving lips, hand gestures, and wrinkles on his forehead showed that he talked to himself, asking questions and answering them himself. He made plans within plans and rejected every plan to start a new plan.

The Boléro Dance

He is surrounded by dark mist, looking at the emerald green pebble lying on the dusty floor in front of him. He recognizes it as his ego. He bends over to pick it up, but before his hand reaches it, a foot comes into his view and kicks it gently out of his reach. He moves forward and bends over again, but another foot moves it away.

He looks up and sees a crowd around him. They are all mannequins with featureless faces, their naked bodies painted with mud.

He hears a faint sound of a snare drum coming from far away - raa ra ra rup, ra ra rup, ra ra rup. The mannequins are moving gently with the drumbeat, kicking his ego like a soccer ball. He falls into step with them, chasing his ego.

Another faint sound joins the drumbeat. It is the shrill wail of a flute, crying in pain. He knows that it is his destiny, calling him to nothingness, devoid of time.

A second flute starts to wail. That is his alternate destiny. He is in a deep well, looking up at the rope hanging over his head. He can reach the end of the rope. The hand holding the rope is that of the drummer, shaking with every beat-raa ra ra rup, ra ra rup.

A clarinet has joined the melody. It mimics the wailing flutes, but the sound is soothing. It pleads with him to hold the rope. He struggles to keep his eyes open as he chases his ego.

The drumbeat gets louder while a caravan of instruments moves in one by one. The strings make their presence felt through a gentle pluck-a cello, a viola, and a harp, as a bassoon enters the melody, flowing like a calm river. He feels the drumbeat reverberation on the surface of the water - raa ra ra rup, ra ra rup.

He follows the pattern to grasp his ego-right foot, left foot, right foot, and stop. He gets into the trance of whirling dervishes.

Suddenly he sees himself in a free fall, and his heart starts sinking. The heavy sound of a saxophone invites him to gain control over himself. It strengthens his resolve to get his ego back. He extends his arms and strikes the mannequins one by one. They fall like dominoes as he makes way for himself.

Violins weep, clarinets wiggle, oboes scream, and piccolos screech. Trumpets, trombones, horns, and euphoniums make him feel like a groom. He is seated on horseback, leading a wedding procession, following a marching band. Bursts of fireworks rise around him as his horse falls into step with the drumbeat. He keeps striking the mannequins.

The music rises to a deafening crescendo and comes to an abrupt stop. He bends over and picks up the emerald green pebble. He clenches his fist to ensure that he does not lose his ego again.

***

Khansab woke up with a start, feeling fresh and resilient. He noticed that the fingers of his right hand were curled into his palm tightly. He looked at his fist and smiled as he extended his arm upwards and shook it. He heard a rooster crow and got up from the bed with a stretch. Nanijan was already up and folding her bed. He greeted her, and she wished him happiness and prosperity. He went to wash up, and when he came out of the washroom, Chhoti Begum was awake. He told her that he was going out.

"Where are you going so early in the morning?" she asked.

"To the mosque."

She was taken aback since her husband had not prayed for many days. She gave her mother a questioning look.

"If someone leaves home at sunrise and goes astray, you cannot call him a lost sheep if he returns before sunset," Nanijan said to her daughter.

When Khansab got out of the house, he felt as if he were ruling the world. The air was fresh and clean. He met several farmers leaving for their fields and responded to their greeting. When he passed Noor Khan's house, he looked at it and kept walking. He entered through the door leading to the mahal and passed it to walk to the mosque. The door was open. He took his shoes off at the stairs and walked into the main hall. It was still dark inside, but he could see that the carpets covering the floor were still clean. He had put those carpets there several years ago and was glad that the mullah had taken good care of them.

After finishing his prayer, he sat there to contemplate. He made decisions and planned his course. Before he realized, the sunlight had spread through the courtyard, and the prayer hall was lit. When he got out of the mosque, he was bubbling with exuberance. He decided to go through the estate's main gate and pass through the fields at the village's back. When he went past his burnt land, he looked at it without any emotion. He had better things to care about.

Fattu, the keeper of Phagna's grave, saw Khansab coming that way. He had not seen him for a long time. He came forward to greet Khansab.

"Is that you, Fattu?" Khansab was looking at a man with a long beard.

"Yes, Khansab."

"I have not seen you for a while."

"I have left worldly affairs and have devoted my life to taking care of Phagna's grave."

"Will Phagna's grave go away somewhere if you don't guard it?" Khansab laughed.

"Still. You made me take care of Phagna in his last days, and I should continue caring for him after his death."

"As you wish," replied Khansab. "I hope people are feeding you."

"I don't have any complaint. Phagna has many disciples."

"I hope you are not selling these mangoes." Khansab looked at the mango trees.

"How can I sell them?" Fattu replied. "You had given them to Phagna. Their fruit is blessed. People take as much as they want. They give me whatever they want, but I never ask anyone for money."

Khansab nodded with a smile and moved on.

***

Munni brought Khansab's usual breakfast: millet bread, hot milk, and honey. Chhoti Begum sat in front of him to give him company.

"I am glad you are cheerful this morning," she said.

Khansab did not respond immediately. She knew that he had been through a lot of stress and had to be allowed to collect himself.

"We are going to Pakistan," he said abruptly.

She thought she heard him say that they were going to Pakistan.

"Did you say that we are going to Pakistan?"

"That is what I said."

Nanijan was nearby. She heard him and was startled. It was on rare occasions that she spoke to her son-in-law. They both respected each other immensely but treated each other formally. Deep down, she was obliged to take care of her in her old age and considered him her own son.

"Have you talked to a tree?" She was referring to his own saying, that one should always seek advice before making a decision, and if one does not find anyone to talk to, he should speak to a tree.

"Yes. I have thought about it carefully. We do not have any future here."

Nanijan spoke to him softly so that he would not think that she was arguing with him. "But your land is here, your elders' graves are here, and your roots are here," she said.

"I now believe Noor Khan, who had told me that our land does not produce grain with our name on it anymore."

"I think it is just a phase that will pass."

"That is what I told him, but now I feel that the future of my son is not secure here."

Nanijan hesitated to respond immediately. She wanted to prolong her silence, giving him a chance to think about what he had said.

"Do you think that your son's future will be secure there?"

"Pakistan is a new country, full of opportunity."

"They say that if one leaves his land, then no other land accepts him and his future generations." Nanijan was careful to be as soft as she could to reduce the severity of her remark. "Once an immigrant, always an immigrant."

Khansab did not like his mother-in-law's remark, but he was too respectful to respond to her.

"I had wished to be buried in my land, next to my parents," she said hesitantly as if she were talking to herself.

Khansab burst into laughter. "Don't worry. We will bring your body back here for burial." He wanted to lighten the mood.

*****

The night was dark. The stars were hiding behind a thick cover of clouds. Even the moon was absent from the night sky since it was the lunar month's first night. Khansab entered Nagla. He remembered that he had been there only a few times in his life, either to visit a sick Brahmin friend or when invited to a wedding. Other than that, there was no business requiring him or any other Muslim to be there uninvited. It was late at night. The village was asleep and silent, except crickets chirping their mating songs. The silence was broken occasionally by a dog barking somewhere.

Khansab was sure that no one had seen him enter the village. He stepped on the stairs to Lala Ishvari Lal's house and entered the faintly lit room where Lala sat on a rug, with his eyes closed and his back resting against a wall. His head drooped, with his chin resting on the chest; it appeared that he was in a deep sleep. A streak of saliva had dried on the side of his lips. In front of him was a writing desk with a set of dip pens, an inkpot, and a blotter placed neatly. Khansab waited for a few moments at the door and then coughed to wake him up. Ishvari Lal opened his eyes and looked at Khansab.

"I was waiting for you," he said, raising his hands and joining his palms. "I must have fallen asleep."

"I apologize for asking you to meet me at this hour," replied Khansab.

"Please sit down. I wish I could stand up to greet you."

"I understand," said Khansab as he sat down in front of Ishvari Lal. "I hope you have the documents ready."

"Yes, I got them prepared this morning." Ishvari Lal picked up the lantern and turned the knob to raise the wick for more light. Then he put the lantern aside, lifted the cover of the writing desk and pulled out a set of papers.

Khansab turned the pages as he read them. He was startled when he reached the last page. "Five thousand rupees? I hope it is the down payment," he said and put the document on the desk and looked at Ishvari Lal.

"That is the price," said Ishvari Lal calmly.

"You must be joking. I am not borrowing money from you. I have never borrowed money from anyone in my life. I am selling what I own." Khansab raised his voice and stood up.

"Listen to me, Khansab. Please sit down and listen to me." Ishvari Lal was still calm. "Let us keep our voices down. You know that even walls have ears, and you want this transaction to stay between us."

"You have not left any room, Ishvari Lal. My house alone is worth five thousand. I am giving you thirty acres of land. That will go for one thousand rupees an acre."

"Then why don't you go ahead and sell it if you can find a buyer."

Khansab was suddenly calm and did not respond. It appeared that the mouth of a balloon had been opened.

"I didn't want this transaction in the first place," said Ishvari Lal. "You will not understand what risk I am taking, but I am doing it because I respect you. These five thousand rupees are for you to travel to Pakistan and be settled there. You know that nobody will buy your property. Even I cannot buy it because it will be declared as evacuee property, and nobody will touch it."

"But I am selling it to you. The title is in your name. So why will it be declared as evacuee property?"

"I don't know. Nobody knows right now. New laws are coming,

and this transaction might not be acceptable to the government."

Ishvari Lal could read hesitation on Khansab's face. "Tell you what," he said. "I will treat your property as collateral for a loan. I can promise you that your servants will keep working in the field and will be fed. When the situation settles down, you can come back and take possession of your property by paying me five thousand rupees plus interest."

"Do you think I will ever come back?" Khansab chuckled sarcastically.

"You never know. Fate might take an unexpected turn."

"Fate is carved in stone. It never takes unexpected turns."

Khansab picked up a pen and dipped it in the inkpot. After he signed both copies of the document, Ishvari Lal opened the desk and pulled out a bundle of hundred-rupee notes. Khansab picked up the money, got up, and walked out with a bad taste in his mouth.

***

The news was out all over the village; Khansab was leaving for Pakistan. People contacted Wafati, the bullock cart driver. He confirmed that Khansab had rented his cart and would depart in the morning before sunrise. They started gathering in front of Khansab's house at dawn, and by the time Wafati arrived, there were hundreds of people in the alley. Khansab came out of the house and greeted them. They were surprised to see that he was embracing the untouchables. They moved closer to him. Everyone wanted to be touched and hugged. Suddenly the crowd parted on one side to give way to Uday Lal, who was approaching to bid farewell to his friend. They came face to face, and Uday Lal raised his hand and joined his palms.

"You, too, Brutus?" Khansab snarled at him with disgust written all over his face and turned to the crowd. Uday Lal was shocked. He stood there for a while, his palms still joined, and then his hands came down gently. He made his way through the crowd and stood at the back, watching Khansab from a distance.

"Namaste, Baba." The voice came from the left. Uday Lal turned and saw his son, face to face with him. They both stood silently, gazing at each other. *Where have you been, my son?* He thought he had said it loudly, but his lips did not open. *My eyes have been searching for you everywhere.* His arms rose to embrace his son as he moved forward. Then he swung his arm and slapped his son on the cheek. Amrit felt the jolt and could not keep his balance; he fell to the ground. People around them were aghast. Some of them moved to help the young man get up but retreated when they realized that, being from lower castes, they could not touch an upper-caste Hindu. Amrit got up himself and massaged his cheek as he left.

"Lala Ishvari Lal is taking over my land," Khansab told his workers. "You will keep working, and your families will be taken care of."

A hush fell over the crowd. Some whispers subsided as Khansab continued.

"I am leaving all my belongings to you. After I leave, you can go into the house quietly and take whatever you need."

"You cannot do that, Khansab," Ishvari Lal's manager, who was waiting to take possession of the house, came forward and protested.

"Go tell Ishvari Lal that he has bought the house, not the contents."

The family had already boarded the cart. Wafati gave a tug to the leashes, and the bullocks moved. Khansab decided to walk behind the cart for some distance. He looked back and smiled when he saw a stampede into his house. People were rushing to get into the house, and Ishvari Lal's manager tried to push them back. Khansab smiled. As his gaze moved, he saw that the street was empty. Uday Lal still stood there, alone, watching the bullock cart move away. Tears flowed down Khansab's cheeks. He had already moved too far to notice that Uday Lal's cheeks were also wet.

***

Azad turned his head back to take one last look at his village. He saw it through the shroud of dust left behind the bullocks. The visibility was cut down further by morning fog. He sat in the back of the cart, gazing at the silhouettes of mud-houses that were drifting away as the carriage moved slowly on the dirt road through a cornfield. His grandmother's lips quivered fast as she recited her prayer, prescribed for travel. "O God, keep us safe from the perils of a journey." He caught the words as she raised her voice while catching her breath.

What perils is Nanijan talking about? he thought. The cart moved at a leisurely pace. He could have walked twice as fast as the bulls, and then there was no other traffic on the dirt road as far as the eye could see. No one had ever seen a bullock cart get into an accident. So what was his grandmother's worry? The carriage was fitted with a wooden frame, around which heavy sheets of jute were wrapped like curtains to keep the heat out and provide privacy to female passengers.

Chhoti Begum had stopped crying, but her eyes were still red and swollen. She had wailed bitterly as she had hugged the pillars under every arch in the veranda. It was not easy for her to leave her Taj Mahal, which her husband had built for her. She had entered that home as a bride and had treated it like her empire. No one could have predicted that her reign would last only fifteen years; no one could have foreseen that she would have to leave her realm, holding the hand of her little boy. She sat quietly, knitting a sweater for him. The speed with which her knitting needles were moving showed the storm's intensity that was brewing within her chest. Azad knew that it was about to blow in the downpour of tears, but she had run out of tears, and her eyes were dry. He lifted the curtain at the rear of the cart and slid it behind his back to take the final look at Birehra.

They had started early in the morning, when birds, perched high in trees, engaged in their daily ritual of a dawn chorus. As the sun rose behind the thick fog, their singing subsided. A lone tateeri flew by, and he looked up to spot it, but all he could hear was its shrill call. *It will be a hot, dry day,* he thought. As they drove past the old banyan tree, Azad remembered that it was the largest and the village's shadiest tree. The two swings that Irshad had tied to the strongest branch of the tree, for him and his friends, were still there. They could spend all day playing under that tree and could even hide behind thick branches when they played hide and seek,

As the dirt road turned around the cornfield, a layer of tears formed on Azad's eyelids, and he tightened his throat to make sure that tears did not leave his eyes. He tried to swallow but felt that the lump in his throat was about to choke him. Despite his effort to remain composed, he swallowed with an audible twitch. "Are you crying, Azad?" He heard the voice of his grandmother.

Oh, no! Nanijan won't like it, he thought. Whenever he cried, she told him that it was okay for men to cry but that they should cry silently.

"It is unmanly to wail and sob," she would advise him.

He tried to camouflage his sob with a cough. "No, Nanijan, I was just coughing." Now that he was leaving the village, never to return, he knew that he would never see his friends again. A tear flowed down into a corner of his lips, and this time, he let himself go. His face was flooded with tears as Birehra disappeared forever behind the cornfields.

Reflections!

Scene after scene appears in the mirror of my memory. And quivers for a blink or two before it fades away.

- Himayat Ali Shaer

Although my father had named me Azad, which means *free*, I have struggled throughout my life to escape from the prison of my nightmares. Ages have gone by, the wrinkles on my face have deepened, and even my eyebrows have turned white as snow, but that dirt road on which my mother was desperately running, still clings like a leech to the depths of my mind. Her sole possession was that gunny sack, which she carried on her head. A few aluminum pots, which had turned black after being used for many years, some ladles and spoons, a pair of tongs, a few enamel plates, and that was all! When she had left home, she had put whatever she could lay her hands on in that sack.

"Hurry up, son!" She stopped from time to time and looked back to call me. I did not have any strength left to keep running with her anymore. How old was I? Just a little over six. How could I keep up with her?

"Wait for me, Mother," I would shout, but she would start running again. In one hand, I carried a tiffin carrier, which had been filled with food when we had started but now was empty. In the other hand, I had my mother's shoes, which she had handed to me when her feet were swollen. She was running barefoot along that track.

There was a flood of people around us-men, women, children, the elderly-with sacks on their heads, bundles under their arms, babies clinging to their chests, and toddlers seated on their shoulders. All eyes gazed toward the front. No one had the courage to look back. Humanity was on the move. People kept passing us, and I was worried that we might be left behind. It would have been better if my mother had kept pace with the others, but she kept on stopping to wait for me. I kept looking back to see if my father was perhaps following us, but he was nowhere in sight. He had been separated from us in the stampede.

We had spent several days on a rocky ground where thousands of people were camping. New crowds arrived there every day and settled wherever they could find an empty spot. The border was closed; there was no way to move forward. No one had the strength to return. We were in no man's land! The blazing sun had baked the ground and everything on it. We could clean the grit on our teeth, accumulated from the dust-filled gusts of hot wind, by wiping them with our tongues, but the only source of water was that hand-pump on a well in the distance, at which hundreds of people were gathered all the time.

My father had gotten four bamboo sticks from somewhere, which he hammered into the ground, and covered over with a bedsheet. That was our home now! Someone gave my father an old bucket, which he took with him to get water from the well. I could see him walking straight ahead until he disappeared behind the crowd gathered around the well. My mother lay beside me with her eyes closed. She had fanned me for a while with her hand fan, but then she had stopped, and the fan lay on her chest. I knew that she had dozed off. I gently picked up the fan to make sure that she did not wake up and sat down to fan her. She was covered with sweat but seemed to be in a deep sleep. No one could tell that she had lost her mother a day earlier.

My grandmother, who had accompanied us, got sick on the way. By the time we reached Amritsar, she had a high temperature and was losing consciousness from time to time. My father carried her on his back as we walked to the border. My mother kept splashing water on her face and trying to keep her cool, but her condition deteriorated until she took one last breath with a gentle sigh and died quietly. I had loved my grandmother. She was the one who had raised me. But I did not cry over her death. No one did, not even my mother. It is said that one way to dampen a pain is to inflict another pain. That was what we were going through at that time. The people around us had been extremely courteous and helpful. They had gathered to arrange her burial. When my father had told them that she did not want to leave her homeland but that he had persuaded her to accompany us since there was no one to take care of her, they had offered him to take her body back and bury her as close to India as they could. They had walked for a mile until they reached the edge of no man's land, where they dug a grave and buried her.

My mother still slept comfortably. Her sweat had dried now. As I fanned her, I kept watching my father moving closer to the well until I could not see him anymore. Perhaps he had already reached the well. The hot wind had numbed everyone. They were all dozing off! There was an eerie silence around us. I felt as if the world had slowed down until it was almost at a standstill.

Just then, I heard a voice nearby, "The border is open!"

"Did you say that the border is open?" came another voice.

"Yes, the border is open!"

Sleepyheads got a jolt; dozing eyes were wide open. "The border is open!" They all stood up. Their sacks went up onto their heads; their bundles got under their arms; babies were picked up, and toddlers climbed on their parents' shoulders.

"The border is open!"

"The border is open!"

The noise around me was deafening! My mother got up with a start, but my father was nowhere to be seen.

The border was still three miles away. Those three miles, which my mother ran barefoot with her swollen feet, were the longest ever three miles, which did not seem to end. At last, we saw a line of buses coming toward us from behind the blowing dust. People started pushing one another to get on those buses. The volunteers were running all over, trying to calm the people down. "Be patient! Be patient! Everyone will get on! There are more buses on the way!" But no one had any patience.

I was left far behind in that pandemonium. My mother had reached close to the bus. The more I tried to reach her, the more I was pushed back by the crowd. Then I gave up trying and wished that she would get on the bus. As she turned around and looked at me, she threw away the sack that she had carried on her head this far and ran toward me. I renewed my effort to reach her, but we were both pushed back by waves of the impatient crowd; we were like helpless ants that keep trying to climb a slippery wall and keep falling. Just when I thought that we were never going to reach each other, she was suddenly in front of me. She picked me up and ran back to the bus. I had lost the tiffin carrier somewhere but still held on to her shoes, as if they were my most valuable possession.

Every bus was overcrowded. People sat on roofs, hung on doors, and clung to windows. By the time we moved from there, it was late at night. Darkness had spread its wings as far as the eye could reach, except for a few twinkling lights here and there. At last, we stopped in front of a huge building. It was a railway station. Someone said that we were in Lahore. When my mother got down from the bus, she picked me up, but then I wiggled out of her hold and stood beside her. I was not a baby anymore and did not want her to keep carrying me. Also, her feet were swollen, and she could hardly walk herself. She let me go but held my arm so tightly that it started aching. She did not want to lose me again. She saw me clutching to her shoes. "Throw them away, son," she said. "I don't need them anymore." But I did not want to give up my possession.

We spent the night on the platform. Everyone sat there since there was no room to stand or move around. Whenever a train arrived, people got up and pushed one another, trying to get on it. My father mentioned that we were headed for Bhoolari Camp, a refugee camp in the south. He had told us that some of my mother's relatives were in that camp. However, my mother did not know where we would go and which train we would take. We kept sitting all night on the platform, watching trains come and go. Thousands of people had left during the night, but many more had arrived.

It seemed that the night would last forever, but eventually, it did. The call to prayer from a nearby mosque announced a new day. The birds started chirping, and the silhouettes of buildings outside the railway station started becoming clearer. While it was raining gold on the eastern horizon, I was trying to keep my eyes open. Suddenly I saw my father coming from the far end of the platform. Heading in our direction, he made his way through people and stared from side to side to locate us.

At last, he spotted me and ran toward us, climbing over people, toppling some, pushing others, and apologizing for causing inconvenience. I ran toward him, cascading through people and their belongings. He was only a few feet away, but it seemed that I would never reach him. Finally, he came forward, picked me up, and held me against his chest. He cried bitterly as he kissed me all over. His beard was soaked in tears. His eyes were crying, but the rest of his body was shaking with laughter. He was trying to say something, but I could not understand anything. He was overcome with emotion, which had slurred his speech. He held me tightly against his chest and kissed me again and again as he took breaks between his broken sentences.

"When shall we get home?" I asked him, looking at him with my sleepy eyes. He laughed uncontrollably as if I had told him a joke. He tried to compose himself.

He extended his arm to the bright horizon and gestured with his hand. "You are asking me about home?" His words were caught in his throat. "I am giving you a whole new country."

I looked up into his face, and all I could see was a shroud of gloom. His expression did not match the enthusiasm in his voice. Was he regretting his decision? Was he thinking about what he would do in the new country to make a living? Perhaps he was trying to look beyond the fog of uncertainty he faced. Maybe my grandmother's words had reverberated in his memory, once an immigrant, always an immigrant.

He shrugged his shoulders and held me closer as he watched the rising sun. A lone steam engine shunted back and forth along with a pair of rails in the distance, spewing smoke that blocked his view. He let me go, and I stood by his side. "When shall we go home?" I asked him again. He did not respond. Holding my hand, caught between hope and despair, he turned back slowly to where my mother was waiting for us.

Epilogue

The memory of Birehra has flashed through Azad's mind at odd times and in odd places. He has remembered his little village while strolling along the Champs-Elysées while grasping the iron gates of Buckingham Palace and looking down at Rome from the top of St. Peter's Basilica. He often thinks about the story of a mountain, which his grandmother told him when he was a little boy:

"As you walk away from the mountain, a voice calls you from behind. You can hear your name clearly, but if you dare to look back at the mountain, you will be turned into stone instantly."

Birehra is that mountain for Azad. It has called to him all these decades, but he has never dared gather enough courage to turn his head.

Sometimes he feels as if he left Birehra just yesterday, even though it was over seventy years ago when he was only six years old. It feels as if he has travelled halfway through the globe-the only way to return to Birehra is to dig a hole in the ground, pass through the centre of the earth, and emerge on the other side. It is only 400 miles away, but each mile is a light-year long.

"Don't ever look back, son," his father had told him as they had crossed the border.

Azad prefers fantasy over reality because fantasy allows him to live without all those obstacles and irritants that come with reality.

There was a time when he lived in reality and was often disappointed when his characters did not behave the way he wanted them to. So he chose fantasy as a way of life and calls it smooth sailing, devoid of annoying crests and ebbs.

He often fantasizes about sitting in a movie theatre centre, watching his life on the big screen. From time to time, he looks through the darkness at the empty seats around him and then turns his gaze back to the screen. As his life follows the screenplay, he wonders how much control he has had over the script. He asks himself if he really needs to have any control, but then he edits the script as he goes along, adding a tear here and a smile there. While he watches events unfold, he reminds himself that he is merely an actor following a script. All thrills, joys, pains, and agonies that he has gone through in life are part of that script; he disowns them in favour of the actor on the screen. This way, he can eliminate the perilous rapids, as he rafts through the serene flow of time and manages to camouflage his pain under the smile of Buddha.

Azad does not believe in borders. If the earth were supposed to be divided into countries, it would have natural walls and partitions separating nations and tribes. When he globetroted through many countries in his backpacking days, he found that all babies cry and giggle in the same language, regardless of their nationality. He discovered that all hearts ache at the loss of their loved ones, and all lovers feel the same ecstasy when they meet, regardless of their race.

As we grow older, we gain wisdom at the expense of agility. Slowly and slowly, we settle down into the age of reflection. Azad knows that the downtown streets are still bustling with crowds of young people on Saturday nights. Movie houses and restaurants are still packed. The City Hall's rink is still crammed with skaters gliding majestically with their hands in their pockets. There are still lineups of excited fans at the box office to get tickets to Toronto Blue Jays games, and crowds still now go wild at every home run. But Azad has had his share of excitement. Now he prefers to spend his evenings sitting in his rocking chair, watching episodes of *I Love Lucy* from the old days.

After planning for forty years, he finally took a trip to his old alma mater. It was like a pilgrimage for him. He visited old labs and classrooms from forty years before. He sat on a bench in front of the old cafeteria, where he used to sit with his friends and engage in hot discussions about Vietnam, hippies, and Mao Tse-tung. He looked around and noticed that the grass on the campus was not as green as it used to be in his day, and the co-eds not as beautiful. Deep down, though, he knew that the grass was even greener, and the girls even more attractive. He simply did not have the same eyes anymore.

At one time, Azad used to search for utopia. He looked from Sparta to Moorish Spain, from the Ottoman Empire to the Soviet Union, and from Maoist China to capitalist America. He followed every *ism*, *ocracy* and *archy,* but always returned empty-handed. Finally, he gave up his pursuit and decided to create his own utopia. He calls it *Birehra*. The life in Birehra is simple. There are simple problems with simple solutions, and it does not take much to be happy. It is not like these countless other places, where we need big things to make us happy, and every little problem looks like a mountain.

Azad believes that Birehra still exists, just as he had left it seven decades ago. He is six years old once again and can clearly hear the dull sound of the bells hanging around the necks of oxen, which are on their way at dawn to plough the fields. He still runs with his friends after dust devils, throwing pieces of paper into them to see whose paper will go highest. He still hears the shrill call of a cuckoo bird perched in a mango tree. As a sudden gust of wind passes through the fluttering leaves, the bird flies away, and the spell is broken.

Azad's friends are convinced that he is at the crossroads of nostalgia and schizophrenia. He erects every mud wall in Birehra with his own hands, puts the characters of his choice in every house, and engineers every event with utmost care. He disagrees with his friends when they tell him that Birehra is just a mirage that he has been chasing all his life. He does not believe in mirages since he knows that every oasis, appearing on the far side of the quivering desert heat, is real. All a weary traveller needs, is the unwavering passion to reach it.

Acknowledgements

First and foremost, I would like to acknowledge the advice and friendship of Zatoon Vania, who educated me about the genre of linked stories and composite novels. She deserves the credit for bringing my manuscript into the current form. She sliced and diced it, cutting, pasting and moving passages around for a smoother flow of the narrative, including the plot and bringing the ending to a conclusion.

Tales From Birehra has been a work-in-progress for fourteen years. The first few stories were written back in 2002, and when asked to critique them, Ron Conrad remarked that he was impressed by their "richness of life and detail." His encouragement compelled me to continue the project. However, over the years, I almost abandoned the writing of *Tales From Birehra* due to other priorities, but I always felt that this story was worth telling, so I kept coming back to it whenever I could.

Sagheer Ahmed Kunwar is yet another friend whose help was inestimable. He compiled the glossary of words from Indian languages, which appears at the end of the book. Sagheer also pointed out several gaps in my understanding of Hinduism and Indian culture. I filled those gaps as I revised the manuscript.

I would like to acknowledge the scholarly contribution of my daughter, Naheed Mustafa, in editing the manuscript. The credit for all the flaws that you do not see in this book goes to her. The creativity of Teresita Hernandez in designing the cover is also acknowledged. It is precisely how I had envisioned Birehra in the monsoon season. Hannah Monteith took the responsibility of promoting the book and educating me about reaching out to my readership. Galia Zavgorodni undertook the task of managing the publication of this book. Acting as a bridge between the team at FriesenPress and me, she never gave me any hint that I was getting on her nerves, even though at times I knew I was. Her patience and professionalism kept the project on target.

I had posted most of the chapters from Book Two and some from Book One on my Facebook page and had invited friends to comment on them as readers. It is difficult to name everyone who responded, but I am grateful to all of them, especially to Syed Hussain Haider, Askari Ansari, Kausar Ali, Penny Fancy, Iqbal Samad Khan, Haroon Shirwani, Adeel Siddiqi, and Darakhshan Siddiqi. My wife, Nighat Mustafa, deserves special mention for being the first to read every page as it was written and offer valuable input. While mentioning all these friends, let me not forget Colleen Kennedy, who strained the manuscript through a fine sieve, and Munir Pervaiz supported and promoted my work on Writers' Forum Canada.

I would also like to thank all the characters in this book who permitted me to intrude into their personal lives. For you, they may be fictional, but for me, they are all real. I can touch them, hug them, laugh with them and cry with them. I can wipe off their tears, and they can wipe off mine. And a final thank you to you for joining me on this journey through Birehra.

Glossary

Abba	Father
Adab Arz	I express my respect to you. Usual expression to greet Muslims by Hindus and vice versa. Hindus usually greeted one another with Namaste and Muslims with Salaam Alekum, which is colloquial for the Arabic expression As-Salaamu-Alaikum
Anna	See Rupee
Azaan	Call to prayer from the mosque
Bahoo	Daughter-in-law
Baqreed	The festival of Eid-ul-Adha to commemorate Abraham's sacrifice of his son
Begum	The title of a married Muslim woman of high rank. Also, see Nawab
Bhagwan	Someone divine; generally used for God among Hindus
Bhangi	A person who collects refuse and cleans toilets; is untouchable and not part of any of the castes
Chaat	A savoury snack, containing yogurt, spices and chickpea balls, typically served on road-side

from food carts

Chabootra	A large patio outside a house where children played in the day and men sat down for evening chats
Chacha	Paternal uncle younger than one's father
Chamar	An untouchable caste whose job is working with leather
Chapati	A thin circular bread of unleavened whole-grain flour
Cheel Gaadi	Cheel: Eagle; Gaadi: Cart; Cheel Gaadi was an aeroplane
Chhoti	Younger, small
Chowki	A large rectangular wooden seat, on which several people can sit at a time
Chulha	A horseshoe-shaped cooking stove using wood, charcoal, cow dung or crop residue
Dharamshala	An inn for Hindu pilgrims
Dhobi	Washerman
Dhol	A large cylindrical wooden drum
Dhoti	Traditional garment worn by Hindu males; a loose piece of clothing wrapped around the lower half of the body
Dom	A member of the untouchable caste whose job is to prepare the body for cremation
Dupatta	A piece of cloth covering the head and the bosom, worn by most Muslim and some Hindu women

Eid	The festival of Eid-ul-Fitr celebrated by Muslims at the end of the month of fasting
Engraze	Englishman; the term was used for any white man regardless of nationality
Gulab Jaman	A milk-solid-based sweet, popular throughout South Asia
Gurh	Jaggery; a traditional non-centrifugal cane sugar
Hajj	The annual pilgrimage to Mecca
Haveli	The home of a middle-class or upper-class Muslim family
Hindustan	A common name for India; derived from the ancient Persian word "Hindu" or the land of abnormal heat
Jai Ho	May he be victorious! Equivalent to He is a jolly good fellow
Janam Patri	A "map of heavens" prepared by an astrologer describing the position of stars at the time of the birth of a child
Jivan Mukti	A philosophical concept in Hinduism: living in a state of self-realization and liberation
Julaha	A Hindu caste devoted to weaving cloth on handlooms
Kaaba	The black cube in Mecca around which the pilgrims encircle during Hajj; it is attributed to have been built by Abraham
Kaana	One-eyed (slang)

Khala	Aunt; mother's sister or cousin
Khan Bahadur	See Rai Bahadur
Khanum	The title of a Pathan woman of respectable rank
Kumhar	Potter
Laddoo	A sweetmeat ball
Lathi	A long, heavy stick, used as a weapon
Mahal	Palace
Maharaja	See Raja; the great Raja; a title reserved for a Raja of the relatively large state; the equivalent title for a female ruler was Maharani
Mahavat	An elephant rider who is responsible for directing the elephant to the destination
Manusmriti	An old text describing the teaching of grand teacher Manu; it outlines the code of conduct of a Hindu. It is considered to have originated around the second century BC
Marghat	Cremation ground
Masha-Allah	"By the grace of God"; the Arabic expression that Muslims use when saying something good, such as praising someone
Mashak	Mispronunciations of mashk, the traditional water-carrying bag, usually made of goat-skin
Mataji	A respectful title to address one's mother
Mithai	Any sweet delicacy of the confectionery or candy type

Musalman	Muslim
Musalmani	Slang for circumcision
Naan	A thick circular bread of leavened flour
Namaste	A standard greeting among Hindus
Nawab	A title bestowed by Mughal emperors upon male Muslim rulers of a semi-autonomous princely state; the equivalent title for a female ruler was Begum
Neem	The most common tree in India
Nilgai	Blue cow; an antelope grazing in herds; it invaded crops and was hated by farmers
Nilghora	Blue horse; orthodox Hindus initially resisted Muslims hunting nilgai, but when the animal did not differentiate between the fields of Hindus and Muslims, the hunters were allowed to shoot it, but call it nilghora or the blue horse instead of nilgai or the blue cow
Paan	A preparation combining betel leaf with areca nut and tobacco. It is chewed for its stimulant effect
Paisa	See Rupee
Pie	See Rupee
Pulao	A dish of rice with meat or vegetables
Pundit	A learned man; an expert in a subject
Qorma	A dish consisting of meat with thick sauce or gravy
Rai Bahadur	One of several titles of honour bestowed during

British rule in India to Hindus for their service to the Empire; the equivalent title reserved for Muslims was Khan Bahadur

Raja   A title bestowed by Mughal emperors upon male Hindu rulers of a semi-autonomous princely state; the equivalent title for a female ruler was Rani

Rakhi   A ceremonial string that a girl ties on the wrist of her brother to show her love for him

Rani   See Raja

Raksha Bandhan   The festival of tying a Rakhi

Ramzan   The month of fasting; a colloquial form of Ramadan

Rupee   The official currency of India and Pakistan; there are one hundred paisas in one rupee. Before metrication, there were sixteen annas in one rupee, four paisas in one anna and three pies in one paisa

Sahib   A polite title used to address a man

Salaam   Greeting

Salaam Alekum   Peace be upon you; common greeting among Muslims; a colloquial form of Arabic greeting As-Salaamu-Alaikum

Sarkata   A mythical headless demon

Sattoo   or sattu; A cereal prepared with toasted ground barley grains; it forms a refreshing drink when mixed with sugar and water

Seer	Unit of weight before metrication, equivalent to approximately one kilogram
Sharbat	A drink prepared by dissolving sugar in cold water
Sheesham	Indian Rosewood Tree
Tateeri	A bird with a shrill sound that appeared in the sky before the rain. Whenever people heard a Tateeri they knew that rain was on the way.
Tweet	A talisman is worn by some Muslims to keep the wearer safe from any evil or black magic and to bring good luck
Thakur	A feudal title used by some Hindu tribes
Thukra'in	The female of a Thakur
Vaidhraj	A Hindu doctor who practices Ayurvedic medicine
Yakka	Also Ikka; a horse-drawn carriage with a canopy
Zamzam	A well located within the Grand Mosque in Mecca; according to Islamic belief, it sprang miraculously when Abraham's infant son Ishmael was thirsty and kept crying for water.

About The Author

Rafi Mustafa earned his Ph.D. in chemistry from the University of British Columbia in 1969. He was engaged in research and teaching at several universities, including the University of Leicester in England, the Universities of Toronto and Windsor in Canada, the University of Sindh in Pakistan, and the University of Khartoum in Sudan.

At present, Mustafa is the CEO of an I.T. company, which he established in 1991. He was on the Advisory Committee of the Muslim Studies Program at Emmanuel College at the University of Toronto. He has also been a part of the International Development and Relief Foundation (IDRF) for the past thirty years as a board member, the president, and currently a member of the Advisory Committee.

Tales From Birehra is his first work of fiction. Apart from several articles and short stories published in online magazines, he is also the author of Ay Tahayyur-e-Ishq, a novel in Urdu, set in the '60s.

www.ingramcontent.com/pod-product-compliance
Lightning Source LLC
Chambersburg PA
CBHW071552030726
47593CB00001BA/131